Reader
series by

Love Comes Silently

"I suggest having tissues close by. I'm not one to get too emotional by the stories I read but I found myself teary-eyed often."
—On Top Down Under Reviews

"Mr. Grey delivers a strong, emotional story that made me breathless and totally engrossed till the very end."
—Love Romances & More

Love Comes in Darkness

"Grey has a very descriptive style of writing that allows the reader to feel what that particular character is feeling."
—MM Good Book Reviews

Love Comes Home

"In typical Andrew Grey fashion, we visit real people in real settings who have real life things happen to them."
—Top 2 Bottom Reviews

Love Comes Around

"The story isn't one filled with action or much angst, but it is one that will surely reaffirm the innate wonder in the love and acceptance of family."
—Prism Book Alliance

Love Comes Unheard

"I really enjoyed this installment and highly recommend it and the series."
—The Blogger Girls

More praise for ANDREW GREY

Eyes Only For Me

"A fascinating look deep into the hearts and minds of two men who never expected the discoveries they made along the way of changing and deepening their friendship to the point they become life partners."

—Rainbow Book Reviews

"This is a good story, with well written, well developed characters. There are some seriously hot steamy scenes, and deeply profound dialogue between the main characters…"

—Divine Magazine

The Gift

"Mr. Grey has given us a wonderful story of love and hope and I hope you each grab a copy and enjoy."

—House of Millar

Spirit Without Borders

"Nobody writes like Andrew Grey. I pick up one of his books and start reading, and I can't put it down. This one definitely was one of those books."

—Inked Rainbow Reviews

"The realistic picture Andrew paints about the conditions, the area, the lives of these people grips you and you become emotionally involved in the story and you won't want to put it down until you finish."

—Rainbow Gold Reviews

By ANDREW GREY

Accompanied by a Waltz
Between Loathing and Love
Crossing Divides
Dominant Chord
Dutch Treat
Eastern Cowboy
Eyes Only for Me
In Search of a Story
The Lone Rancher
North to the Future
One Good Deed
Path Not Taken
Saving Faithless Creek
Shared Revelations
Stranded • Taken
Three Fates (Multiple Author Anthology)
To Have, Hold, and Let Go
Whipped Cream

HOLIDAY STORIES
Copping a Sweetest Day Feel • Cruise for Christmas
A Lion in Tails • Mariah the Christmas Moose
A Present in Swaddling Clothes • Simple Gifts
Snowbound in Nowhere • Stardust

Art
Legal Artistry • Artistic Appeal • Artistic Pursuits • Legal Tender

BOTTLED UP
The Best Revenge • Bottled Up • Uncorked • An Unexpected Vintage

BRONCO'S BOYS
Inside Out • Upside Down • Backward • Round and Round

Published by DREAMSPINNER PRESS
www.dreamspinnerpress.com

By ANDREW GREY (CONT.)

Published by DREAMSPINNER PRESS
www.dreamspinnerpress.com

By ANDREW GREY (CONT.)

Published by DREAMSPINNER PRESS
www.dreamspinnerpress.com

Love Comes to Light

ANDREW GREY

DREAMSPINNER PRESS

Published by

DREAMSPINNER PRESS

5032 Capital Circle SW, Suite 2, PMB# 279, Tallahassee, FL 32305-7886 USA
www.dreamspinnerpress.com

Love Comes to Light
© 2016 Andrew Grey.

Cover Art
© 2016 L.C. Chase.
http://www.lcchase.com
Cover content is for illustrative purposes only and any person depicted on the cover is a model.

ISBN: 978-1-63477-128-3
Digital ISBN: 978-1-63477-129-0
Library of Congress Control Number: 2015960371
Published March 2016
v. 1.0

Printed in the United States of America
∞

This paper meets the requirements of
ANSI/NISO Z39.48-1992 (Permanence of Paper).

To Lisa Carlton Guertin and my amazing fans everywhere.
I couldn't do this without each of you.

CHAPTER
One

ARIK SAT at his easel, canvas in place, staring at the blank whiteness. He hated that color, the one that mocked him with nothingness. He blinked a few times but couldn't stop the tears that spilled from his eyes and rolled down his cheeks. It was time to say good-bye to his dreams and to move on with another chapter of his life. His head knew that, but his heart ached as though he'd lost the love of his life. And maybe he had. Lord knew he'd never met anyone he wanted to spend the next fifty years with, but the canvas and his paints? He'd thought that would be a lifelong love affair. He'd learned differently, watching, looking at the whiteness waiting to be brought to life, but nothing came. Not that he could do a fucking thing about it.

He turned away, lashing out, the easel and its contents falling to the floor with a crash. The canvas went sailing and landed facedown near the wall. At least it was no longer mocking him. Arik wanted his anger to build, more and more, and maybe then, in a fit of rage, he could end it all. But once the sound settled and things became quiet, his anger went as well, replaced by despair and self-loathing. There was fuck all he could do, and making a mess wasn't going to help.

He gathered everything up, put it all away, and then left the tiny second room of his apartment. It had been meant to serve as the bedroom, but that was where the light was, so he slept in the main room so he could take advantage of the light—the place's one true amenity. Now it was just a room the sun hit during the day. Nothing more. It would never be the room where his mind and body became one and he made art, where he could let his soul shine through.

As soon as the door clicked closed, Arik deflated like a balloon. What little energy he'd seemed to have the past few months was spent and gone, long gone. Curling up under a blanket on the sofa, Arik closed his eyes to try to sleep. That was the one escape from this whole mess. He could dream about spectacular landscapes and capturing the essence of the little girl, Cassie, who lived next door, the way he had in the painting that hung in their living room, the one he'd done for Cassie for her seventh birthday. Feel that rush, the energy of creation coursing through him, knowing he was seeing something others didn't and needing to get that on canvas the way the rest of the human race needed to breathe. It was part of his soul… at least it had been. Now that was gone. Arik only felt that way in his dreams now, so he slept as much of his life away as he could.

ARIK STARTED awake, blinking, to find the apartment bathed in morning reds and oranges. He heard the vibration of his phone somewhere. He wanted to let it be, but it vibrated insistently, and Arik almost fell to the floor before getting his legs underneath him. He found the ridiculous piece of technology and answered it, surprised it hadn't gone to voice mail.

"Hello," he said quietly, trying to think who could be calling.

"Is this Arik Bosler?" an assertive, confident voice said.

Arik wondered if this was one of those sales calls. "Yeah…," he said half questioningly.

"Good. I'm Ken Brighton. You entered the Great Lakes Regional Arts contest last year."

Arik's heart sped up, and he sat straighter on the sofa. Ken Brighton was calling him. Arik had studied his work in school, and here he was talking to him on the phone. "What can I do for you, sir? I wasn't the winner of that contest."

Arik remembered working for weeks on his entry. The first prize had been a chance to spend two weeks working directly with the man he was talking to now. Arik had wanted to win that prize so badly he'd been able to taste it.

"I'm aware of that. The thing is, I was very impressed by your contest entry. There was a panel of judges, and we didn't always agree on the definition of art, or much else, for that matter." Ken cleared his throat. "Be that as it may, as I said, I was impressed with your entry, so I decided to call you and see if you'd be interested in coming up here to work with me for two weeks. I know the contest prize included board, and we have an extra room here that you're welcome to use during your stay."

Arik's mouth went completely dry and his hand shook as he held the phone to his ear. "That would be so awesome!" he exclaimed before he remembered, and the momentary burst of energy drained away.

"Excellent. Do you still have the same e-mail address?"

"Yeah, but...."

"Very good. I'll send you the address. Do you have transportation? If I remember from your entry, you live in Pontiac—that's a good drive to Pleasanton."

"I have a car," Arik said automatically.

"Great. Does a week from now work for you? I have a project that will be finished by then, so I thought we could start something together and take it through our artistic processes, so we can learn from each other."

Ken Brighton wanted to learn something from him? Arik's breath escaped, and he nodded before remembering that he had to speak. "I can be there." He had nothing else going on.

"That's wonderful. Like I said, I'll e-mail you all the information, and please don't hesitate to contact me if you have any questions. I'm really looking forward to working with you."

"Thanks," Arik said without thinking. The line went silent. He pulled the phone from his ear and stared at it for a few seconds, wondering what he'd just done. He had agreed to spend two weeks with Ken Brighton, his hero. He was going to get to meet him. It was like a dream come true.

In art school, he'd taken a class in currently working artists and art trends. They'd studied Ken Brighton's work in class, not because what he was doing had been particularly groundbreaking—Ken's work was actually quite traditional—but because his technique and talent were outstanding. Arik had taken notice, and he'd even adjusted his own personal style to move closer to Ken's. But how could he do this? Working with him would be a waste of Mr. Brighton's valuable time. Arik knew he should simply call him back and explain that he wasn't able to come after all.

Instead, he was so excited about meeting him that he got off the sofa and rummaged in the coat closet for his suitcase. Then he began packing his things to get ready for the trip. He hadn't been excited about anything in so long.

THE DRIVE through Michigan a week later was beautiful. Late June, summer was in full swing, and as Arik went farther north, the heat of the Lower Peninsula dissipated, the air freshened, and he turned off the struggling air-conditioning in his car and rolled down the windows to let in the clean air.

Arik knew he should have simply called Mr. Brighton and told him that he couldn't come. But he figured since he didn't have anything better to do, he'd make the drive, meet Mr. Brighton, maybe be able to see his work and talk to him. Then, once he'd explained that while he would have been thrilled to work with him, it just wasn't possible, he'd leave. Maybe he'd spend a few days in town before driving home to figure out what he was going to do with the rest of his life. For now and the next few hours, he was thrilled that he was going to meet one of his heroes.

He crossed the Mackinac Bridge, watching the water, calculating how he could recreate that exact color of blue. Not that it mattered, but by the time he reached the Upper Peninsula side, Arik was fairly sure he could get the color right if he tried. Not that he ever would again. He paid the toll at the far side and continued on, passing Castle Rock as he headed north toward Lake Superior.

As he drove, Arik enjoyed the scenery, but as he got closer to Marquette and then Pleasanton, he began to regret not calling Mr. Brighton and calling off the visit. But it was too late now. He was already there.

At the edge of Pleasanton, his nerves began to get the better of him. He pulled into a gas station and up to the pumps, then turned off the engine. He needed gas and a chance to think. He should have stayed home and not put himself through all this.

A tap on the doorframe pulled him out of his thoughts. Arik turned and squeaked at the huge man half leaning into his window. "You want some gas or what?" the man asked gruffly. Arik was belted in or he'd have scooted into the passenger seat to get away.

"Yeah," he answered shakily. Arik watched as the huge, bald-headed man, dressed in jeans and a plaid shirt with a leather jacket hanging open over the top, stared back at him with eyes that said he wanted to tear Arik apart. At least that was what Arik saw in them. He shivered and tried not to look scared. "Th… thank you?" God, he hoped this guy worked at the station.

The guy didn't move—he just watched Arik for a few seconds as Arik chilled and willed his legs not to shake while hoping the guy wasn't about to reach in and grab him.

The huge man pulled back, and Arik breathed a sigh of relief.

"You need to open your gas cover," the man said, and Arik pulled the gas-cap lever, fingers shaking. He reached over and raised the passenger window. He also raised his partway and felt a little safer. Arik adjusted his rearview mirror, watching the man and wishing like hell he could get out of here. He reminded himself that the two of them had never met before, and the guy pumping his gas had no reason to hate him. That still didn't stop Arik's insides from churning. When he heard the sound of the gas nozzle being removed, he pulled out his wallet, checked the pump for the amount, and got out some bills.

"That will be $27.53," the man said gruffly.

Arik handed him thirty dollars. "Thank you," he said hastily, and then he raised the window and started the engine. The man might have said something, but Arik pulled away and turned back onto the main road, following the directions his GPS system gave him.

It took a good ten minutes for his breathing to return to normal. He hated that the gas station guy had intimidated him, but he hadn't been able to help his reaction. He pulled his mind away from his fear and concentrated on his driving, making the turns indicated until he pulled up in front of a well-kept home on a tree-lined street—the kind of place anyone would want to live.

A riot of color lined the walk and the front of the house, flowers in every hue. All Arik wanted to do was get to work… but that wasn't part of his life any longer. He had to realize that and move past it. Still, he could enjoy something as beautiful as the rainbow of color that went perfectly with the Craftsman-style home. After taking a steadying breath, Arik opened the car door and stepped out. He closed the door and walked across the street, down the beautifully lined walk and up the steps, where he rang the bell and waited.

It opened, and a stunning man with eyes the color of heaven stared back at him.

"I'm Arik Bosler. Mr. Brighton is expecting me."

The man nodded and motioned for him to come inside. He closed the door behind him without a word and motioned him farther into the house. Arik got the idea from the way he used his hands that the man couldn't talk. He seemed to hear okay, or at least read lips. Arik wasn't sure what else to do, so he followed the man through the house and toward the back. The man opened a door, and the scent of paint, familiar and warm, wrapped around Arik.

"Mr. Brighton," Arik said, and Ken Brighton turned around, breaking into a smile.

"Arik, I'm glad you made it." He set his palette aside and walked toward Arik, extending his hand. Arik hesitated, then pulled his right hand out of his pocket. He could tell instantly when Mr. Brighton noticed. He looked into Arik's eyes, meeting his gaze straight on. That alone was different. So was the gentle, yet firm, way Ken gripped his damaged hand. "It's good to meet you."

Arik looked away. "I should explain. I really wanted to meet you, but I thought about calling to cancel because—" He looked down at his hand. "Well, I'm not an artist any longer. I was so thrilled when you called, and I wanted to meet you so badly, but… I probably shouldn't waste your time."

"Slow down. And please call me Ken." He reached over, grabbed a stool, and moved it closer, motioning for him to sit. "Let's take things one at a time. This is my partner, Patrick," Ken said, and Arik extended his hand. Patrick nodded and shook it. "He isn't able to speak because of an accident, but he's very adept at other forms of communication."

"It's nice to meet you," Arik said, and Patrick smiled, his eyes warming even more. Patrick lightly patted Arik's hand and then released it. Patrick then left the room, closing the studio door. "Like I said, I shouldn't have come and wasted your time."

Ken didn't say anything, just walked to the corner of his studio and returned with a painting that Arik instantly recognized as his contest entry. "All of the entries were sold at a charity auction, and yours was the only one I bought. It spoke to me in a way that went right to my heart. I had to have it."

"I did that a year ago...." He looked down at his hand and slid it back into his pocket. He hated seeing it.

"Your work is gorgeous and shows great talent," Ken said.

"Well, it shows what I once had."

Ken continued looking at the painting.

"That was my grandmother's home," Arik said. "The contest guidelines were for us to paint a memory. I chose a time when I was happiest. My grandmother had a house on the lake in Muskegon. There was a swing in the backyard under a tree, and she and I used to sit in it and she read me stories."

"She must have been a gardener."

Arik nodded. "She loved flowers and even bred roses. The purple ones and the orange ones in the picture are ones she bred herself. She loved the color, but I think she was after scent more than anything. I remember her always smelling like roses. They were her passion."

"You didn't put her in the picture," Ken remarked.

Arik smiled. "She's there." He pointed to the row of color that disappeared along the side of the house. "She's in those flowers. She told me once that after she was gone, she'd live on as long as someone grew her flowers."

"That's really nice."

"It is." Arik hadn't even realized he'd pulled his hand out of his pocket. He slid it back inside.

"There's no need to hide," Ken said.

Arik slowly withdrew his hand. "I finished the painting and sent it off to the contest."

"When did that happen?" Ken tilted his head toward where Arik rested his hand in his lap.

"Six months ago," Arik answered. "I can use it for most things, but the skin is tight and a lot of the nerves are gone. So I don't have the fine movements any longer. Like I said, I'm sorry I didn't tell you sooner. I know working with you the way you offered isn't possible, but I have admired your work for some time, so...."

"Take it easy," Ken said with surprising gentleness. "You seem to be under the impression that your artistic ability rests here." He took Arik's burn-damaged hand in his. "It doesn't. Your talent is in your head and heart. That's what came through in the picture. Not how steady your hands are."

"But...."

"Yes, I can see that the fine motor skills you needed to create art like this might be gone. They could also only be on hiatus, waiting for you to redevelop them. Have you tried working with your left hand?"

"Yes. And it was a disaster. I've never been very good with that hand, and trying to do something as exacting as painting didn't work at all. I've tried so many times." Arik felt tears welling like they had a million times before. He stopped them. There was no use crying over what he couldn't change. "My heart has always been with painting. It's what I've loved since Gran got me my first set of crayons. You know how kids color in the lines? Well, I used to color one over the other to get the exact shade I wanted. Gran bought me watercolors when I was eight, and I made her picture after picture. Then when she got me acrylics, I was in heaven. I worked with those through junior high, and then in high school I discovered oils and learned to use them. After that I painted all the time. It was all I ever wanted to do, especially after Gran died."

"What about your parents?" Ken asked.

"They're still around." Arik's hand began to hurt. He knew it was only a phantom, a symptom of his mind rather than anything going on in his hand. He tried willing it away. He slid off the stool. He stood and turned slowly so he could take in the entire studio. A painting leaned against the wall, a portrait of Patrick. Before he could stop himself, his feet had carried him over for a closer look.

He didn't touch the canvas, just stared at it. Love—pure, hot, all-possessing—looked out from the image. A tingle ran down his spine at the intensity in the eyes. They bored into the viewer the way Patrick must've looked at Ken while he was painting. There was no way that was from imagination. The heat and soul-deep yearning had to have come from real life.

"That's what I wanted to be able to have," Arik said, unsure if he was referring to the ability to paint like that or to have someone look at him that way. He figured both were lost to him now, his mutilated hand taking them both away in one swoop.

"You know you can. Like I said, your talent isn't gone."

"A lot of people have told me that. But every time I try to access what I see, to put it on canvas, nothing comes out but crap. My hand shakes, and when I try to do something intricate with a brush, it comes out different. It's like my hand isn't attached to my brain any longer."

Ken stood, grabbed a brush from the pot, and held it out. Arik stared at it and finally accepted it. He tried to place it in his fingers, to hold it the way he'd been taught.

"Forget what you've been taught. If the will is there, then you need to learn a new way to hold the brush and a new way to paint."

"I've tried," Arik said, handing back the brush. He put his hand back in his pocket. "I do appreciate what you're doing, but I think it's hopeless." Arik walked to the studio door. "I've taken up enough of your time." There was nothing anyone could do for him now. He was beyond help.

"Arik," Ken said softly, and when he turned, Ken indicated the stool once more. "Do you always give up so easily?"

Arik shrugged.

"You came all this way. At least we can talk."

Arik nodded and took the seat Ken offered. "How do you get so much emotion in your portraits?"

"Just like you," Ken said, motioning. "I put some of myself in each piece I do. This isn't a portrait of your grandmother, but the way it's painted and the way the flowers seem to sway in the breeze tell me a lot about how you felt about this place. There are memories there, hidden behind those windows." Ken picked it up. "Look at the glint in the glass, resembling eyes, but only from a certain angle, as though the owner's soul still resides there."

"I like to think that Gran is still happy there because she made me happy."

"See, that comes through, and that came from inside you, working its way out through your brush. It wasn't a product of your hand, but you."

"I know. I can still feel things and see them, but my hand doesn't work like it did." Arik pulled it out of his pocket and laid it on his lap. He'd stared at it many times. "I don't have much feeling in these fingers. A lot of the nerves were damaged." He moved his fingers. They did what he asked, but only because he could see them and concentrate on the movements. There wasn't anything that was automatic or easy about it.

"I'm not a doctor, but I do know the artistic temperament. There have been men who have painted with their teeth and even with their feet. If you want this badly enough, you'll find a way." Ken turned back to the painting Arik had done. "This wasn't the way I expected this morning to go. I had thought we would talk, then I'd watch you work to get a feel for your technique. Then after lunch, I had hoped that you and I could devise a project we could collaborate on."

"I guess that's out of the question," Arik said.

"I think that's up to you." Ken's eyes held a challenge Arik found hard to dismiss. "Patrick and I have arranged for you to stay here with us." Ken stood and pointed across the yard to a small building down a path near the corner of the yard. "Why don't you take your things down there and get settled. A friend is coming over this evening for dinner, and we'd like to have you join us."

"What do you want me to do?"

"Instead of collaborating right away, I'd like to start with you doing a piece for me."

Arik was already shaking his head, but Ken continued. "I'm not expecting this level of work, but you need to move forward. I won't watch over your shoulder, and you can work on your own. There's a small studio space with a garden view that you can use, and it gets great light. All I want you to do is try."

Arik nodded, because what else could he do? He'd come all this way and Ken was being so nice, so he wanted to make him happy. Besides, he figured it couldn't hurt. Maybe this time something would happen and his results would look something like what he envisioned in his mind. "Okay."

Ken smiled, and, dang, Arik knew he'd made the right choice.

"Go ahead and get your things. Patrick and I will help get you settled." Ken checked his watch and then led Arik back through the cozily neat house. Arik unlocked the car, and Ken and Patrick helped him get his supplies and suitcase out of the trunk, then led him through the side gate into the yard.

Arik stopped in the backyard, taking in the even more riotous color of the gardens. Plants and flowers of every color caught his eye. It was like a rainbow everywhere Arik looked. The colors weren't random but arranged in large patches in various shades of yellow, red, orange, blue, purple, and white. It was stunning, and Arik longed to paint it. "Is it okay if I work out here?"

"Of course," Ken said brightly, picking up Arik's suitcase from where he'd dropped it. Arik barely noticed Ken and Patrick as they continued on. Images filled his mind of the color around him and how he wanted to paint it. Energy and creative juices filled him to the brim for the first time in months. After a few seconds, he followed them inside the small garden house.

There was a tiny living room/kitchen combination, with a solarium off to the side. Patrick set Arik's art supplies in there. Arik followed Ken into the bedroom. It was also small, but with a built-in double bed that had drawers under it. All of the furniture was gorgeous in warm wood tones.

"Patrick made all the case furniture and built the cabinets," Ken explained. "The sofa cushions lift and there's storage under them. We wanted this to be efficient and comfortable."

Arik was a little overwhelmed. "Thank you." He continued looking around and wondered if this was how Van Gogh felt about his little rooms in France, and if that was why he painted them so lovingly.

"Feel free to make yourself comfortable and set up wherever you like." Ken smiled.

Arik nodded and jumped slightly when a heavy hand settled on his shoulder. Arik turned, intent on pulling away, but Patrick smiled gently at him, his eyes warm with comfort. He patted his shoulder lightly, and somehow Arik knew the silent man understood his pain. How, he had no idea, but Ken had been right—with a brief look, slight tilt of his head, and a gentle lilt to his lips, Arik knew Patrick understood. Then, before Arik could react, Patrick pulled him into a hug, the kind a dear friend might give. Arik closed his eyes, remembering what it felt like to be held, almost cradled, in simple kindness. After a few seconds, Patrick released him and stepped away. Arik nodded, trying to keep from embarrassing himself by breaking into tears.

Patrick turned and left the room.

"I'll come get you for lunch in an hour or so and we can talk some more if you like," Ken said.

Arik nodded and began setting up his supplies. He left his suitcase where it was; he could unpack later. He set up the easel he found in the sunroom and got his paints and a small canvas from the ones he'd brought. He'd packed supplies against his better judgment, and he was glad now that he'd gone ahead and done it. He'd fully planned to turn around and go back home—heck, he still might—but for now, he'd do what Ken asked.

There was a stool in the studio area, and he carried that outside as well, setting up at the edge of the shade where he could see the entire garden. He opened his paints and began mixing colors so he could get to work.

HIS BRUSH fell to the ground for the third time since he'd started. It didn't feel right in his hand. They never did now. Arik picked it up and wiped off the tip. Once he'd ensured it was clean, he returned to work. He had decided to use smaller brushes than he usually did, hoping that would give him some control. But his frustration grew by the minute.

"Do you want to come in for lunch?" Ken asked as he walked up to him, and Arik nodded. His head ached. He'd only been at this for an hour, but it seemed like he'd been working for much longer, with nothing to show for it. At least nothing he was remotely happy with.

"Thank you." Arik stood, bending each way to take the slight crick out of his back. Then he went inside to take care of his brushes. Painting was an exercise in futility. He'd let Ken give him hope that he'd figure out some way to do what he loved again, but what he ended up with looked worse than what he'd done in high school. There was no control, no finesse.... He thought about throwing everything aside, but he didn't want Patrick and Ken to see his show of temper.

Once he had things set so he could come back to them, Arik walked from the garden house to the main house and was greeted by a stunning beauty with the most incredible eyes. "You must be Hanna," Arik said. "I've seen the paintings your dad has done of you."

"I am," she said with a smile.

"I'm Arik. He's working with me."

"I know. Dad said you were coming." She turned and closed the door. "We're eating on the side porch. Pop has already brought the food out there."

"So Patrick is Pop?" Arik asked.

"Yeah. Pop's great. He can hear, but he can't talk. But I bet you figured that out already. We use sign language a lot with him, but Pop's pretty expressive, so you won't have any trouble understanding what he's trying to communicate." She sounded very grown up, even though he guessed she was fourteen at most.

"I found him," Hanna said as she pushed open the door off the kitchen. The porch was small but fully screened, with a round table and comfortable chairs. The breeze blew through, creating a great indoor, yet outdoor, space.

"How is it going?" Ken asked as he stood, motioning to an empty seat.

"Much like I feared," Arik answered honestly. "I can't seem to hold the brush anymore. There are times when I'm not able to feel it at all. I'd be better off painting with my feet."

"All right. Don't give up."

"But what if it's not possible any longer and I *should* just give up?" Arik asked. Ken sat down, but it was the tap on the shoulder that caught Arik's attention. He turned, and Patrick stared at him.

"Oooh," Hanna crooned.

"What?" Arik asked without looking away.

"That's his not-happy-with-you face." Hanna sat down.

"I'm trying, but not having any luck."

Patrick's hands moved very quickly. "He says you need to keep trying. Giving up on a gift should never be done lightly," Ken interpreted. Patrick pulled out his chair when he was done signing and sat down. Arik did the same, wondering once again if he should simply go home and crawl back into his hole.

"Uncle Connor called. He said he's going to the children's home because there are some repairs he needs to make," Hanna told Patrick. "He was wondering if you were free to give him a hand." Patrick nodded and pulled out his phone. He texted, and Arik was grateful that the attention had shifted from him.

Ken began passing the dishes.

"Can I go to Sophia's this afternoon? She's playing soccer too, and we want to practice together."

Arik got the idea that this was a busy house.

"As long as Gordy and Howard are fine with that."

Hanna took some chicken salad and passed the bowl to Arik. "Sophia said they were okay with it. Uncle Howard is going to be home. Uncle Gordy was going to be out."

"It's fine," Ken said. "I have to go that way, so I can take you."

"Thanks, Dad." She smiled and began to eat. Arik was ready to offer to take her—anything so he didn't have to spend the afternoon staring down a canvas and brushes that weren't working. He took some of each dish as it was passed. Arik felt a little like he was there under false pretenses, and as he listened to them talk and sign through lunch, he realized he truly wanted what they had. They were a real family. There wasn't any fighting—they talked things over, no huge drama and yelling. With his own family, those were his primary memories. Arik's only relief from that environment had been his gran. Once she died, even that was gone.

"Where do your parents live?" Hanna asked between bites.

"Detroit," Arik answered and took a bite, figuring he couldn't talk if he was eating.

"Do you see them much?"

Arik shook his head. If he ever saw them again, it would be too damn soon. But he wasn't going to say that to the earnest young lady sitting next to him. They didn't need to know his awful family situation. He ate with fervor, and when he was done, Ken told him he could go back to work if he wanted. Arik carried his plate into the kitchen and returned to the backyard. He sat down to take up his nemesis once again.

He worked hard, trying to master a way to hold the brush so he could get the effects he wanted with the paint. After two hours he was ready to throw it all away. Nothing was working.

Ken came out to check his progress. "Let's see."

Arik shook his head. "I hate it." He reluctantly showed Ken what he'd done and then turned away from it. "I used to love to paint. I spent hours and hours working and was never happier. Now it feels like it hates me. The brush and I used to be friends, but now we act like enemies."

Ken looked at the work and then at him. "I can see that." He handed the canvas back. "Will you give me a little time to think things over?"

"Yeah. It's too late to drive all the way home tonight."

"No. I'd like you to stay for a few days. You still have talent." Ken pointed. "Look what you did with the patch of flowers over there."

"I wasn't finished with them," Arik said. "That's just the start."

"Maybe, but it shows potential." Ken kept looking at what Arik had done. "I'm not willing to give up if you aren't."

"Why?" Arik asked. "You don't know me from Adam. Why should you care? There are other people who could use your guidance to take them to the next level. You don't need to spend your time on a guy who may never do anything decent ever again."

Ken's gaze was straight and powerful. "Let's just say I have my reasons." Ken stepped back and looked up at the sky. "I think you need to pack it in. The wind is shifting, and the clouds are going to roll in. So the light is going to fade, and we're likely in for some rain." Arik began packing up. "Patrick is going to help a friend of ours. You're welcome to stay here if you like, but I was thinking that if you wanted, you could ride along with him."

Before Arik's eyes, a bank of clouds rolled in. They were low and thick, obscuring the sun within minutes, spreading dampness where seconds before there had been sunny warmth. "I'll try to help if I can. He was going to some children's home, right?"

"Yes."

Arik thought for a few seconds. A place like that should be pretty cool. "When should I be ready?" The wind came up, and he shivered slightly.

"I think he's leaving in ten minutes."

Arik nodded and gathered the rest of his things. The day certainly had shifted on a dime. The clouds thickened by the minute—by the time Arik got his things inside, dampness seemed to permeate everything, so he closed the windows. He got a sweatshirt out of his bag and pulled it over his head. Then, once he was ready, he got his keys and closed the door behind him before walking through the garden. The flowers seemed to have braced themselves against the coming weather, and he wished he could paint the scene. It was evocative and moody. But he wasn't ready to try to face all that again.

Patrick stood on the deck, motioning to him. Arik followed him through the house, where Patrick got a jacket, and then they went out. Arik got in the passenger side of Patrick's huge, dark blue truck, and they drove in silence into town. There were a lot of things he wanted to ask the large, quiet man, but he wasn't sure how to phrase them or how he'd actually understand his answers, so Arik sat quietly, looking out the windows as they drove through the rural roads, past fields of crops just beginning to reach for the sun and thick green forests that looked as though they'd been there forever.

"I want to paint all this," Arik said, breaking the silence.

Patrick glanced at him and nodded.

"I want to be able to work the way I used to," he confessed, holding his scarred wrist in his other hand. "Why can't things be the way they were?" Patrick blinked at him a few times, and Arik knew he was being stupid. Nothing was ever going to be the same again.

Patrick pulled the truck off onto the shoulder, and once it had stopped, he reached into the door beside him. *You have to stop feeling sorry for yourself,* Patrick wrote on a small notepad, then jammed it in his direction. *What happened, happened, and it's in the past.*

"I know. But painting was the one thing I was good at."

Patrick ripped off the top sheet and began writing frantically. *Singing was my gift, and that was taken away from me too. I thought that was all I could do. I was wrong.* Patrick handed him the pad, then put the truck back in gear and pulled out onto the road. Arik stared at the note and then his feet for the rest of the trip.

He hadn't figured out how to say that he was sorry to Patrick by the time they parked in front of an old, stately building that had seen decades of weather and use. Patrick got out and Arik did the same. They were greeted by a man carrying a tool belt.

"I'm Connor," he said, shaking Arik's hand without squeezing or pausing. One of the things Arik was coming to hate were the looks of pity he got when someone first saw his injury.

"Arik."

"You're the artist working with Ken," Connor said. "He's been looking forward to your visit."

"I'm afraid he was disappointed." Arik waved his hand and then slipped it back into his pocket. "I'm pretty useless now."

Patrick rolled his eyes and then shook his head.

"Let's get to work," Connor told Patrick. They headed up the steps and inside the Victorian-era building. "I've been working to try to replace some of the worn-out floors. In some cases I was able to sand and refinish, but in others, it's a complete replacement, and that's what I need help with."

Patrick nodded.

Arik kept quiet, listening. "I can help if you need it," he said finally.

"Reg is coming in too, and between us, I don't think we have room for someone else to work in there." Arik got the feeling Connor was being polite and worried about his hand. He was about to argue when the front door opened and the huge man he'd seen earlier in the day at the gas station lumbered inside. Connor smiled, but Arik took a step behind Patrick. The guy seemed even bigger now, his sleeves rolled up, showing off tattoos running all up his arms.

"Patrick, you know Reg," Connor said, and Patrick nodded. "This is Arik. He's working with Ken."

He nodded, staying quiet and hoping this Reg guy had forgotten all about him. Arik hated that he felt this way, but guys like Reg scared the crap out of him. He'd been around enough of them in his life and been intimidated and bullied more than once. Reg looked at him hard, and Arik took another step behind Patrick, swallowing the squeak that threatened as his stomach did unhappy loops.

"Let's get started," Connor said, leading them down one of the hallways. Arik watched them go and then leaned against the wall, hand over his heart, trying like hell to catch his breath.

"Are you okay, sweetheart?" the young lady behind the desk asked gently. She had a kind look, and some of the trepidation he was feeling slipped away.

"Yes. I'm sorry." He felt like a fool, scared of his own shadow, and wanted to get the hell out of there. This had all been a mistake, and it would definitely be best if he just went home.

CHAPTER
Two

THE WHIR of the circular saw cut through the air, the whine echoing off the walls of the small room. Reg Thompson placed the boards, set them, and then used the gun to nail the floorboards in place. Snap, snap, snap. The task was going well, and they expected to be done in an hour or two. The hard part had been ripping out the old flooring and hauling it away. This work was tedious because of all the measuring, but with the three of them, it was progressing quickly.

"Let's take a break," Connor called after the saw whined down once again.

"Good idea," Reg agreed. Patrick nodded and grabbed a bottle of water, then left the room. Reg followed him with his gaze, waiting until he'd left to ask, "What's with that kid who's staying with them?"

Connor shrugged. "I just met him, but I saw the way he acted."

"Like he wanted to crawl inside a wall to get away from me. He stopped at the station for gas, and I expected him to make a run for it any second, acting like a scared rabbit." Reg grabbed two bottles of water from the cooler and handed one to Connor.

"Did you see his hand?" Connor asked. "Maybe that has something to do with it. Those burns aren't that old." Connor grinned. "And let's face it, you don't project love and happiness, or have little bluebirds landing on your fingers."

"Fuck no, I'm not a princess," he growled and then sighed. "But that kid is cute as a button." Reg knew it would be best if he put Arik out of his mind. The guy was scared as hell of him.

"Yeah, the growliness is the perfect way to keep the kid from running for the hills."

Reg did it again. "I am who I am. Never claimed or tried to be anything but." If he was big and strong, then no one messed with him and that was just fine. He'd taken more than his share of shit in his life, and he was done with that. "I'm going to hit the head. I'll be back in a few, and we can finish this project." He checked his watch. He had to be back at the gas station by six, but that should leave plenty of time to get this project done.

Reg knew the way. He went to the restroom off the entrance, waving to Claire, who was sitting behind the desk, as he passed. She was a biker chick at heart, and when he stopped by, they usually talked Harleys for a few minutes. He pushed the restroom door open and went inside. After taking care of business, he washed his hands and pulled the door open. Childish laughter rang through the hall. Reg glanced at Claire, who pointed to the activity room. More laughter followed, and Reg followed the sound. He peeked into the room.

"Mr. Reg!" Bobbie Jo raced over to him. "I heard you working." She imitated the saw. "I didn't bother you because that's going to be my room when you're all done." She grinned, showing her missing front teeth. He lifted her into his arms and watched as Arik turned toward him and then quickly looked away again. "He's showing us how to draw a bunny." She pointed to a paper on the table, all smiles and unbridled energy.

"That's great, sweetheart," Reg said, carrying her back to her place.

"He has a hurty hand like me. See?" she said, pointing to Arik and then lifting her own right hand.

"Does it hurt today?" Reg knew she sometimes dealt with a lot of pain, particularly after the surgeries or when she was having a growth spurt.

"Nope." She smiled and wriggled her thumb and the next two fingers. That alone was a miracle and a half, as far as Reg was concerned. Bobbie Jo's little fingers hadn't grown right and ended up twisted and curled. She'd had surgery on three of her fingers to correct it, and there were still two to go.

"That's good, honey," he said, setting her back in her chair and handing her the pencil.

"I'll drawed a bunny for you," she said and looked to Arik. "Would you tell me again?"

"Sure," Arik said gently, but Reg felt his gaze on him and saw the fear and nervousness in his eyes.

Reg thought about leaving the room, but that would upset Bobbie Jo, so he knelt on the floor next to her to seem less threatening… he hoped.

"First you draw the face," Arik said, going slowly as he demonstrated, letting the others keep up. "Then the ears." He drew the first one. As he made the second ear, the pencil dropped from his hand, rolling along the table and onto the floor in front of Reg. He picked it up and held it out to Arik, who looked at it as though it were on fire. Then Arik slowly reached for it, gently taking it from Reg's fingers. "Thank you."

Reg nodded, and Arik continued with the lesson. "That's so good."

Bobbie Jo's tongue stuck out slightly as she concentrated, making the shapes Arik showed her. It didn't look as fluid as his, but Bobbie Jo was obviously pleased as punch as she added the whiskers.

While she worked, Reg took a few seconds to study the tiny man across from him. He had to be only a little over five feet and maybe a hundred pounds soaking wet. Arik had this little swooped nose and two of the biggest, bluest eyes he'd ever seen. He even might have said Arik was girly but for the cut of his cheekbones, which added power and appeal to his face. Wheat-blond hair that fell nearly to his shoulders softened his jawline.

"What color do you want the bunny to be?" Reg asked.

Bobbie Jo looked up at him, sliding one finger into her mouth as she thought. "Reg-colored… so maybe pink." She giggled, and Reg handed her the pink. He had no idea why that was Reg-colored. There wasn't anything pink about him, but if it made her happy, he'd go with it.

"Choose whatever colors speak to you," Arik suggested, and Bobbie Jo nodded, reaching for the brown crayon. She began coloring, and Reg watched her work. When she was engrossed, Reg let himself glance at Arik. He had his head down, drawing carefully. He could see that Arik's movements weren't practiced or fluid.

A tussle broke out between two boys who wanted the same color. "That's enough," Reg said calmly, staring at each of them in turn. They settled right away and decided they could use another color.

"Don't be mean," Bobbie Jo scolded.

Reg smiled at her. "I wasn't," he said to her in his gentlest tone. She set down her crayon, and Reg took that opportunity to tickle her. She giggled, and he did it again, holding her as she squirmed and laughed. When Reg looked at Arik, he saw him smiling. That was a beautiful sight—all white teeth and perfect lips, eyes shining, losing some of their darkness and fear.

"Are you going to help us finish up?" Connor asked from the doorway.

"I have to go back to work," Reg told Bobbie Jo. "But you finish your picture, and I'll see you before I leave."

She wound her little arms around his neck and gave him a big hug. "Okay."

Reg released her and stood up. He saw Arik watching him, stiffening like he didn't know what was going to happen next, as if he expected to be hit or worse. Fear filled Arik's eyes, and Reg hurried out of the room to where Connor waited for him. "I'm ready when you are," Reg said, glancing back at Arik, wondering what in the hell had happened to him and who could have hurt him so badly.

"Patrick is already back at work."

They strode down the hall to the room they were working in, and Reg went back to placing boards on the floor. Patrick and Connor cut and measured. Between the three of them, they made good time and quickly had the boards in place.

"I'm going to clean the floor and then get the stain on so it can dry," Connor said, once they had put the tools away. "You were a huge help." Connor shook hands with them, and then Patrick and Reg left together, returning to where Arik was still working with the kids. They had moved on to colored paper and glue, with Arik helping them make trees.

"Is it time to go?" Arik asked from where he was sitting, and Patrick nodded. Arik stood and paused. Then he shook his head ever so slightly and approached them both. "I'm ready when you are. I was giving the kids an art lesson."

"Will you come back?" asked Kyle, a boy about eight, who in Reg's experience never said very much at all, as he hurried up to Arik.

"Yes. I'll come back. I promise."

Reg knew these kids didn't get enough attention and love. The staff cared for them and did their best, he knew that, but they weren't their parents. And that's what each of these children needed more than anything—someone to love them. Reg walked over to Bobbie Jo, said good-bye, and gave her a gentle hug. She held up her drawing of the bunny.

"It's beautiful, sweetheart." He never liked having to leave. "I'll come to see you again soon," he told her. She nodded and threw her arms around his neck. Reg did his best not to tear up, but it was fucking hard. "Be good."

"I will," she promised, like she always did, and then Reg released her and let her go back to her artwork. He walked to the doorway, stopping to look at her one more time before leaving. Leaving her was getting harder and harder each time he had to do it.

Patrick pulled a small notepad from his pocket and wrote. *Are you going back to town?*

"Yes. I need to check on the station."

You're coming to dinner tonight, remember? Patrick wrote.

"Right. What time?" The thought of another night of frozen dinners alone in front of the television wasn't particularly appealing.

Seven, Patrick wrote, and Reg said that would be fine. He said good-bye to Patrick as well as Arik, shaking his hesitant hand and being as gentle with it as he could. Then he hurried out of the building and got on his electric-green Harley with purple and white detailing. He loved that bike. He took off to get it home before the threatening rain arrived.

Normally Reg drove like a bat out of hell. When he was on his Harley that was how he felt—free, as though nothing could stop or catch him. It was so awesome: the wind over his head, whipping through his leathers, the power under and around him. It was almost better than sex, and given the fact that he hadn't had any in a while, it was as close as he got.

Dark clouds built on the horizon ahead of him, getting closer and closer by the second. He approached town and sailed into the gas station as the first drops fell around him. One of the bay doors was up, and Reg drove inside, pulled to a stop, and turned off the rumbling engine as the sky opened up.

"I said you were taking a chance taking the bike," Slasher, his head mechanic, said as he slid out from under the Cadillac he was working on. "I'm glad your timing was good."

"So am I," Reg agreed, looking outside as sheets of rain soaked the concrete. "Are you about done for the day?"

"Yeah. Finishing up this repair. I swear Mrs. Clark takes these things off-road. You should have seen the crap I found up in here."

"You know her. She may be seventy, but she has a lead foot and a need for speed." Reg grinned. Livia Clark had been his customer for years, and there were times the repairs to her cars had kept the wolves at bay.

"I should be done in half an hour. Is Derrick coming in tonight?"

"Yes." As Reg answered, Derrick pulled up in his car and raced inside.

"Man." The high school senior came in, shaking off the water. "God's sure pissed about something."

"Maybe it's about you talking like that," Slasher teased.

"Ha-ha," Derrick said as he went into the station office to man the register for the night. Slasher chuckled and slid back under the Cadillac. The station itself was old but really solid. Reg wanted to get a lift system installed, but money had been tight for a few years. He hoped to add one in the next few months, but until then they did things the old-fashioned way.

"Do you need anything?" Reg asked, sticking his head into the office, where Derrick sat behind the desk with a book open on the counter.

"No. I'm good. You want me to lock everything up like I did last time?"

"If you can." Reg popped the register drawer and took out most of the money and the credit card receipts. He got a bag and put the day's receipts inside. "I don't expect much business tonight. With weather like this, most people will be hunkered down inside."

"No problem."

"You have my number if you need anything."

"I won't," Derrick said with a confident grin. "I can handle things." That was very true. Derrick was built like a linebacker, and when he pulled himself to his full height, he was more than enough to intimidate anyone who might be contemplating anything untoward. "But I'll call if anything comes up I can't handle. Now go have fun and let me get back to work."

Reg stared at the book. "Work?"

"There's only so many times I can straighten the candy bars and soda cooler." Derrick looked through the windows. "And like you said, we aren't going to have a rush on gas or anything."

"Fine."

"Don't worry, I'll sweep and mop the floors and stuff. This place is always a mess when it rains."

"Okay," Reg said, relenting. "I'm having dinner with friends."

"Go have some fun. I plan to after I close up. There's this girl I have my eye on, and she's going to be down at Gordon's tonight, so I'm going to show up and see if I can interest her in all this." He flexed his muscles and flashed a smile.

"She'll be more interested if you're nice and act like a human being rather than a mindless gorilla." Derrick glared at him, and Reg glared back. "You're always reading, and I know you work hard in school, even though you don't want anyone to know it because of the reputation you have, but a time is going to come when you'll realize that being big man at school will end. You have one year left of high school, and then all that is over and you're a has-been. An Al Bundy dreaming of what you did in high school while you're sitting on the sofa getting a beer belly, wondering what the hell you did with the rest of your life."

Derrick swallowed. "That's not going to happen to me. I've got big plans…."

"Like college," Reg pressed. "No one can take what you know away from you."

"Did you go to college?" Derrick asked.

"No. And I damn near screwed up my life. I was just like you—big dreams and a bundle of talent. Instead, none of it happened and I did whatever I wanted. Spent years riding across the country, did all kinds of dumb stuff, almost ended up in prison. I got lucky, but you can do better than I did, and it starts now!" Reg deepened his voice, and Derrick jumped a little. He knew he could intimidate, and he wasn't above doing it.

Derrick swallowed hard and looked away. "Okay…. So what do I do?"

"First thing, you acquire a little humility and treat this girl with respect. That is, if you really want her to notice you. Listen to her."

"What would you know about getting girls to put out?" Derrick asked.

"Is that all this is about? Is that what this girl means to you?" Reg asked sharply.

Derrick shook his head. "Not really. Marcie's kind of different. She's quiet and doesn't usually go out. But some friends of hers convinced her to spend the evening with them, and they told me she was going to be there." Derrick really was just a huge kid.

"Then take my advice and see if you don't find something other than what you usually get. Because it sounds like this girl isn't going to be impressed by the usual routine." Reg lifted his eyebrows and then checked his watch.

"Thanks, Dad," Derrick replied with sarcasm. "Now get outta here so you're not late." Reg waved on his way out.

Slasher was finishing up and had closed the overhead doors. Reg returned to the bays and stowed his bike in the back. He and Slasher left together, each heading to their vehicles.

Reg drove home and hurried inside, dodging the rain. He went right to the bathroom, took off his sweaty work clothes, and got under the spray. He washed quickly, trying not to give his mind a chance to wander. But as soon as he was under the water, Reg found himself wondering what Arik had under those baggy clothes of his. Reg knew that was a bad road to go down. After all, Arik paled and backed away whenever he was near him. But dammit to hell, something about his eyes and lips, as well as how good he was with the kids, caught his interest. Besides, he was the cutest guy Reg had seen in years.

He had to hurry, but he lingered under the water for longer than he needed because images of Arik refused to fade. In the end he took himself in hand, imagining Arik's legs wrapped around him and his sleek body sliding down his. By the time he was done, breathing hard, he was in danger of being late. Reg dressed quickly in a pair of jeans and a black button-down shirt before hurrying to his truck and over to Patrick and Ken's.

The rain picked up as he pulled into the driveway, pounding the windshield and hood of his truck. Reg sat for a few minutes, but it didn't seem to be letting up, so he opened the door and stepped out. His shirt was soaked through before he got to the front porch. Reg rang the bell and was surprised when Arik opened the door, though not half as surprised as Arik seemed to be. At first Reg thought he'd scared the cutie again, but Arik seemed intent on staring at his chest—or the shirt that clung to it.

"Um. Come in. Ken and Patrick are in the kitchen, and they asked me to get the door," Arik mumbled and stepped back, taking refuge halfway behind the door.

"This weather…," Ken said, walking up as Arik closed the door. "Patrick, Reg is going to need to borrow one of your shirts. He's soaked," Ken called into the other room. "Dinner will be ready in a few minutes. We thought about building a fire, but even though it's wet, it's too hot, so the AC is on to take out the dampness, I hope…."

Patrick walked through and up the stairs, returning a few minutes later with a dry shirt and a towel. Reg took off the shirt he was wearing, dried himself off, and shrugged into the dry one. His pants weren't as bad, thank goodness, and he hoped they'd dry on their own.

"Hanna is with some friends," Ken said, motioning to the living room chairs. Reg followed, noticing that Arik hung back, staying out of the way. "Make yourself comfortable. Dinner shouldn't be long."

Ken and Patrick left the room, and Reg sat down, waiting to see what Arik would do.

"I'm not the boogeyman," Reg said after it seemed Arik was ready to stay in the corner of the room, as far away from him as possible. "And I don't bite."

"I know that," Arik said. He slowly came closer, choosing to sit in the chair farthest away. He stared at Reg and then looked away, studying the portrait of Hanna over the fireplace.

"How long have you been here?" Reg asked, sitting back to get comfortable on the cushy sofa.

"I drove in today," Arik answered without looking at him. "I'm supposed to be here for two weeks to work with Ken, but"—he turned from the painting but seemed to be looking over Reg's shoulder rather than at him—"I don't think things are going to work out. I don't want to waste his time." Arik placed his burned hand on his lap and mostly covered it with the other one.

Reg wanted to ask what happened to him, but he doubted Arik was up to telling the story. From the looks of the burns, the injury was fairly recent. The scars hadn't had a chance to fade like they would if the injury was old. "I doubt Ken thinks you're a waste of time."

"Yeah, well. He invited me here to work with him, but I can barely hold a brush or a pencil, as you saw this afternoon." Fire shone in Arik's eyes, and Reg smiled, glad there was something other than fear in the kid.

"Can I bring you something to drink?" Ken asked as he swooped into the room. "I should have asked earlier but forgot my manners."

"Wine is fine," Reg answered, and Arik asked for the same.

"All right," Ken said and hurried out. He returned with two glasses. "I hope this is okay. I got some red, and I hope it's good." A timer rang in the kitchen, and he raced back.

Reg smiled. "So what sort of art do you do?"

"I paint... or I used to paint."

"He does amazing work," Ken said from the other room.

"I used to," Arik said softly, holding his hand once again. "The thing is, I can't do it any longer. The nerves and…."

"Go on," Reg encouraged.

"There's nothing to say. I need to accept things as they are and go from there."

"Why the hell would you want to do that?" Reg asked a little more loudly than he intended. "You don't get shit in this world unless you're willing to fight for it or throw yourself into the thick of it. Giving up doesn't get anyone anything."

"And neither does wishing for what was yanked away." The fire was back, combined with anger. "You don't know anything." Arik waved his arm, and a little of the wine slopped out of his glass. Reg grabbed some napkins, and Arik did as well. They wiped up the spill, Arik watching him warily.

"I know what it's like to lose something precious and special," Reg confessed, his hand brushing against Arik's.

"Yeah?" Arik asked. "I lost—" He stopped and sat back in the chair. Reg did the same, and they settled into silence. Reg wasn't sure how comfortable it was, but he did see Arik watching him a few times.

Finally, Ken called them in to dinner. They were placed next to each other at the table, and Reg could feel the tension washing off Arik.

"Do you have any interesting projects going?" Ken asked Reg as he sat down and began passing the food.

"I have a bike I'm working on for one of the guys. Klapp has a thing for wings, so I'm detailing a set on his fuel tank. I have this idea to carry the theme through the entire bike. I was thinking I could do wings on his helmet, like Mercury."

Arik tilted his head slightly. "What sort of work do you do?"

"Customized bike detailing. I don't build the bikes, but I design and execute custom paint. I started off doing my own after I took over the station, and some of the guys in the club liked it and asked me to do theirs. Now I'm booked for the next six months, and everyone wants something unique." Reg turned slightly in his chair. "I like designing something that fits each rider's personality. You can only do so many skull or flaming devil bikes before it gets to be dull. So I never do the same design twice."

"What's the most interesting bike you ever did?" Arik asked.

Reg hesitated, a little surprised that Arik had willingly spoken to him. "One of the ladies in the club had a dog for many years, a

Dalmatian named Harvey. After he died, her bike went a week later, and when she got a new one, she asked me to do something special. So I painted the bike white, added spots, and had a custom seat done for her. Louise cried when she saw it."

Patrick signed to Ken. "He says he's seen her in town, and the bike is awesome."

"It is. I don't think I've ever seen another one like it. But now Louise has a golden retriever. I hope that dog lives a long time." A Dalmatian bike was one thing, but he'd hate to try to make a bike look like a golden. Maybe he'd have to add yellow fringe to everything. The thought made him shiver.

"Do you do a lot of bikes?"

"It takes a few weeks to do each one because I make the seats as well as paint the designs. Sometimes I have to fabricate custom parts to add to the bike. It's a very detailed process, and I want them all to be perfect." Reg took some sliced beef and passed the plate. "Are you working on a project at the moment?" Reg asked Ken and Patrick.

"Arik and I will be collaborating on a project that should be amazing," Ken said and turned to Patrick to answer for him. "He's working on an oak-and-walnut bedroom set for a bed-and-breakfast in Marquette. They wanted something stately for their largest suite."

Attention fell to Arik, who seemed uncomfortable. "I'm trying to figure out how I can paint again so Ken doesn't end up doing all the work."

"I told you before, art is up here," Ken said, gently touching Arik's head.

Reg stifled a growl and wondered where in fuck that was coming from. Yeah, he'd wondered what Arik's blond locks would feel like threading through his fingers, but Ken was just being nice.

"You know what I think?" Ken asked. Arik turned to Ken with hope springing in his eyes. "When you went to art school, you started at the beginning. You took drawing and charcoal classes to develop basic skills. That's what you should do again. Instead of trying to paint, let's build up your skills from the ground."

"But...."

"Your brain is used to working with your hand the way it was before you were injured. So we need to reteach your brain and hand to work together. Tomorrow you and I are going to start a project together, and we're going to sketch it out. I'm thinking something large and impressive."

The look of aghast surprise on Arik's face was precious. Reg smiled and turned away so Arik couldn't see his amusement.

"But why would you spend all this time on me?" Arik asked.

Ken stood and left, dropping his napkin on his seat. When Ken returned, he carried a canvas along with him. "Look at this," Ken said, holding the painting out to Reg. "Is that stunning?"

Reg stood and took the canvas. "You must have loved this place very much." He looked around the side to Arik. "Who is it that's inside these windows, looking out at you?"

"There's no one in the painting," Arik said.

Reg looked intently at the image. "That's not what I meant. In your mind, who was watching you through those windows? Who lived there and took care of you?" Reg went back to the painting. A simple portrait of a house, but filled with emotion, overflowing with love, the door open slightly as an invitation to come inside and be a part of the warmth. It was nearly irresistible.

Arik sniffled. "My gran lived there."

Reg continued looking, staring at the windows, wanting to see inside, wishing there was more. "That's why you need to figure out how to paint again. This isn't about technique, but putting what you feel and what's in your heart on a canvas." Reg reluctantly handed the painting back to Ken. He didn't want to let it go. He'd never had a place like that in his life, and he'd longed for it so many times. "Ken does that in his work."

"And you do it in yours," Ken said, turning to Arik. "That's why I wanted you to come here. I wanted to take an artistic journey with you. So maybe we take a different one than we planned. The journey of a thousand miles starts with a single step, so we'll take our first ones tomorrow and see where they lead us."

"But...," Arik began and stopped, nodding slowly. "I guess we'll have to see."

"You bet we will," Ken said. Reg saw him smile and was reminded again why he liked him. He'd met Patrick and Ken about two years ago. Patrick had needed some work done on his truck and brought it in. They'd shared signals, signs, and notes to communicate, and after that Ken started bringing in his car too. They'd begun talking, and after that he became part of the circle.

What Reg liked most was that Ken, the famous artist, didn't look down on him. Instead, he considered Reg an equal, a working artist. "I can help."

Ken looked up from his plate. "Yeah, you can. Do you still have that airbrush set that you let me borrow last year?"

"Airbrush?" Arik said.

"Yeah. Working with it takes real control and a special touch, but it's different from holding a brush. The movements required are different, so I was thinking we could explore that kind of work while you're here. Maybe toward the end of the week."

"I could show you," Reg offered. Arik held his gaze, and then he nodded. It was only once, but that was enough. Once again he wondered what had happened to Arik. Reg hadn't been particularly forward or even spoken very loudly to Arik, yet he seemed in a constant state of agitation and low-grade fear around him. He was surprised Arik had accepted his offer of help. "Just let me know when you need it, and I can bring over the set."

"Wonderful," Ken said.

The conversation drifted away from art to the weather, and Arik seemed to relax a little. He never said very much, but he was always engaged and listening. Reg helped Ken clear the table and joined Arik and Patrick in the living room. He sat next to Arik on the sofa, wondering how he'd react. Arik tensed and moved a little closer to the arm.

"Is business okay in general?" Ken asked when he joined them.

"Yes. It took more time than I expected to build up a regular clientele." He looked down at himself. "I guess some people were afraid of me." He glanced at Arik and then at his cup of after-dinner coffee. "My friends were always supportive, but they weren't enough to keep me going. Now I have a lot of regular people who bring in their cars. That keeps Slasher really busy, and between that and the detailing work, I can take a few nights off every now and then."

Reg finished his coffee and stood. "It's probably time for me to head home. I have to be at the station early in the morning. If you want to give me my shirt, I'll...."

"It was still wet when I checked it. Keep that one for now, and we'll drop your shirt off the next time we see you." Ken stood and gave him a hug. Patrick did the same. When it came to saying good night to Arik, he wasn't sure what to do. He thought about shaking hands, but instead, he gently drew the smaller, timid man into his arms.

"Good night," he said softly, holding Arik for only a few seconds before letting him go. "Hopefully I'll see you later in the week." Reg left the house, thankful the rain had let up, and walked to his truck. He drove carefully on the wet roads, driving by the station, which was closed and looked fine. Then he went home.

Reg thought about watching television for a while, but nothing interested him. Instead, he sat at the table and began working up drawings for some of the bikes he had coming up. His mind kept running to Arik and how he'd felt in his arms, warm, and yeah, slightly tense, but at least he had returned the hug. That was something. Reg wanted to beat the living hell out of the person or people who had made Arik afraid of the world.

He set down his pencil and then picked it up again. He got a clean sheet of paper and got to work.

An hour later, feeling tired, he looked at his idea for a bike. Only that wasn't what he'd drawn at all. It was Arik, eyes bright, like he'd seen in those few unguarded moments when he'd laughed and forgotten to be worried or scared. Reg knew it was time to go to bed or he'd never make it through the day tomorrow. He used the table to push himself upright. Then he checked that the doors were locked, turned out the lights, and climbed the stairs to his bedroom.

THUNDER WOKE him in the middle of the night. Reg got up and looked out the window, watching the lightning as it danced across the sky. Realizing he wasn't likely to be going back to sleep anytime soon,

Reg wandered naked down the stairs and found his pad on the table. He grabbed the pencil and paper, then returned upstairs to his room. Reg got back into the bed, pulled the covers over his legs, and began to draw. The outline of Arik's cheeks and lips took shape, followed by his amazing eyes. He didn't draw his hair right away, concentrating on his face. After a while his pencil stilled, and an image of Arik in the throes of passion came into his mind. Reg flipped the page and began to draw, his hand skimming lightly over the page, shaking a little as he got caught up in the passion his mind was conjuring.

Reg knew this was all his imagination and none of it was real. It wasn't likely Arik felt anything for him at all, but the alluring images his mind kept conjuring were too good not to get down on paper, so he drew long into the night, then lay back on his pillows and closed his eyes, the sketchpad resting on his lap.

CHAPTER
Three

ARIK SAT in Ken and Patrick's garden house in the dark, surrounded by quiet that was broken only by the sound of his own breathing. He checked the small clock on the other side of the room. It read two in the morning but he was wide awake. Images and feelings ran through his head in a nonstop parade of inspiration that seemed to clog his brain. Before, he would have worked to get them out and onto canvas and paper, but now they stayed where they were, his outlet gone. Sweat poured down his forehead as he shook, wanting to curl into a fetal position.

He picked up the pencil and concentrated, holding it in a fist instead of between his fingers, moving his entire hand. It seemed like a ridiculous way to work, but his hand obeyed what he wanted to do, even if his fingers weren't able to. Slowly, the form in his mind took shape on the paper. It was Reg, the guy who both scared and fascinated him. He had to work through these feelings. He hated having them, and he sure as heck refused to go through the rest of his life afraid of some guy he'd never met simply because of the way he looked. Before his injury, he worked out all his emotions through his art. If he had feelings he didn't understand, he painted them. Now he wasn't sure what to do, and he was an emotional mess and fucking scared of his own shadow.

Arik wasn't sure how long he worked at the single drawing, but it slowly took shape. Light began to appear in the windows as Arik finally set down his pencil. He looked at what he'd drawn, smiled, and then slowly put his head on the table, sleep overtaking him.

He jumped when someone touched his shoulder. Arik whirled around. Patrick stood behind him, a plate and glass in his hands. He held them out, and Arik nodded. "Thank you," he said with a yawn. Arik turned and saw the drawing he'd been working on last night still on the table.

Patrick patted his shoulder and smiled, nodding when he turned to look at him.

"It took me hours to do a simple drawing."

Patrick gave him a thumbs-up and then left. Arik stared at the drawing while he ate, his stomach rumbling at his first taste of food. He wasn't sure how long he sat staring and eating, feeling a little like some of the mental constipation that had built up for months was finally working its way out. At least it was starting to. There was still a lot there, and it was only a single drawing, but it felt good to have produced something he was pleased with. Progress. That was all it was. Just a little progress.

He turned at the sound of a knock and motioned for Ken to come inside. He held up the drawing and handed it to him. "It was hard as hell to do."

Ken nodded as he looked at it. "You like him."

Arik swallowed even as his cheeks heated. "He scares me."

"Maybe he does, but there are other emotions coming through in this. If there was only fear, this image would be darker and his expression more sinister. Instead...." Ken sat down. "See how you gentled his eyes? And the corners of his lips are—"

He reached for the drawing. Maybe it had been a bad idea to show it to Ken. Arik should have known he'd have been able to read the picture as though it were a manuscript to his emotions.

"This is why I wanted you to stay. See? It's still there just waiting to come out. Now show me how you did it."

Arik took a fresh sheet of paper and began work on another, simpler drawing to demonstrate the technique. "It won't work with a brush."

"No. But it means you're starting to think differently. People have painted with their toes, so you can certainly learn to use your hand differently to hold a brush, or anything else you want to use." Ken handed him back his drawing and then passed over another one.

"I was thinking we could work together on something like this. It's the concept for an entire installation. There would be eight works, and each would show the steps in a journey."

"But there are sixteen places."

"Yes. Eight for your journey and eight for mine. As people, we all grow and change, so I thought what we could do is put them together to show that while some of the steps along the way may be the same, each of us takes our own individual journey. What do you think?"

Arik's eyes widened. "You want me to do eight pieces in a few weeks?"

"No. We'll develop the concept, and then I'll get my agent to book a joint show. By the end of the next few weeks, I'd need your commitment, and we'll develop a timeline for completion."

"Isn't that putting the cart before the horse?" Arik looked at his hand. "What if I can't do it?"

"You'll know in the next few weeks." Ken sounded so firm and confident, and Arik didn't want to let him down. "Give it some thought and continue working. Maybe shift from standard to colored pencils. Take it one step at a time and see where it leads you." Ken patted his drawing. "And hold on to that."

"It's just a drawing," Arik said with a shrug.

"No. It's progress, and that's more important than anything. This isn't going to be a quick road back. You need to find your own way, and those kinds of things are always difficult." Ken leaned forward. "When Patrick and I met, Hanna had leukemia, and we didn't know if she was going to live. She's okay now and has been disease-free for a few years. But that required adjustments in my life and a reevaluation of priorities. You're going to have to do the same."

Arik huffed softly, knowing Ken was right. "Is there an art store in town?"

"There's one in Marquette. You probably drove by it on your way here. It's right on the main street of town. Art and Light. The owner is an old friend. Just tell Charlene that you're working with me, and she'll make sure you get fixed up with anything you need."

"Okay." There was no time like the present. If he wanted to redevelop his talent, he needed to get moving. "I'll be back later, and we can talk more about how we see this project going."

"Sounds good," Ken said. "And keep up this energy. It's good for you."

Arik hadn't even realized he'd been smiling until Ken had pointed it out. He was happy, at least happier than he'd been in a while. He grabbed his keys and practically bounded to his old Nissan. He got out his GPS, and to his surprise it had the art store in its directory. Arik turned on the radio, found a classic rock station that played cool songs he could sing along with, and made the drive to the store.

He arrived a lot more quickly than he'd expected. He parallel parked in front of the store, perfectly the first time, and went inside. The smell of paint, oil, thinner, and creativity assaulted him. It felt like home, and he stood just inside the door, breathing it in.

"Now that's an artist's reaction if I ever saw one," the woman behind the counter told him with a smile.

"Are you Charlene?" Arik asked.

"The one and only. I've never seen you before. I would have remembered."

Arik saw her looking at his hand. He went to hide it but stopped himself. He needed to accept what had happened and who he was.

"What can I do you for?" Charlene asked.

"Ken Brighton sent me in. I'm working with him for a few weeks and… well… I need some artist pencils. The biggest set you have." There was no use going halfway.

"I've got a set of 72. Does that work?" Charlene asked, already leading him through the store to the section. "Do you need paper?"

"Give me the works," Arik said brightly, picking up the set of pencils and then looking up and down the aisles.

"Is this your usual medium?" she asked as she began leading him to the artist paper.

"No. I'm…." He looked at his hand and then back at her. She nodded and her gaze softened. "I used to work in oil, but now…."

"Starting over, as they say," she supplied, and Arik nodded, relieved he wasn't going to have to explain.

The bell on the front door rang, and she straightened and looked in that direction. A familiar rough voice rang through the store. "Hey, Charlene."

"Reg, I'm back here," Charlene called. "I'll be with you in a second." She helped Arik find the paper, and he picked out what he wanted, trying not to look around to see where Reg was. Part of him said not to give in to the butterflies of fear in his belly. But then it dawned on him that the flutters he was feeling weren't fear at all, but something very different.

"Hi, Reg," Arik ventured in a soft voice when he saw Reg's bald head over the counter.

"Arik," Reg said, his lips curling upward in a huge smile. "What are you doing here? Is Charlene taking care of you?"

"Yeah." He held up his new supplies. "I have what I need. Now it's only wishful shopping." He'd been standing in front of the tubes of oil paint, longing for the days when he used to…. That was enough of that. "What are you here for?"

"The box is in the back," Charlene said. "You need to check that all the colors you wanted are there."

"Great," Reg said and then turned back to him. "I get my enamels and things here. I could order them direct, but the minimum order is pretty big and Charlene has a good supplier, so I support her and she has her bike work done with me."

Arik wandered up to the counter with Reg so he could pay. Charlene plopped a medium-sized box on the counter, and Reg leaned over it, hugging her gently and kissing her cheek. "I appreciate you doing this for me."

"No problem at all," Charlene said. "I'll add it to your bill."

"Perfect." Reg lifted the box. "See you soon, Arik." He smiled again, and the butterflies turned from a few to a swarm. This was bad—Arik knew it—but dang, it was nice too.

Charlene rang him up, the bill coming to just under a hundred dollars. Arik did a mental check of his account balance and handed Charlene his card. He was going to have to get a job before he was totally out of money. He signed the slip.

"Don't be a stranger, and if you need something special, just call and I'll make sure I have it on hand for you."

"That's so nice. Thanks." Arik took his bag and carried it out to his car. He didn't realize until he got to the car that he'd been carrying it in his bad hand. He shifted it and moved his fingers to work out the ache. This was the part he hated—the pain in parts of his fingers that the doctors had said had no nerves. Phantom pain, they'd called it, but hell, it hurt as much as the real thing, and there was damn little he could do about it other than try to ignore it and hope to hell the crap went away. Doing just that, he unlocked the car and got inside, then pulled into traffic and turned back toward Pleasanton.

A few miles out of town, he passed a farm with a sign for a carousel as well as a gift shop. He saw some people milling about, so he pulled in. Pine-scented air instantly surrounded him, as did calliope music and the laughter and happy screams of children. Arik followed the sound to a barn.

"Can I help you? Arik," Connor said with a smile. "What are you doing here?"

"I was in town and I saw the activity, so I stopped." He watched as the carousel went around, animal figures slowly going up, down, and around. "Did you do this?"

"I restored it. The process took me years. Patrick helped me with some of it. I open the farm and carousel for tourists. There's a gift shop and a few other rides and attractions. We also have a Christmas village." He motioned across the yard, and Arik followed him. Connor walked right into the house, and Arik began looking around the small gift shop. "I'm going to give Arik a tour," Connor called out to someone in the house. "Call if you need me."

"Okay, Dad," Arik heard, followed by a hum, and then a boy, maybe thirteen or fourteen, rode out in a wheelchair. He wore jeans and a nice shirt along with a smile that showed crooked teeth and eyes filled with warmth. "Is it okay if I bring my things in here?"

"Sure, Jerry. I'm not going to be far. Joan is out by the carousel."

Jerry exaggeratedly rolled his head and eyes the way only a teenager could. "I'll be fine. What is someone going to do, steal stuff from a kid in a wheelchair?" Jerry wheeled himself away and returned with pencils and paper on his lap, like the ones Arik had just bought.

"Just call if you need anything."

"Are these yours?" Arik asked, his attention drawn to the framed flower drawings hanging on the walls.

"Yes. I did them. Dad says we have enough of my drawings at the house, so I made some for here and they sold."

"I can see why." The lifelike detail was extraordinary. "They're beautiful." Arik carefully plucked a picture of a pink peony off the wall. He held it up to the light and then put it back, choosing one of an orange rose instead and taking it to the counter. "I'd like this one."

"You don't have to do that," Connor said softly from behind him.

"This is stunning," Arik said, his hands shaking as he paid for the work. "I'd buy them all if I could." He meant it.

"Thanks," Jerry said, beaming as he finished the purchase.

"You can pick this up on your way back if you like," Connor explained as he looked at his son with obvious pride.

Jerry put the framed work behind the counter and then wheeled up to a small table, took out his pencils and paper, and slowly began to work. Arik looked at Jerry's curled hand and then down at his own scarred hand. "Fucking hell," he muttered under his breath and then shook his head. It was long past time he took control of his life again.

"Ready for the tour?" Connor asked, and Arik nodded, following him out of the gift shop and across the yard. "There are nearly a hundred acres of trees. The area over to the west was purchased a few years ago. The trees were overgrown, and we cut them for garlands and boughs, then we started replanting. Every year we clear a new area and replant. In a few years the first trees we planted will start to come up to size, and then the area over here will start to be cleared. It's a never-ending process."

"You really seem to love it."

"It keeps me close to the earth, and…." Connor inhaled. "I love that scent. On days like today when the air is still, the entire place smells like the world's best pine-scented air freshener."

"I love it." Arik looked all around. "Is that corn?"

"Yes. For the maze. In the fall we have a pumpkin patch. The kids can wander through the corn maze, pick out pumpkins, and all that. Jerry, Lila, and Janey all come out here to work. They have so much fun."

"You have three children?"

"Yes. My partner, Dan, adopted Lila and Jerry. He and I adopted Janey together a few years ago." Connor looked as happy and contented as Arik had ever seen anyone in his life. "They love it out here, and we do a lot of this for them." Connor lifted his sunglasses and wiped his eyes. "Jerry told me once that he wanted to ride a horse. Of course riding a real one was impossible, but that was what drove me to finish the carousel. The black horse is Jerry's. There's even a brass marker attached with his name on it. Lila has the tiger, and Janey has yet to stake her claim on one of the figures, but when she does, she'll get a marker as well."

"That's so cool." Arik turned away under the pretense of looking around. He didn't want Connor to see the pain he knew would show in his eyes. Connor's story got him to thinking about his family, and those thoughts were always a source of pain.

"The Christmas village is right over there, next to the carousel house. I made cutouts in the wood shop, and there's a path that families can take. We light it when we're open at night. Jerry painted some of the presents and the Christmas tree for me."

"He's gifted," Arik said. "There's no doubt about it. He has a great eye for detail, and each flower, while true to life, has a personality."

"I know. It takes him many hours to make each one. At first I wasn't sure about putting them in the shop, but he makes so many of them our walls at home were going to overflow. Garret, a close family friend who works here, first suggested we add his drawings to the store. He's sold a number of them, and each time, Jerry is over the moon."

"I can understand that." He remembered the first time he'd sold a work of art to someone he didn't already know. It was pretty heady. "I really appreciate you showing me around. I know you have things you need to do and you weren't expecting me to stop by, but I saw this place and had to drive in." He was pretty anxious to get back and get to work.

"I'm glad you did." Connor smiled. "Don't forget your purchase."

"I won't." Arik smiled, thanked Connor again for the tour, and went into the gift shop. Jerry was still at his table and looked up from his work. He stopped what he was doing and slowly handed Arik his package.

"Thank you," he said brightly, his words very slightly slurred.

"Thank you," Arik said as he took the package and left the gift shop, heading to his car. He pulled out of the farm and turned toward Pleasanton. Two miles down the road, his car began to shimmy. He slowed and the movement lessened, but if he tried to speed up, the entire car shook. He knew something was very wrong, and he slowed even more, limping along.

There were other cars right behind him. Arik put on his caution lights and gripped the wheel tightly. He kept going as fast as he dared, sweat rolling off him as the engine light came on and the car began to lose power.

Never in his life had he been so happy to see the edge of a town. A familiar sight shone ahead, and Arik put the car in neutral, coasting to a stop near the gas station office. He pressed the brake and turned off the engine. He got out because he wasn't sure how bad off the car was.

"What happened?" Reg came racing out of the garage, his expression changing when he saw him. Arik thought he might have seen concern.

"I don't know." He explained what he'd experienced. "I was trying to get back and not be stranded."

"Okay." Reg turned. "Slasher, can you come out and take a look at this?"

A man as huge as Reg came out, hurrying toward him. Arik tensed without thinking, and Reg stepped closer, between him and Slasher. "What's going on?" Slasher asked.

"Arik's car is having problems. He limped in here. Was it a power fall-off?" Reg asked, turning to him. Arik nodded and explained about the shimmying. "Okay. He'll take a look. You can leave the car here, and I can give you a ride back to Ken's."

Arik nodded slowly, all the while hating that he was scared of both of these men just because of their size. "Thank you." He got his things out of the car and handed his keys to Slasher. It was an old car, he knew that, but he didn't have the money for a new one. He hoped this wasn't the end of it because otherwise he wasn't going to be able to get home.

"Slasher is the best. He'll figure out what's wrong." Reg didn't seem to be worried, but then, it wasn't his car.

"Don't worry, little guy. I'll get it running again." Slasher pulled open the door of his car as Arik saw red. He ground his teeth, forgetting about his fear, and poked Slasher in the back.

"Yeah?"

"Little guy!" Arik mocked. "Just because I'm not as big as a house doesn't mean I'm a child." He seethed. All his life people had discounted him because of his size, and he was tired of it. "How would you like it if I called you fatass?" Slasher whirled around. "Because what you got bringing up your caboose sure isn't going to be described by anyone as dainty."

"Chill out. I didn't mean anything by it."

"My name's Arik."

"It's okay. Slasher has all the manners of a porcupine sometimes," Reg said. "But I don't think he meant anything." Then he started to laugh. "But Arik does have a point—your backside could use some work."

"Jesus," Slasher said, slamming the car door closed. "Is that all you do, spend your days looking at my ass?"

"I hope not," Arik piped up. "Though it's been a while since I saw one that big. And for the record, no, those pants do not make your ass look big. Your ass makes those pants look big." Once he engaged his mouth, he seemed to have forgotten how to turn it off.

"Okay. I think we've exhausted the topic of Slasher's big ass. And I don't think anyone is going to call you little again." Reg was trying to make peace, so Arik closed his mouth. "If you've got what you need, I'll take you on to Ken's, and Slasher can look at the car."

"I'm not sure I want to," Slasher said, folding his arms over his chest.

"Stop teasing and get to work," Reg said right away.

Slasher broke into a smile. "I'll get it running."

"And I'll stop making comments about your ass," Arik said.

"Thank God. I was beginning to get a complex." Slasher walked back toward the garage.

"Say no to crack," Arik called, and Slasher held up his hand, extending his middle finger without turning around.

Reg shook his head as Arik followed him to his truck. He got in and buckled up, staring out the window. Now that the anger and adrenaline had dissipated, he kept looking over at Reg, sitting stiffly in the seat.

"Why are you afraid of me?" Reg asked after starting the engine. "You look like you're about to dive out the door at any second. I'm not that mean, I hope."

"I guess not," Arik said. It was hard for him to put his feelings into words, and he didn't want to go into all that crap.

"You weren't afraid of Slasher."

Arik laughed. "I was shaking in my Nikes. But…."

"You got angry."

"Yeah, and I forgot how big he was."

"Is that it, then? Big guys frighten you?" Reg asked. "Because I can't make myself smaller, any more than you can make yourself taller…." Reg glanced over at him and stumbled over his words. "You know what I mean."

"Yeah, I suppose." Arik really didn't want to go into his entire background, so he tried to come up with the easiest explanation possible. "Let's just say I became very familiar with the inside of my own locker. I think at one time I was some rite of passage for the football team. You couldn't be in the group unless you stuffed me in my locker. One guy shut the door and locked me in. I spent an entire class period yelling for help." Arik instantly wished he'd kept his mouth shut. "One of the teachers let me out once she heard me calling."

"Did you tell her who'd done it?" Reg asked.

Arik shook his head. "I said I didn't see him. But I knew. Mike sat next to me in Algebra. A big, dumb kid who got through by looking on other kid's papers. Most people let him, and I did the next time, only I made sure he got all the wrong answers. Then I changed mine before I handed in my paper. I passed the test, and he got caught for cheating and was suspended for a week. Of course, that cost me more harassment once he got back. After all that, I got good at staying away from them and trying not to be seen."

"What did your parents do?"

Arik laughed. It was the only reaction possible other than breaking into tears. "You don't want to know." Arik turned to look out the side window as they made the turn onto Ken and Patrick's street. He was relieved when Reg pulled into the drive. He didn't want to talk about any of that at all. "Thank you for the ride." Arik opened the door and got out of the truck as soon as Reg pulled to a stop.

"Hey," Reg said. Arik skidded to a stop on the gravel out of habit. "I was thinking that maybe we could have dinner sometime."

Arik slowly turned around, thinking Reg must have lost his mind or at least that he'd gone crazy. "You're asking me out? Why?" Arik searched Reg's expression for some sort of answer but saw nothing. The only explanation he could come up with was that Reg was making fun of him. "Thanks again." He turned back around and hurried to the side yard.

"You didn't give me an answer."

"Sure. I'll go to dinner with you. But first I have to know: What's the adult equivalent of being pushed into lockers? Just so I can be prepared." Arik raced around the side of the main house and hurried into his small quarters, closing the door behind him. His heart pounded hard, and he leaned against the door, the bag from the art store clutched to his chest. He slid down the door, wondering what was wrong with him. He'd been up most of the night with images of Reg floating through his head, and now, when Reg asked him to dinner, he ran away like some scared rabbit. He'd stood up to that Slasher guy without thinking about it, but having dinner with Reg made his insides shake. "I'm pathetic."

It was too late anyhow. After that little display, there was no way Reg would want to have anything to do with him. And as Arik got a chance to think, he clamped his eyes closed and groaned. Reg was helping him with his piece of shit car, and he'd been nice enough to give him a ride, and how did Arik repay him? By insulting him and running away. Definitely not his finest hour.

"Arik, was that Reg's truck?" Ken asked from outside the door.

"Yeah." He straightened up and set the supplies on the table before opening the door. "My car broke down, and Reg brought me home." He didn't mention the rest.

"Okay, and I see you got what you needed."

"Yeah, and I'm anxious to get to work." He pulled out the drawing he'd bought. "I met Connor's son, Jerry."

"I can see that," Ken said with a smile. "I have a number of his works. I've worked with him some. He's very talented."

"Is that why you want to help me?"

"You saw the obstacles Jerry has, and he doesn't let that stop him. I think you have the same fire inside and all you need to do is let it out. That's why I'm helping you."

"Okay." Arik wasn't sure what else there was to say. "I should go to work now."

Ken shook his head. "There's just one more question I have. Why is Reg sitting in his truck, staring at my garden house?" He smiled wickedly. "I think you need to go talk to him, and this time try not to pull the rabbit routine."

Arik colored. "You saw that?" Dammit. Now he looked stupid in front of Ken. "He sort of startled me, and—"

"Just go talk to him. I promise you, Reg is not mean, and you have no reason to be afraid of him."

"I guess I know that."

"Then at least find out what he wants, so he can go back to his garage and you can get to work." Ken turned and walked back to the main house. Arik couldn't see for sure, but he was willing to bet that Ken was either grinning like an idiot or trying like hell not to laugh out loud. He glared after him until Ken went inside, and then he stomped around the side of the house and out to Reg's truck.

Reg got out, arms crossed over his chest, but this time Arik wasn't afraid for a second. "What are you still doing here?"

"Giving you a chance to come to your senses." Reg glared at him for two seconds and then broke into a smile that completely destroyed the bad-boy effect he'd had going on. "Besides, I wanted to make sure you were okay. I really didn't mean to frighten you."

"I'm fine." He knew Ken was probably watching from inside. "Guys like you scare me, okay?"

"I get the feeling this has very little to do with guys pushing you into lockers," Reg said, and Arik looked down at his shoes. "You don't have to talk about it, but whatever has you scared, just know that it's not me. I'm just a guy like you."

Arik shook his head. "No, you're not." He looked up. "You're huge and you have all these tattoos and you scare me… and I can't stop thinking about you." There, he'd said it. Now Reg could laugh at him.

"You like me?"

"Yeah." He felt like a twelve-year-old admitting he liked a girl for the first time. Hell, he wanted to turn away in complete embarrassment.

"Then why the rabbit act?"

How could he say that he was both frightened of and attracted to Reg at the same time? Guys like Reg were what he fantasized about at night when he was alone. The men he envisioned were always big and strong, but his fantasy men were also in his mind, at a distance, and safe. Reg wasn't distant—he was right here, and he had this look. He also pushed all Arik's fear buttons. Arik ended up shrugging.

"Okay. I can take no for an answer." Reg turned and walked back to his truck.

Arik realized this was his decision moment. Reg wasn't going to run after him like a lovesick teenager. If he let him get back in his truck and drive away, he wouldn't get a second chance. He had to figure out what was most important and how he wanted to live his life. "I didn't say no, exactly."

"Then you'll have dinner with me?" Reg asked as he turned around.

"Yeah." It was only dinner, Arik told himself. Not a lifetime commitment. He rubbed his injured hand nervously. "I'd like to go, and I'll try not to let this whole fear thing take over."

Reg walked closer and gently took his hand, the injured one. Arik was about to pull it back, but Reg stroked his skin gently. "When was the last time someone touched you?"

"You mean when they weren't yelling or screaming?" Arik clarified and tried to remember. "No one ever touches my hand. They think it's yucky."

"Does it feel strange when I hold it?" Reg looked him straight in the eye, and for a second Arik forgot about anything other than holding Reg's gaze. He shook his head and swallowed hard, trying to keep his racing heart under control.

"No. Other than me, no one usually touches it other than to shake hands, and most people hesitate."

"I won't hesitate to touch you," Reg said, his voice soft and deep enough to send ripples running through him. "And while I can't say I won't yell, I won't hurt you either."

"When do you want to go to dinner?"

"How about tomorrow night?" Reg moved closer, and Arik thought he might try to kiss him. He wasn't sure if he was ready for that. At least his head wasn't. His body, on the other hand, had its own ideas. He thrummed with energy and shifted so his dick, which had decided to wake up in a huge way, was more comfortable and less obvious.

"Okay," he answered breathlessly. Part of him couldn't believe he was having this conversation, and that after the drama of the last little while—all his fault—he'd somehow ended up with a date for dinner. "I need to get some work done or Ken is going to be angry with me."

"And I need to get back to the station because I have a project I need to finish." Reg stepped back slightly but was still close enough that when the wind stilled, Arik could smell his heady, earthy scent. "Give me your phone a second." Arik pulled it out of his pocket, and Reg dialed and his phone rang. "We're all set. We have each other's numbers. I'll call you with the exact time."

Arik nodded, feeling a little speechless and slightly overwhelmed. "Okay." He'd been saying that a lot lately, but it was all that came to mind. "I'll see you tomorrow."

"And when Slasher has some word on your car, I'll let you know what we can do."

Arik nodded and stepped away from the truck. Reg got in and pulled away. As soon as he was out of sight, Arik bounced on his feet a few times and then bounded back to the garden house and right inside. With his energy, he wanted to work outside to take advantage of the light he still had. So he carried the small table outside, along with a chair, then laid out his supplies and got to work.

He had pretty much thought he'd go back to the idea of the garden scene that he'd tried to paint. He used a pencil and carefully sketched out the rough idea for the drawing, then shifted to the colored pencils. He didn't want to outline anything; the colors should flow from one to the other.

He lost himself in the work, creating the garden scene. After a while, Arik realized he was no longer drawing the scene in front of him, but his grandmother's garden. The house had disappeared from the picture altogether, with only flowers and a garden path showing. The technique he'd used with the pencil seemed to work with the colored pencil, but it was slow going. Arik really didn't notice until he began to lose the light. Then he groaned and began packing things up.

Once he had everything inside, he wandered over to the main house. He found Ken in his studio, standing in front of a canvas. Arik doubted Ken even realized he was there, his concentration was so complete. Arik jumped when Patrick touched his shoulder, but he kept quiet and followed him into the kitchen. "He gets like I used to when I was working."

Patrick nodded and reached for a pad. *Did you forget everything?*

"Yes. I'd stand with my paint and work for hours, letting it flow, the brush an extension of my hand and mind."

Is it like that with the pencils? Patrick wrote.

"No. I can use them, but I don't feel that same connection. Maybe it's because I want to paint again so badly that I don't want to use anything else."

Patrick stirred a large pot and then motioned toward a chair. Arik sat down, and Patrick took the chair next to him. *Sometimes we don't get to choose what we want. I used to sing opera.* He pushed the paper over so Arik could read it. When he got to the final sentence Arik's mouth fell open. *I will never sing again. I know that, but I spent two years wishing I could. The thing is, you may never be able to paint again. But you can't let that stop you.*

"I'm trying."

No. You're wallowing, Patrick wrote and met his gaze. *Stop feeling sorry for yourself and let yourself learn something new. I work with wood now, and I'm good at it. I have a family who loves me and cares for me above everyone else. That makes my life complete. I can't sing any longer, but my heart does each and every day. That makes everything worth it.* Patrick held Arik's gaze in his amazingly powerful eyes and then stood and went back to the pot on the stove.

"I'm going back to the garden house." He had the urge to work again.

PATRICK BROUGHT him dinner, setting a plate on the table next to where he was working. Arik thanked him and barely looked up. He'd abandoned the garden scene for now and was working strictly from his imagination. Reg stood in front of him, shirt off. He didn't have all the information, but that didn't stop his mind from filling in what he hadn't seen. His pencils flew over the paper, and he changed colors with an ease and urgency he'd never expected to feel again.

He ate, working between bites, and continued well into the night. Arik wished more than anything that he really had Reg here with him just so he could get him to take off his shirt. Granted, if that did happen and Reg seemed as eager as Arik hoped he was, maybe Reg wouldn't stop at just his shirt.

Arik began filling in the top of Reg's pants, just before they disappeared off the page, and dang if he didn't have the button open, Reg's warm skin showing just a little. He changed colors and began to fill in the hint of denim at the very bottom of the picture. His hand came to a stop, and he pulled away, staring at the half-completed image. Arik wasn't sure how late it had gotten, and he was getting tired. But he wanted to finish his work, so he continued on.

Arik sat down to look at what he'd done and woke later, his neck aching. He turned out the light and went to bed. He was asleep again almost as soon as his head hit the pillow.

ARIK SPENT the morning and afternoon immersed in his work. He finished the picture of Reg and kept it hidden because it was too private to show anyone, so as soon as he was done, he returned to the garden scene.

"Are you progressing?" Ken asked quietly as he approached across the lawn.

"Yes." Arik smiled and continued without stopping. He was motivated to finish.

"What's got you so driven?"

"Patrick," Arik answered, looking up from his work.

Ken nodded, and the contented heat on Ken's face told him all he could ever want to know. "Patrick is a special man."

"Yeah, he is. He tried to help me understand that I have to accept things the way they are, and he's right." Arik put down the pencil he was using. "I may never be able to paint the way I did before, and I have to move on."

"So what does this mean?" Ken pulled one of the lawn chairs closer and sat down.

"I guess it means that I need to find a new medium. I don't want to work with colored pencils all my life. So I need to search for something that speaks to me." He turned what he was working on so Ken could see it. "I need something that flows more seamlessly between colors, the way paint does, but it has to be something I can control. I like these, but there isn't enough fluidity."

"Then we'll find something." Ken smiled as he looked at what Arik had done. "This is gorgeous, though."

"It is, but you can see that the spark you saw in the work you bought isn't there."

"That's true. It's technically good, but…."

"I know. For now I need to work on technique because I'm going to have to develop something new." Arik inhaled. "Oh crap"— he pulled out his phone—"I forgot to call Reg. He's taking me to dinner." He tried to suppress a smile, but it couldn't be stopped.

"Go ahead." Ken sat back in his chair, soaking up some sun while Arik made his call.

"Are we still on for dinner?" Arik asked hopefully when Reg answered, his heart fluttering.

"I hope so," Reg said. "I have to work a little later than I expected. Derrick called and said he's going to be a little late. I was going to pick you up…."

"I wish I had my car. Then I could just meet you there."

"I can take you," Ken volunteered. "I have to take Hanna to a soccer game tonight, so I can drop you off on the way."

"Ken says he can drop me off, so we can go to dinner when Derrick gets there." Arik was so excited he could hardly sit still.

"I'll see you then," Arik said and hung up.

"Someone has a date," Ken teased with a grin, and Arik nodded, almost too happy to believe it.

CHAPTER
Four

REG WAS exceedingly glad he'd brought a change of clothes with him, just in case. Things tended to happen around the station that resulted in changes of plans, so he'd long ago gotten used to preparing for it.

"Derrick's going to be late?" Slasher asked as he slid out from under the Oldsmobile he was working on. Most of the cars in the area were old, and this one was almost a classic.

"Yes," Reg groused. "I understand, but dang it." He wanted to kick something.

"Did you forget about the club rally tonight?" Slasher asked, and Reg shifted his gaze to the blackened, beamed ceiling of the garage bay. "I thought so. It's one of the summer weekend camping trips. Some of the guys were going a day early to set up, and I think they were expecting you to join them."

"I never said...."

"You know Cross. He gets an idea in his head, and everyone is supposed to fall in line. The big control freak. It isn't that important. You can always go tomorrow."

"How?" Reg asked, standing over Slasher, looking down at his prone form. "You're going, and Derrick can't watch the station all weekend." No one else thought about things like that. It was one of the crappy parts about owning his own business. He had responsibilities that couldn't be shirked.

"I could...."

"No. You go like you planned. I didn't have you on the schedule, and you deserve the fun time." Reg tried not to fucking sigh, although he did want to kick something. He'd missed the last campout with the guys, and he had to stay behind for this one as well. "Is that car almost done?"

"Yeah. Give me half an hour. Then I'm going to start on that one." Slasher indicated Arik's. They'd managed to move it, but there was something majorly wrong with it, and they hadn't wanted to start it until Slasher had a chance to look at it more closely. "I should take a look at it so your friend will know what's wrong and how much it'll cost."

"Thanks. Once that's done, you might as well take off." That got Slasher moving, and he slid back under the car. Reg went back to work himself, listening for the ding of someone driving in while he took apart a bike and prepped it for paint. He wasn't going to do the actual painting until he had some quiet time, but prep could be done now.

Not that he got much done. He had a steady stream of customers all afternoon. Reg helped the ones who needed it. Even though the pumps were self-serve, there were some customers that he helped because they needed it, and they were all very loyal.

"Here's the list of what Arik's going to need," Slasher said. "Overall it isn't as bad as I thought. His fuel pump is shot and will need to be replaced, and we'll need to do some work on the front end. It got out of alignment a while ago, and it's gotten worse over time."

"So it wasn't one thing?"

"Nope. What I really think is happening is that the poor car is coming to one of those points where things start to go wrong because the car's wearing out. We could fix this and he'd be fine for a while. Or something else could go wrong next week. It's hard to know."

Reg looked at the list and began adding up the costs in his head. He'd need to have a more exact estimate, but the cost wasn't too much. At least to him. Maybe to Arik it would be a huge amount. He had no idea.

"Thanks. You might as well take off and have some fun. I'll see you tomorrow."

"Cool." Slasher put away his tools and locked everything up. Reg cleared away what he'd been working on before closing the overhead door. "I'll look after things out here while you change, and then I'll go."

Hopefully Derrick would be there in a few minutes, but Reg thanked Slasher and went into the restroom to put on nicer clothes and clean up well enough that he wasn't covered in grease smears. Heavy-duty soap worked wonders, and by the time he emerged, Derrick had arrived, sooner than expected. Reg said good-bye to Slasher and told Derrick what needed to be taken care of that evening.

Ken pulled up as he was finishing, and Arik got out of the car, an excited smile on his handsome face. "You really like that guy, don't you?" Derrick observed.

"Yeah. You have a problem with that?"

"No," Derrick said, but he obviously did from his tone. "I guess I never saw you actually looking at a guy like that before. I mean, I knew you were gay and all."

"It going to be a problem?"

"No. You're as cool as they come. It's just different actually seeing it." Derrick chuckled nervously. "And watching you looking at him like he was breakfast."

"Stop it," Reg said firmly.

"Come on. You're practically drooling. I mean, the guy is cute, if you go for that sort of thing." Derrick cringed. "I never said that, and if you say anything, I'll deny it." Derrick was beet red, so Reg decided to give him a break.

"My lips are sealed." Reg left the office to meet Arik, who had wandered over to his car.

"Is it really bad?" Arik asked worriedly.

"No. Slasher gave me the details a little while ago, and I haven't had a chance to work up the cost, but it isn't too bad." It could have been a lot worse given the problems the car seemed to have when Arik brought it in. "Are you ready to go to dinner?"

"Yes." Arik smiled slightly. "Are we taking your truck?"

"We can. It's a nice night. We could take the bike if you'd like to ride." The thought of Arik sitting close to him was exciting. "I have an extra helmet."

"Me. On a motorcycle?" Arik asked, looking down at his khaki pants.

"We can take the truck."

"If you promise you won't go too fast...," Arik continued.

Reg raised the garage doors and walked out his large touring bike. He closed the door and handed the extra black helmet to Arik, who looked it over.

"I was expecting skulls or something."

Reg laughed. "My fully detailed bike is at home, but no skulls. The first bike I customized was my own. I got it done and I sold it right away. One of the guys in the club offered me a lot of money for it. I bought this bike, but never got the chance to do anything with it because I'm always so busy with other guys' bikes. Someday I want to do something with it, but right now I don't have time in my schedule." Reg put on his own helmet and then helped Arik with his. He looked hot with his blond hair peeking out under the edge of the helmet.

Reg steadied the bike while Arik got on, then he mounted and started the engine. Once he was ready, he got into position and brought Arik's arms around his waist, tugging him closer. Then he released the clutch, and they began moving forward.

Reg turned onto the main road and drove toward town. This was going to be a short ride, and he wished it was going to be longer. He loved having Arik pressed to him. "Do you like it?" Reg yelled.

"Yeah," Arik answered, tightening his hold. "It's pretty awesome." Arik shifted closer to him, and Reg groaned into his helmet. Arik was excited, truly. There was no doubt about that. Reg felt plenty of evidence pressing against his ass and lower back. "Can we go faster?"

That was all the permission Reg needed. He turned at the light in town, and as soon as he passed the edge of town, he opened the bike up, letting them fly over the country roads.

"Jesus. It's like the engine is right under my balls," Arik said.

"It is, in a way," Reg yelled, hoping Arik could hear him. He drove for a few minutes and then slowed, turned around, and sped back to town. He slowed at the edge of town and drove to the restaurant. Reg waited for Arik to get off the bike and then parked it.

He dismounted and turned just in time to see Arik adjusting himself. Reg smiled as he followed Arik inside, noticing he was walking a little unsteadily.

"That was wonderful."

Reg placed his hand lightly on the base of Arik's back, guiding him to the hostess station. They both carried their helmets with them. "I'm glad you liked it." Reg slid his arm around Arik's waist, and they stood close together when the hostess approached.

He saw the first moments of her discomfort as they approached the podium. "We'd like a table for two. I called yesterday and made a reservation. The name is Thompson." He knew he was intimidating the hell out of her, and at that moment that was his goal. He wasn't going to put up with any comments or difficulty.

"Of course," she said and reached for menus. She walked briskly through the restaurant to a table against the side wall. After placing the menus on the table, she hurried back to her post. Reg paid no attention to her once she left. He waited for Arik to sit before he took his own seat.

"I wanted to bring you someplace nice," Reg told Arik. "I don't normally eat here."

"Where do you go when you eat out?"

"Marge's Diner or the coffee shop across the street. I'm not a fancy food kind of guy."

"Then why come here with me?" Arik asked.

Reg had asked himself the same question. "I wanted you to know that I thought you were special."

Arik smiled at him brightly enough to light the dimly lit dining room. The candle in the middle of the table flickered on the white tablecloth, and even in the low light, the china and silver glimmered. Crystal chandeliers glinted from the ceiling. The entire dining room glistened with elegance, and Reg felt more than a little out of place. He picked up the menu and began reading, wondering what the dishes were.

"I can't read most of this," Arik whispered. "Who puts a menu in French way out here?" He began to chuckle. "Talk about pretentious."

"I guess there's English descriptions," Reg said.

"Boeuf Bourguignon," Arik said. "I know what that is. Beef stew in red wine. That should be nice. There's also a quickie." Reg looked up from his menu. "That was Gran's joke. It's quiche."

"I'm going to get the chicken and a salad." He felt very out of his depth, but Arik seemed to be having fun decoding the menu.

"There's duck too," Arik said. "I've never had that before."

"What kind of food did you grow up on?" Reg asked.

"Blue-box macaroni and cheese. Mom always had it in the house, so I learned to make it when I was young, and I had a lot of it." Arik made a face. "That and Hamburger Helper. If it was cheap, Mom bought it, and I had to cook it if I wanted to eat."

"Where was she?" Reg asked.

Arik gazed down at the table. "My folks went out a lot." Their water glasses were filled, and Arik picked up his, drinking most of it right away. The glass was refilled, and then the man in a white coat left the table. "This place is really fancy."

"Are you uncomfortable?"

Arik shrugged and leaned over the table. "I don't want to do anything to make you unhappy or wish you hadn't brought me."

"Just relax and be yourself. I bet half the people in here are trying like hell to be on their best behavior. Is there anything that looks good on the menu?"

"Do you have any questions?" their server asked in a soft but richly deep voice. "I can recommend the coq au vin or the trout almandine. They are both spectacular tonight."

"I like fish," Arik said. "I think I'll have the trout."

The server talked him through the rest of his selections, and Reg decided on the beef with a salad. They both decided on water. Reg didn't think either of them was comfortable enough to try ordering wine, and Reg was driving anyhow… so water was best for him.

"I guess we made it through that trial," Reg quipped.

Arik grinned. "Do you ride bikes a lot?"

Reg nodded. "I like to. Of course, winter is impossible, so I have the truck for that time of year. The thing is, up here, where summer is rather short, I like to make the most of the time I can ride. I take it out whenever I can. I have saddlebags and even a really small trailer at home. It's big enough for a small tent and sleeping bags, so I can go camping with it. The club is going this weekend, but I have to stay and work."

"Can't someone watch the station for you?"

"Slasher is already going. When I first started working at the station, my uncle would watch it sometimes. It was his for years, and instead of leaving it to me when he died, he brought me in as a partner when he couldn't run it anymore, and we did things together. As he got older, he did less and I did more. It passed to me fully when he died."

"Is it doing well?"

"It's okay. Uncle Ron let things go because he couldn't do them any longer. So I've had to build up the business. The pumps were really old and I had to replace them. Then the bathrooms needed a lot of work." Reg made a face that said he was not going to describe that in detail at dinner. "At that point I started doing more. Next on the list is a lift. I'm hoping to get that next month. I want to have the place painted and brightened up."

"You know. The building is from the twenties or thirties. It's got those art deco details on the corners. You could come up with a color scheme that would highlight them, and then people would remember the place."

"I was going to paint it white."

"No. You should go with an off-white, and you could do deep blue and gold accents. You've got that chevron pattern up along the roofline—that could be brought out with color, and so could the doors. It would look amazing, and it wouldn't cost much more to do. Paint everything a base coat and then add the rest of the color once it dries. No one would be able to pass the station then. I bet you'd have tourists stopping to take pictures."

"Maybe," Reg hedged.

But the excitement in Arik's eyes was contagious. He practically bounced in his seat. "I bet the town has grant money for things like that. Especially since you'd be restoring a property to its former glory. Stuff like that helps the entire town, not just the business owner."

Reg chuckled as the server brought their salads.

"What's so funny?"

Reg waited until the server left. "You. Well, you're not funny, but you're happy and bouncy. I like that."

"It's been a long time since I've been bouncy about anything." Arik tucked into his salad, and Reg did the same, not watching the difficulty Arik had eating. The way he gripped his fork meant he spilled sometimes. It brought into relief how hard life must have been right after his injury and how hard Arik must have worked to get back the mobility he had.

"I was planning to go over to the children's home on Sunday. Derrick will come in for the afternoon, and I usually spend part of it there. I was wondering if you'd like to go since you were so good with the kids. They need more people to stop in and spend time with them."

"I'd like that," Arik said after swallowing. While Reg watched, Arik shifted his fork to this other hand, resting the injured one on his lap.

"You don't have to hide."

Arik glanced around. "The people behind you were staring at me," he whispered.

Reg whipped around. Sure enough, the older couple seemed to be watching Arik. Reg glared at them, growling under his breath. The woman squeaked and the man turned back to his dinner. "Manners, young man," she said.

Reg leaned closer to their table. "I think you need to take your own advice." He glared at her and then turned back to Arik.

"You didn't need to do that." Arik's face was red, and he looked down at his lap. "I need to get used to people staring. It happens all the time now, and it isn't going to stop. I had a lady stop me in the grocery store a few months ago and tell me all about her son who was burned. I know she meant well, but it was overwhelming. I don't want to be the object of pity."

"She was…."

"Not her. I can take people like her. I've dealt with them my entire life. I don't want pity from you."

"But… I was standing up for you."

"You don't have to. I don't need you to stand up for me. I just want you to like me."

Reg didn't know what the hell to say. "I said something because those people were disrespecting my date, and in case they and you haven't noticed, I'm here with the best-looking guy in the place. No pity. I don't feel sorry for people. I don't have the time or the patience for it." It was Reg's turn to lean over the table. "But I will stop anyone who makes you feel uncomfortable or self-conscious. That's part of who I am." Reg reached across the table and took Arik's hurt hand in his. "You are who you are, and I like the whole person."

"But you don't know me."

Reg shrugged. "And you know little about me. That's why we go out, to get to know each other." He couldn't help wondering why Arik was so tentative around him and others.

"I know that. It's just that people don't...." Arik paused. "It's nothing."

"They don't what?" Reg asked. "You can't start something like that and stop." He took a bite of his salad with the mustard vinaigrette and stifled a moan. Dang, that tasted good.

"Most people don't want to get to know me. When I was growing up in Ann Arbor, the other kids didn't come over to play. My mom didn't ever want strangers in the house, and my dad...." Arik shivered. "They were gone a lot, and when they were home, it wasn't very good. So none of the other parents wanted their kids to come over."

"It sounds like you weren't very happy." Reg had had his own rough upbringing, but he figured he couldn't expect Arik to open up if he wasn't willing to. "My parents worked hard all their lives. They gave me and my sister what they could." Reg finished his salad and put down his fork. "I had a sister, Marianne. She was the princess, but when she died suddenly at fifteen, my mom never recovered. She couldn't work any longer, and Dad was never home because he was working extra jobs. I worked in high school and barely graduated."

"You said you got the station from your uncle," Arik said.

"Yeah. My mom's brother took me in. I was flunking out of school, and my dad couldn't deal with me and my mom. So Uncle Ron and Uncle Jack took me in. I stayed with them through high school, and then I went right into the Army. My parents moved to Florida while I was deployed—sold the house and got out of town. Mom is doing better there without being surrounded by memories and things."

"Do you see them often?"

"Not really. I was closer to my uncles, and in some ways really lucky." Reg pulled out his wallet and took out a picture, then handed it to Arik. "This is Uncle Ron and Uncle Jack on Hilton Head that last summer." Reg swallowed. He didn't talk about this much. "I got a few weeks' leave and we all went down to have some fun. That's when they told me Uncle Jack had brain cancer and that treatment had been ruled out. They had decided to make the most of the time they had."

The server took their salad plates and brought the entrees, so the conversation died off for a while, which was fine with Reg. He hadn't talked much with anyone about his family history, not even with Slasher, who knew most of it. They just didn't talk about it.

Reg swallowed a bite of his beef, which was amazing, but suddenly the food didn't taste as good. "Neither of them wanted me to worry, so they didn't tell me until they had to." Reg wiped his mouth. "I was so angry at them."

"I know how you feel." Reg noticed that Arik had set down his fork and was rubbing his hand.

"Are you hurting?" Reg asked, and Arik stopped rubbing instantly and shook his head. "It took me a few days before I realized that the time at the beach might be all we had left. So I had to get over it."

"Was that the last time you saw him?"

"No. I got home six months later in time to say good-bye." Reg blinked and held his breath. Arik took another look at the photograph and handed it back. "I missed the funeral, but Uncle Ron had a memorial service when I came home again. Once my tour was up, he asked me not to reenlist and made me the offer on the station. He was the only real family I had left." Reg shrugged and went back to eating. The food didn't taste like much, but he didn't want to be a total downer. "Mom and Dad are still very involved with themselves. Mom is on a lot of medication and sometimes she doesn't remember me anymore. She has seizures that have wiped portions of her memory, so in her mind, she only had one child, who died."

Arik held his fork still, halfway to his mouth. "I'm sorry."

"I'm not. I had my uncles, and they were amazing parents. They loved each other so much. I also learned not to hide when I was with them. I kept quiet about who I was because the Army was still a pain in the ass, but once I was out of the service, I was out of the closet and happy… sort of. I had Uncle Ron, but he wasn't the same without his other half."

"I can imagine," Arik said. "Having the other half of yourself for a long time and then losing that and having to go on."

"I guess that's as good a description as any. Most of Uncle Ron's close friends understood, but a lot of people in town didn't. They thought of them as good friends and nothing more. My uncles played by the rules. They'd been together for more than thirty years, so they kept quiet, never showed any affection in public, worked, and gardened. They never caused waves and basically ignored it whenever anyone said anything mean or unkind."

"God. I can't imagine doing that."

Reg nodded slowly. "I can't either now. Though in the service I did plenty of it. I had to stay quiet and keep to myself. So that's what I did. My uncles were proud of me and of the man I became. Uncle Ron told me so once, and I wanted to believe him." Reg's throat constricted. "Sorry. I guess this wasn't the best conversation to have at our first dinner out together." Reg wiped his mouth and took a second to collect himself. He had never considered himself an emotional guy, but talking about his uncles made his heart ache. They'd been gone for some time, and he still missed them.

"Why did you tell me all this?" Arik asked. "I can tell you don't talk about it much."

"I figured if I told you something about me, then when the time came and you felt comfortable, you'd know you could tell me about you and what happened to you." Reg picked up his fork. "I know you aren't ready yet, but when you are, I'll listen."

"Thanks," Arik said, and they returned to their dinner.

"So what are you working on?" Reg asked to change the topic of conversation. He needed to talk about something lighter.

"I'm using the colored pencils. I have a garden scene in the works that I like. But I need something more than the pencils will allow me to do. They're very precise, and I can control them well, but I need something more flowing. Paint always gave me the freedom to let one color flow and mix into the other. I didn't do it all the time, but that freedom was there and it's gone now, at least with this medium. Realism works very well, but the expressionism I want isn't quite there, at least for me."

"All right. Have you tried acrylics?"

"Yes. Actually they're worse than oils because of how quickly they dry. What I need is something more forgiving."

"Then let's follow Ken's suggestion and try airbrushing. It's a completely different technique and one that could work for you. I have a couple sets in the paint area in the garage. Maybe you could come over on Sunday and we can go to the home to visit the kids, and afterwards you can spend some time learning to airbrush."

"I did it some when I was in school."

"Then it should be easy to get the technique back. You can see how it works for you now."

"Okay… let's give it a try." Arik's smile lit the room.

THEY FINISHED their dinners and Reg paid the bill, over Arik's objections. Then they put on their helmets and got back on the bike. Arik was much more relaxed this time, but he stayed as close as he had earlier. Reg loved the closeness and thought about making a number of wrong turns just so the ride would last longer than necessary. He loved Arik's hands around his waist, his chest pressed to Reg's back, and the way Arik rested his head lightly on his shoulder at the light. All of it made him want more than just a cycle ride.

Reg's entire body thrummed with energy and heat that only increased every second they were together. When he pulled into Ken and Patrick's drive, Reg waited while Arik got off the bike and handed him the extra helmet. Reg turned off the engine and secured both helmets before taking Arik's hand and walking him around the side of the house and out back. The door of the garden house loomed ahead like a huge, green The End sign.

He tugged Arik into the shadows and held him to him, soaking up the heat from Arik's chest.

"Reg, I...."

He gently stroked Arik's cheek and saw his eyes flutter closed. Reg took that as permission and leaned in, kissing Arik gently and then deepening the kiss when he couldn't hold back any longer. God in heaven, he wanted Arik so badly. He ached for a taste, and he took it. Parting Arik's lips, he surged forward, dueling with his tongue for just a second before pulling away. He held Arik closer, cupping his head in his hand.

Reg's heart pounded in his ears as it soared on eagle's wings. This was what he'd been waiting for all these years. Instantly he knew what his uncles had felt for each other and how they must have felt that first time they'd been able to be alone together, because he never wanted this to end, even as he broke the kiss and pulled away, looking deeply into Arik's magnificent eyes. He saw reflected back the unexpected joy that welled in his own heart.

"My uncles used to tell me that someday, when I least expected it, I'd meet someone special. They said it would be when I wasn't looking and would take me by surprise. I guess I never really thought about it. But I think they were right." Reg stepped back but refused to break the lock that held their gazes. The evening air had chilled, but Reg hardly noticed it. He was surrounded by a bubble of warmth. "Good night," he whispered and took a single step back, and then one more. Arik stayed where he was until Reg turned the corner of the house and couldn't see him any longer.

CHAPTER
Five

ARIK THREW himself into his work for the next two days. He finished the picture of Reg as well as the garden scene and even tried going back to brushes and paint, trying to transition some of the techniques he'd mastered to that medium. He was moderately successful, and once he'd done a few pieces, he could see that while his eye hadn't changed, his style of painting had definitely morphed. Maybe that was how it should be. He couldn't do the extremely fine detail work any longer, so he had to let the color and shading do more of the heavy lifting.

"That's really nice," Ken said as Arik worked out in the yard on Sunday morning.

"There isn't any of the—" He searched for the word.

"Spark... that the other had, but that isn't the point. You're working on basic technique."

Arik nodded and flexed his injured hand, setting down the brush. His entire hand ached something fierce, and Arik knew he'd overdone it. "Reg is going to be here soon, so I need to clean up."

"I'll help you," Ken said, and he began carrying things inside. Arik washed out his brushes and set aside his work to dry. Ken brought in the last of what Arik had dragged out into the garden, then said to him, "You're supposed to leave in a week."

"Yeah," he agreed, not sure he was ready to go. The invitation had been for that time period, but he was making such huge strides here.

"I was thinking that you could stay longer if you wish. We haven't had time to get to work on our project, and I don't want to rush you."

"I can't impose," Arik said even as his heart raced. He'd have to make some arrangements, but it wasn't like he had deep roots back in Pontiac. He'd brought along with him most of the things he had that were of any value. His biggest worry at the moment was how he was going to pay for having his car fixed. The bill was less than a thousand dollars, but that would pretty much wipe out the small amount of money he had in his savings account. Somehow he'd figure it out.

"You're not. Actually it's been good for me to have you here. Because you've taught me some things, especially about perseverance." Ken sat at the table. "My work has been stale for a while. I can see it and I certainly feel it. So I'm trying for something new, and I think you might have shown me the way."

"You're going to work in colored pencils?" Arik teased.

"No. But I've been doing the same kind of work for nearly a decade. Now I think I need to try something new. So I'm going to try to turn some of my works into sculptures. I want to add a third dimension. I haven't done it before, but I think I want to try. So I'm going to learn and develop a technique. I don't know if it will work, but...."

"I think it would be cool. Are you going to do Patrick and Hanna?"

"I don't know. I need to start simply and work my way up, but I'm excited about it. I love my work, but real, deep-down excitement, the kind that keeps you up at night—that's been missing for a while."

Arik finished washing the brushes and set them out to dry. "I wouldn't have noticed."

"I doubt anyone has, but it's how I feel. If we don't grow and change, we become stale." He stood. "I should let you get ready for your day with Reg."

"I have time." Talking like this with Ken was part of what he'd come here for. He wasn't going to lose that chance. He sat across from Ken.

"When I first met Patrick and with all we went through with Hanna, I was motivated, and my life was so churned up that it showed in my work. But I've been settled and happy for so very long that my work has settled along with it."

"I don't think that's bad. All of us can't go through our entire lives balanced on the edge of a knife just so we can make good art." He'd give anything to have the contentment and happiness that Ken had.

"And I don't want to be unhappy, just challenged." Ken stood once again, and this time he went to the door. "Have fun today. Patrick and I are taking Hanna for an outing this afternoon, so we won't be home until this evening. If you need anything, you can call my cell."

"I should be fine." He would be with Reg most of the time anyhow.

"Have a good time." Ken left, and as soon as the door closed, Arik rushed to get changed so he wouldn't be late when Reg came to pick him up. Arik undressed and jumped into the tiny shower. He thought about what it would be like to have Reg with him, water pouring over them while Reg held him tight, sliding against him. Arik's cock reacted right away, and he closed his eyes, letting his imagination take over. He stopped himself before he went too far. Reg was going to be here in a few minutes, and he could maybe have the real thing to hold as opposed to a fantasy.

Arik finished showering quickly, laughing at himself, because as small as this shower was, there was no way Reg would fit along with him. As soon as he was clean, he turned off the water, dried off, and dressed. He finished just as he heard a knock on the door. With a smile, he slipped on his shoes and pulled open the door.

His mother stood outside. Arik swallowed, his mouth dropping open in near total shock. "What are you doing here?" His throat went dry, and he instantly cradled his right arm in his left as a low, throbbing ache traveled down his arm with the speed of molten lead.

"I came because I had to see if you were all right." She wiped a crocodile tear from her eyes.

Arik had seen that act before, many times. "I meant what I said all those months ago." He straightened himself, pulling up to his full height. She was still taller than he was, but he wasn't going to let that intimidate him.

"Sweetheart...."

"How did you find me?"

"I called where you live, and the landlord told me you were here to study. It didn't take much work to find you after that. When I asked at the main house, I told them I was your mother, and they sent me back here."

Arik would have warned Patrick and Ken if he'd had any inkling his mother would try to find him. "And you came here because...? I don't have anything to give you," he added hastily. "I'm staying in a friend's garden house and my car is in the shop. The last of my money will go to try to get it fixed, and I have no idea how I'm going to live when I have to leave here." Arik swallowed and lifted his right arm. "I'm trying like hell to figure out how I can paint again and rebuild my life." He was nearly crying and shaking with anger at the same time. "So what is it you want?"

"Arik." Reg raced across the yard and stood next to him, filling the doorway. "Are you all right?"

"Reg, this is my mother, and she was just leaving." He vibrated from head to toe. Leave it to her to show up as he was beginning to rebuild some semblance of his life. "I suggest you go back to Dad and the two of you have a good, smoke-filled, drug-hazy life." Arik stepped back inside and closed the door. It took him two seconds before he realized he'd left Reg outside too, but he wasn't going to spend another second with her. "Is she gone?" Arik asked when Reg came inside.

"She's leaving," Reg answered. "Are you okay?" he asked and turned toward the door. Arik followed his gaze and saw his mother walking through the yard toward the front of the house.

"No," Arik answered honestly, still shaken from the unexpected visit. "I will be once she goes back to where she came from." He clenched his fists, his injured hand aching once again. He had thought his mother and father were out of his life. There had been months of silence between them, and then she turned up again like a bad penny, a counterfeit mother as useful as fake money with equal potential to cause pain and suffering.

"Can we go now?" Arik asked.

Reg hesitated and then nodded. "If you want."

Arik wound his arms around Reg's waist and pressed against him, resting his head on his shoulder. All he wanted to do was hide. But that wouldn't do him any good. His mother knew where to find him, so short of leaving, he was stuck with whatever crap she wanted to fling his way. "I don't want to move."

Reg stroked his head. "Do you want to talk about it?"

Arik shook his head and stood still. It was nice to be comforted for a change. "We should go." Or he was going to chicken out and end up staying here for the rest of the day.

"All right." Reg tightened his hug. "We can go whenever you're ready."

Eventually Arik stepped away. "Did you bring the bike?"

Reg smiled. "I take it you like riding?"

"With you, yeah." It was exciting and felt kind of decadent, given the way he got to hold Reg. "Did you bring it?"

"You'll see," Reg said with a grin.

Arik got a jacket and carried it with him as they left. He rounded the corner of the house, half expecting his mother to be waiting for him, but she was gone. That alone added a spring in his step, but then he saw the large black motorcycle with the extra helmet attached to the back.

"Let's go. I want to feel free." He needed that so much right now.

"Then put on the helmet and let's go. They're expecting us at the children's home in an hour. Until then we can ride as much as you like." Reg grabbed his helmet and slid it on his head.

Arik did the same and climbed on the bike behind Reg, holding on tight. "Kick it," Arik said.

Reg took off, riding down the residential street and out of town, where he opened up and they soared over the country roads.

"That's Connor's farm," Arik said as they zoomed past ten minutes later.

Reg nodded and made a turn, heading through the country until they reached the lake. He pulled off onto the beach road, and they roared near the water, the crash of the waves adding to the power that thrummed through Arik. He pressed closer to Reg, his erection bursting in his pants, and it felt good pressed in the warmth between them, the engine roaring under them. Arik's mind began to cloud as lust and desire built and warred inside him. He wanted Reg in the worst way, but even with Reg being nice to him and having kissed him and all, he still couldn't see why he'd want anything from Arik other than some fun.

Reg pulled the bike to a stop right near the beach at a wide point in the road. "What's got you thinking so hard?" Reg asked, turning around. "I can feel the tension rolling off you."

"It's nothing," Arik lied and leaned closer to Reg as they looked out at Lake Superior, water as far as they could see.

"I know that's not true," Reg said.

Arik could tell Reg was a little hurt that he wasn't being forthcoming, but Arik wasn't ready to bare his family history... not yet.

"But you don't want to talk about it," Reg said.

"It's a great day, and I don't want to spoil it." Arik forced a smile and got off the bike, then went to stand at the very edge of the beach, watching the water that in places seemed blue and in others as deep and gray as the abyss that Arik sometimes expected to open and swallow him whole.

"You can't," Reg said, slipping his arms around Arik's waist, pressing to his back, surrounding him with warmth against the cold wind from the lake. "I used to come out here all the time and just watch the water. My uncles always knew where to find me. The lake gave me a place to think."

Arik looked up at Reg. "I suppose." He turned back to the water, watching the waves crash against the shore.

"There's a storm out there somewhere," Reg said. "That's what makes the waves so fierce. It can be just off the horizon, but we still get the effects here."

Arik nodded, still watching. In so many ways his life felt like the lake: dark, mysterious, with hidden depths that he didn't understand. He understood the storms just off the horizon. He had long thought that he should have learned how to see them coming, but so many things still took him by surprise. With his parents, Arik should have been ready for anything at any time. He'd become a very independent child and had done his best to avoid his family's mistakes in his own life. "Why can't I get away from them?" he said out loud. He hadn't meant to and hoped he'd actually uttered the words softly enough that the wind and water would drown them out.

"Is that what you really want?"

Arik sighed and, realizing Reg had indeed heard him, simply nodded and pursed his lips together.

"If you could have anything at all, what would it be?" Reg asked.

Arik stilled and thought and let a scene develop in his mind. He was in a cabin, rustic and warm, a fire in the room. He didn't see himself there, more like he felt the warmth and quiet all around him. As he stood, watching, a brush in hand, strong arms wrapped around his waist, adding additional warmth. Arik began to paint, his mind filling with energetic images that slowly turned amorous. The man behind him seemed to read his mind because the unseen figure gently took the brush away from his now-perfect right hand, and then Arik was lifted off his feet and carried to the sofa.

"You can see it, can't you?" Reg whispered in his ear, and Arik nodded. "What is it?"

He blinked, reluctant to let the fantasy go, especially when it was getting really good. "I want to be safe and warm." He wished he could reach out and touch that image. "I want to paint it," he whispered.

"Will the image dissolve, or can you hold on to it?"

Arik leaned back into Reg's solidity and heat. "I think it's going to stick around for a while." He certainly hoped so.

"Is this really about the image in your head?" Reg whispered, his hot breath caressing Arik's ear.

Arik turned slowly, meeting Reg's gaze. "I don't know."

Reg growled and pulled him close, locking his arms behind him and splaying his hands firmly on Arik's back. "Maybe this will help you decide."

The kiss curled Arik's toes—deep, hard, possessive. He held on to Reg's arms for a second and then slipped his hands around Reg's neck, returning a kiss he could easily get lost in.

"Did that help?"

"Maybe," Arik smirked.

"Maybe." Reg mugged slightly. "You mean you need more information to make up your mind?"

"Yeah. I need more data to make a proper decision." Arik would have giggled at saying such a thing, but Reg closed the distance between them again, this time sliding one of his hands down to cup Arik's butt. Arik groaned and pressed closer, hips thrusting slightly. Reg lifted him off his feet, and Arik wound his legs around Reg's hips, locking his feet and wishing they were in his fantasy place—safe, warm, naked, in front of a fire on thick bedding where Reg could bury himself inside and drive him to the pinnacle of forgetful happiness. He pressed his hips to Reg, grinding shamelessly against him.

"Sweetheart," Reg crooned into his ear. "Damn, I guess you got what you needed."

Arik pulled away and immediately blushed. "I'm sorry." He slowly climbed down off Reg and stood back on the ground, blinking a few times to reorient himself to where he was. "I was gone for a while. Lost in a fantasy that…."

"Hey. Whatever fantasy you were in, I liked it, and maybe we can go there a little later, but"—Reg turned as a car whizzed past them—"doing this out in the open is not the best idea."

"Oh God," Arik breathed. "Maybe we should go." He inhaled deeply and turned back to the lake, opening his jacket, letting the cold wind rush closer to his skin. He needed the bracing chill to help pull him back. "Sometimes the images of what I feel become so real and overpowering that I forget where I am, and…." It was so hard to explain. "It doesn't happen very often, but sometimes I get so carried away…." What he really wanted to do was go back to the house and paint. But a throb from his hand brought him back to reality like a clap of thunder.

He walked back to the bike and put his helmet on. Reg joined him, and he climbed on the bike after Reg, holding him as they made their way back to Pleasanton. This time he just rode. There was no excitement or energy in it. When they pulled up in front of the children's home, Arik mustered up some energy. These kids deserved more than to have him mope around while he was there. He took off the helmet and waited for Reg before following him inside.

"Mr. Reg!" Bobbie Jo cried and raced down the hallway, jumping into Reg's arms. She was all smiles and laughter. "You came back." She hugged him, and Arik watched the two of them.

"I told you I would," Reg said.

Bobbie Jo nodded solemnly. "People don't always do what they say they will." She crossed her little arms over her chest, glaring at Reg while he held her. The scene would have been adorable if she hadn't been so earnest.

"That's true, but Mr. Reg always tries to keep his promises," Arik said. "And I promised I'd come back so we can make more pictures."

"Hi, Maggie," Reg said as a woman approached them.

"I have the activity room all set up for you," she said, looking at Arik. "The kids had an amazing time when you were here last." She smiled at him, and some of Arik's funk lifted. He knew all of this was inside his head and he needed to let it go.

"That's great." He turned to Bobbie Jo. "Do you want Mr. Reg to draw with us?"

"Yes!" she answered happily and squirmed to get down. When Reg set her on her feet, she took his hand and began leading him down the hall.

"She has him wrapped around her little finger," Maggie said.

"Can I ask why she's here? I mean, she's so cute. I'm surprised she hasn't been adopted."

Maggie sighed. "Most people look at her and only see her hand. She's scheduled for another surgery that will fix her last two fingers. At least for now. The doctors are afraid that her hand might not grow right as she gets older and that more surgery will be required. We hope not, but we don't know. Most people are afraid to take on that uncertainty. And they want babies."

Arik looked at his own hand and nodded. "It's not right." Laughter filtered in from the other room. "I should get going so I can train the artists of tomorrow." He smiled and walked to the room where Bobbie Jo and Reg had disappeared. Maggie had set out paper and art supplies. Arik passed some over to Bobbie Jo. "Do you want to draw a picture of Mr. Reg?"

Bobbie Jo nodded and got to work. "Will you do one too?" Bobbie Jo asked, handing a crayon to Reg.

"I will if Mr. Arik will."

Of course Bobbie Jo looked at him with huge puppy dog eyes and there was no way he could refuse. Not that he would have for a second.

"I brought some more artists for you," Maggie said, holding the hands of two little boys Arik remembered from last time. "This is Colin and Joey."

"Come on in and sit down."

"What are we going to make today?" the older of the two, Colin, asked as he rushed to a chair, the other boy following.

"We're drawing pictures of Mr. Reg," Bobbie Jo said.

"You can draw whatever you like, and in a while I thought we'd make flowers that you can put on the windows in your rooms," Arik said.

"I wanna make Batman for my room," Joey piped up.

"Superman," Colin added, putting his hands in the air.

"How about you draw Superman, and you draw a picture of Batman. Say, do you think Reg here could be either of them in a movie?" Arik smiled at Reg's mock grumpy expression.

The boys looked at each other and then grinned and shook their heads. "He looks too mean," Colin said.

"He could be the Joker," Joey offered, and both boys nodded. "I'm gonna draw Mr. Reg as the Joker." Joey grabbed a box of crayons and began drawing, head down, tongue between his teeth as he concentrated on the important task ahead of him.

Colin didn't seem as convinced. "Draw Superman," Arik said, lightly touching his shoulder. Colin nodded and solemnly got to work. He didn't have any of the energy Joey did and remained quiet for the next half hour while Bobbie Jo and Joey both chattered away. "That's very good," Arik said, looking at Colin's drawing. There was detail and even perspective in what he'd drawn.

Colin looked up for a second and then went right back to work. Arik turned to Reg for some guidance. He could see so much of himself in Colin. There was definitely talent, but the pain in the little boy's eyes was almost too much for Arik to bear. It reminded him of his own hurt and how he'd been at Colin's age. Arik stood up from the low table and walked around to where the others that had joined them were all drawing and having a good time.

"I'll be right back," Arik said softly and left the room. Maggie met him in the hall.

"What happened?" she asked right away and stuck her head in the room. When she turned back to him, he saw nothing but confusion. "Are you all right?"

Arik nodded. "I will be."

"Sometimes this can be a rather sad place for folks."

"That's just it. I was wondering if I wouldn't have been better off if I'd been raised here."

Maggie's eyes softened. "Oh, honey. We do the best we can for all the children in our care. And we love them all in their own way, but every child is better off with a family of their own."

"Not me," Arik said.

"Honey. You have to let it go. Not all our kids will be adopted. Though we try to find homes for all of them, some have spent much of their lives either here or in the county home. When kids graduate out of the system, we try to help them build their own lives. And it's not easy for them because the only support system they had is gone, and it was relatively artificial. At least you had a family who cared about you."

Arik shook his head. "I wish I had."

"Mr. Arik." Joey hurried out to him, a paper waving behind him. "This is Mr. Reg as Batman." Arik knelt down and took the paper. He could barely make out anything other than a figure on the page, but Joey looked so proud.

"That's awesome. Why don't you sign it like an artist, and I bet Maggie will help you put it up in your room?"

Joey shook his head. "It's for you." He hurried away, leaving Arik staring at the newest addition to his art collection.

"They're all such wonderful children," Maggie said, wiping her eyes. "There are days when I want to take all of them home with me. My husband Jack told me once that he figured we should just move into the home here and adopt them all. That way he'd know I'd be happy." She sighed. "We're hopeful that Joey will be adopted soon. There's a family who has visited him a number of times, and the director, Gert, and I pray they want to give him a home."

"I hope so," Arik said and turned to where all the kids were climbing on Reg. "I better go rescue him from the hordes."

"Call if you need anything, and I'll check back soon. The older kids are going to a baseball game this afternoon." She grinned. "Jerry, one of our adoptees, arranged it."

"Connor's son? I met him the other day."

"He's an amazing young man," Maggie said and hurried down the hall. Arik went back inside the room and got the kids settled around the table once more. This time he demonstrated how to make flowers. He drew the outlines for them and then had the kids color them in. They had a lot of fun, and once Arik and Reg cut them out and they'd all made stems and leaves together, the kids had brightly colored decorations for their rooms.

"Those are so pretty," an older lady said as she came in.

"This is for you, Mrs. Gert," Colin said, handing it to her. She took the flower as though it was the most precious gift she'd ever received, hugging him gently.

"Can you thank Mr. Arik and Mr. Reg for coming in to do art projects with you?" Gert said. A chorus of thank-yous followed as Gert helped escort the kids out of the room, and Arik began cleaning up.

Bobbie Jo stayed behind, standing close beside him. "Will you come have a tea party with me?" she asked Reg, her pretty eyes as huge as saucers.

"Mr. Arik and I have to go, but we'll be back again, and when we come we'll have a tea party," Reg told her.

Bobbie Jo stuck out her lower lip, and her eyes darkened slightly. She turned to Reg and buried her face in his shirt. Arik knew she was likely crying or trying her best not to cry.

"Honey, I'm sorry, but we do have to go."

"I know," she said, her voice muffled. "Everyone has to go." She stood up straight. "It's because I'm not pretty. That's what Kyle said yesterday outside. He said I wasn't adopted because I wasn't pretty, and that no one was going to want me with my ugly hand." She stuck her hand behind her back.

"Your hand is just fine," Arik said, hurrying over to her before he could stop himself. "See? I have a hurt hand too, and it's okay. They make us special, and only the most special people are the ones who understand." Bobbie Jo wiped her eyes, and Arik found he was doing the same. "And you are pretty. You're the cutest, prettiest little girl I've ever seen. So next time Kyle says something, you walk away from him because you know better."

Arik looked at Reg, his heart aching.

"Where's your tea set?" Reg asked.

"In my room. I got it for my birthday."

"Then go get it, and we'll have a tea party right now," Arik said. Bobbie Jo raced out of the room, and Arik sat back down, holding his head in his hands, trying not to fall to pieces. "I can't tell her no."

"Hey. It's all right. I was only interested in getting the airbrushing tools so we could work. If you want to stay here, we can do that." Reg held him. "I didn't know."

"I didn't know how these kids would affect me."

"They touch me too."

"I got it, Mr. Reg," Bobbie Jo said, returning with an unopened box containing a plastic teapot and four cups and saucers.

"I came to see if—" Maggie said, entering the room. Arik looked at her, and she held up her hand and backed out again.

Reg opened the package and helped Bobbie Jo set out tea for three. "You'll have to show us the proper way to have tea," Reg said, and Bobbie Jo set them each a place, putting a plate in the center of the table for imaginary cookies. Reg was patient with her, helping her set everything just the way she wanted. Each of his touches was incredibly gentle and caring. It was clear that Bobbie Jo adored him. Arik wondered how he could ever have been afraid of Reg.

"Mr. Arik," Bobbie Jo said, pulling his attention from his thoughts. "You're supposed to put your pinkie out like this," she instructed, and Arik did his best. He noticed she had a little trouble doing it, but he did his best to imitate her, his own pinkie only cooperating so much. She seemed happy, and they drank imaginary tea for fifteen minutes.

"Bobbie Jo," Maggie said. "It's time for you to have a snack, and then we're going to the park."

Bobbie Jo immediately began gathering up the dishes and putting them back in their slots in the box.

"We'll come back to see you soon," Reg said. Bobbie Jo smiled and turned to him, setting her dishes carefully on the table, as though they were made of the finest china. Then she hugged him tight. "Good-bye, sweetheart," he said, and Bobbie Jo kissed him on the cheek, a big smackery one that sent her into a fit of giggles. "Go give Mr. Arik a hug too."

She rushed over, and Arik got a hug as well, along with a loud kiss. He hugged her back, closing his eyes as he sent his best wishes for her out into the universe. Once he released her, he helped her pack up the tea set. Then she said good-bye and carried it out of the room. Arik watched her go and blinked a few times.

"I wish I could help them all," Reg said.

Arik agreed with him and got up. "We should go. This place…."

"I know. It can be sad sometimes."

Arik shook his head and started putting away the supplies they'd used for their projects. "It's more than that. I know these kids don't have families, but the people here care about them." That was more than he'd had most of the time. He truly believed what he'd told Maggie, that he'd have been better off in a place like this than he had been in his own home, especially after Gran died.

"They do, but it isn't the same."

Arik took a deep breath. "Yeah. But what if it's better than the alternative?"

Reg didn't seem to understand how to take his remark, and that was okay. To be truthful, Arik wasn't sure what he was feeling at the moment. His emotions were all jumbled up, and he swung from hurt to anger like a pendulum. "Let's go. We can get a late lunch, and then we can head to the paint room. I bought some canvases and things for you to work with. There's also some boards and things you can use to get the hang of things."

"You did all that for me?" Arik asked.

"Yeah," Reg said as though it were nothing, leading the way out of the room and toward the front door. They waved to Maggie, who waved back before entering the dining area, where the snacks must have been put out. The sound from in there was deafening, but happy with laughter.

Arik pushed his way out into the afternoon sun and began getting ready to ride. He wasn't in the mood to talk, and Reg thankfully sensed that and didn't press him. He climbed on to the motorcycle behind Reg and held on tight. He wasn't sure if it was to keep from falling off the cycle or to stop himself from falling apart.

Reg drove fast, and less than five minutes later, they pulled up to the closed filling station.

"Thank you," Arik said as he got off the bike.

"I can get us something to eat," Reg offered. "I thought with as quiet as you've been that maybe you needed to work. I can take you home if you like."

"No." The real problem was that yes, he needed to work, but he didn't know how he was going to do that. Everything was as jumbled and stopped up as it had been when he'd first arrived. "Can we start?" His hands itched. Reg locked up the bike and took care of the helmets. Then he unlocked the station and led Arik through to the paint room.

"Give me a few minutes to get things set up." Reg set about getting the airbrushes ready. "You probably already know the limitations. You can only use one color at a time."

"Yeah. And there's limited drying time."

"Do you know what you want to do?" Reg asked.

"I think so." Arik used one of the boards to test out the brushes.

"I'm going to leave you alone and go get us something to eat. I won't be gone long, and you can't hurt anything in here, so just have fun."

"I'll try," Arik said, smiling at Reg, watching as he left and listening for the fading sound of the motorcycle. Then he turned back to the sample board and stared at it. Color lay on top of color, splotches with no particular pattern or reason. They were just there. Arik stared at them, letting them morph together in his mind, rearranging them in his head until they came together just the way he wanted them. Without thinking, Arik used the airbrush to bring his vision to life.

Time slipped away, and he didn't stop working, changing out color after color as quickly as he could. The bang of a door brought him back to reality.

"I'm sorry it took so long," Reg said. Arik checked the clock on the wall. He'd completely lost track of time. "Can I see what—" Reg's words fell away, and Arik followed his line of sight back to his work. "Did you just do that?"

"Yeah. I was just playing around, but… I think I like it," Arik said, putting the airbrushes down on the nearby bench.

"Wow, is that how you feel right now? It's chaotic and jumbled, but there's an order to it that binds it together somehow. I wonder what Ken would say about it."

"I'm calling it artistic constipation," Arik said. He meant to be flip, but that was exactly what it was. "I'm all bottled up inside, and I don't think I know who I am anymore." He stared at the result of his artistic tantrum and figured he'd set it aside. Maybe he'd see what Reg saw in it eventually. But right now, it was like seeing his own confusion staring back at him.

"Come and eat. Then you can go back to work," Reg said, and Arik nodded, following him out of the paint room. They went through the garage work area and into the office, where Reg had laid out napkins and sandwiches. "I got you egg salad. I hope that's okay? If not, you can have the chicken salad one. Just take your pick."

Arik sat at the counter and began to eat the egg salad. He hadn't realized how hungry he was until he took that first bite. Then he was starved, downing the rest of the sandwich with a speed that suggested he hadn't eaten in days. "Get what you'd like to drink," Reg told him, motioning to the Coke cooler. Arik got a Diet Coke and one for Reg before returning to his sandwich with a vengeance.

"I bet you're feeling better now," Reg said, stroking his arm. "You need to eat better."

"I eat."

"What did you have for breakfast? It's nearly two now."

"I ate." Arik protested but Reg fixed him with a glare. "I had some potatoes."

Reg held his gaze. "Let me guess. You had a handful of potato chips and then went right out into the garden to work." Arik set down what was left of his sandwich. "Don't act surprised. I know you because I act the same way, working when the spirit is on me until I'm ready to fall over."

"I guess no one has ever bothered to care before."

Reg reached across the counter, lightly touching the underside of Arik's chin. "I care." He leaned over the counter, kissing him. Arik closed his eyes and leaned into the kiss, letting it happen. He wanted to believe that things would get better and that what Reg told him he felt was real. The warmth of his eyes and the heat in his kiss made him want to believe so very much. Arik wound his hand over Reg's bald head. He deepened the kiss, finally giving himself over to Reg. That kiss, the intensity, the heat and desire that it raised in him were no illusion.

"You do," Arik said. "I believe it, and I care about you too."

Reg smiled against his lips and then kissed him harder, curling Arik's toes. He loved the way Reg took command of his lips and mouth. He'd been afraid of not being in control, but this was a gentle surrender, one he hoped was safe.

"We should finish eating," Reg said, pulling back with a wide grin.

Arik nodded slowly and picked up the last of his sandwich. He blinked a few times to clear his head. "Yes, we should, and then you and I are going to have some fun with airbrushes." Arik smiled and took the last bite.

"What do you want to do?" Reg asked as he finished his lunch and wadded up the paper into a ball.

"I'm not sure. This really isn't my medium. What I did before was sort of from my gut, and I don't know if I can get back there." He was too excited… and more than a little turned on.

"You have to do what's in your heart," Reg said.

Arik giggled like a kid. "Well, things are sort of feeling naughty right now," he explained. Reg raised his eyebrows. "It's all your fault… with your incredible toe-curling kissy lips. How can I think of anything else?"

"Do you want to pack up the airbrush set and take it back to Ken's? We can do other things this afternoon." The insinuation was there. Arik could have what he wanted. All he had to do was nod.

"Okay," he answered breathlessly, feeling his cheeks heat. "They said they'd be gone, but we can sit in the garden, or…." He gulped, unable to say the words about what they could actually do. "How are we going to get all the stuff back? It isn't like it'll fit on your bike."

"True. I can bring it over later when I've got the truck." Reg threw away the trash. "Come on. I know you're itching to get to work, and it isn't with airbrushes. You've been jumpy, and what was the term you used? Artistically constipated." Reg chuckled. "Let's see if we can change that."

Arik made sure that everything was cleaned and put away. Once they were done, Reg locked up, and they rode to Ken's. This time Arik felt more settled and less jumpy.

The yard was quiet and the house closed up when they arrived. Not that Arik expected anything different. "You should put the bike under the overhang near the house," Arik said, looking up at the sky. "They weren't calling for rain, but the clouds are getting thicker, so you never know."

"One of the joys of living on the lake—sunny one minute and cloudy the next." Reg walked the bike close to the house. There was a large overhang on one side of the garage. Reg left his bike there, and they walked through the yard and out to the garden house.

"I keep expecting my mother to show up again."

"Did you find out why she came?"

Arik shook his head. "I didn't give her the chance." He felt a little guilty about that, but she should have known he wasn't going to give her the time of day. As far as he was concerned, he and his mother had said all there was to say to each other.

"Do you think you should have?" Reg asked.

"Would you give your mom another chance if she showed up on your doorstep?" Arik retorted with more heat and vitriol than he intended.

"My mom is mentally ill. She'll never get better, and my dad takes care of her. It isn't like she has a choice in how she feels or what she remembers."

"I didn't mean it like it sounded." Arik sighed. "I have a lot of anger and unresolved issues when it comes to my mother. She and my dad pretty much ignored me for years. I grew up on my own with only my grandmother who really cared. More than once she threatened to take me away from my parents, but she was in her late seventies. I used to hope she would, but now I know that I'd have ended up in the foster care system because of Gran's age. So I suspect she did what she could for me, and everyone hoped for the best." Arik unlocked the door and went inside, waiting for Reg.

"What if your mother has changed?" Reg asked.

Arik had asked himself the same thing. "I don't know if I care."

"Damn, that's cold," Reg said.

Arik ignored the comment. He knew it might appear that way, but he couldn't bring himself to feel any differently, not after all that had happened. "It may seem that way," he finally answered, after Reg's comment gnawed at him. "But it's an improvement for me." He closed his eyes and ignored the phantom ache that raced through his hand and jumped slightly when Reg touched it.

"You carry your pain and worry here, don't you?" He slowly rubbed the mottled skin of Arik's hand.

Arik closed his eyes and tried like hell not to shiver. Other than the doctors, very few people touched his hand, and Arik wasn't used to it. Sometimes when others touched his hand, it tickled or he had the sensation of mild pinpricks. His nerves were all over the place, some ultrasensitive while others barely registered at all.

"Do you have some lotion?" Reg asked.

"In the bathroom," Arik answered.

"Sit down and get comfortable. I'll be right back." Reg took the few steps to the bathroom as Arik sat on the sofa. When Reg returned, he sat right next to him and reached for Arik's hand once more. "Lay it on my leg," he said gently and splopped some lotion onto his hand. Then he began rubbing it into Arik's hand, slow and gentle, massaging each finger along with his thumb.

Arik sighed loud and long and closed his eyes, his entire body decompressing like he'd just stepped out from under a mountain of stone pressing down on him. "Dang."

"I knew it. Whenever you get tense or nervous, you rub your hand. You try to hide it, but I've watched you."

"I feel it there first now. When I get excited, the blood rushes and my hand throbs and aches."

Reg continued his slow, methodical movements as he moved closer. "Does that happen only when you worry, or when the excitement and heart pounding is for a very different reason?" Reg continued coming closer. Arik felt his breath on his lips. He kept his eyes closed, soaking in the attention on his fire-ravaged hand.

When Reg's lips touched his, Arik almost pulled away as heat shot through him, the warmth settling in his hand first and then zinging south. He groaned into the kiss and would have hugged Reg tighter, but the gentle caresses continued to his hand, and he didn't want to stop them.

"Dang," he moaned, afraid to move, not wanting either amazing sensation to end. Reg pressed him back against the cushions and released his hand, wrapping Arik in his strong arms.

"Well, do you feel it in your hand first?" Reg rasped when he pulled back.

"I did, but not the same way. Now I most definitely feel it someplace else." Arik wrapped his arms around Reg's neck, holding on while Reg slid a knee between his legs, parting them.

His pants were way too damned tight, and his cock throbbed like there was no tomorrow. Reg slid his hand down Arik's chest and then along his hips and the side of his leg. Arik's breath hitched, and he silently hoped to all that was holy that Reg didn't stop there.

"You know I want to be with you," Arik whispered. He lolled his head back when Reg released his lips and licked along his jaw and tickled his tongue over his throat. Shivers raced through him, and he thrust his hips forward, rutting against Reg's leg.

Arik was breathing hard and halfway to release when Reg pulled away. His eyes flew open and he sat up, wondering what he'd done wrong. Just when he was willing to trust someone again, they pulled away. Arik tried to hide how much Reg had affected him and sat up straight. "I guess we were moving too fast?" God, he hoped that was it.

"No," Reg said. He leaned over him, scooping him off the sofa. "I thought we'd be much more comfortable in your bed rather than making out on the sofa like teenagers. I don't know about you, but I'm a little old for that, and my back needs something more comfortable."

"Oh," Arik said, and then he giggled. "I'm perfectly capable of walking." He tried his best to appear stern, but he probably came off looking ridiculous and gave up. Not that Reg had far to carry him.

Once Reg put him on the bed, Arik scooted up to the head and crossed his arms over his chest.

"What's that for?" Reg asked.

"I don't want to miss anything," Arik said, raising his eyebrows. "And I mean *anything*." When Reg didn't move, Arik got onto his knees and began undoing the buttons on Reg's shirt. "Wow," he whispered when he got the fabric open. Once it parted, Reg did the rest until he stood in front of him, a shirtless, tattooed buffet, big enough that Arik didn't know where to start.

"Like what you see?"

"Yeah. This...." Arik's mouth went completely dry. He ran his hand lightly over Reg's chest, ripped muscle dancing beneath his touch. "It's even better than I imagined."

"You thought about me without my shirt on?" Reg had to be teasing, but Arik went with it.

"Actually I thought about you with a lot less than that." He grinned and watched as Reg's blue eyes darkened to deep sapphire. "I might even have put my fantasies down on paper." *Take that, Mr. Hot Smugness.* "I will admit I didn't get the tattoos right because I didn't know about this one." He traced the design on Reg's right pectoral. "What does it mean?"

"Peace," Reg answered.

Arik traced the intricate symbol with the very tips of his fingers. "I like that," Arik whispered and tilted his head upward. Reg drew him close, kissing him hard and fast, overwhelming Arik with sheer power. Reg tugged at his shirt, pulling it over Arik's head and off his body.

"Damn, you're pretty," Reg growled and licked down his chest, then sucked on a nipple. He was gentle at first, but with each of Arik's moans, Reg increased his suction, scraping the skin with his teeth as Arik shook like a leaf in a gale. "Wow."

"What?" Arik gasped.

"You're so responsive. Are you like this with everyone you're with?"

Arik swallowed hard. "You make it sound like there's a revolving door on my bedroom. I haven't been with anyone since…." Arik slipped his hand under one of the pillows.

"Don't," Reg snapped. "No hiding from me. I've seen your hand, and I've touched it, rubbed it. I know what it looks and feels like, both in my hand and against my skin. It's part of you, nothing more or less."

Arik pulled his hand out, and Reg cradled it in his and brought it to his lips. "You don't…."

"It's part of you," Reg repeated in a whisper, and then he set Arik's arm and hand on the bedding before slipping his fingers along the waistband of Arik's pants, tugging open the belt and then the catch. Arik hadn't expected things to happen this quickly, but within a minute his shoes hit the floor and the rest of his clothes followed. He didn't have time to be self-conscious before Reg wrapped one of his big hands around his shaft, pumping and stroking to Arik's delight.

"I…." Oh God, he needed more air, and he gasped as Reg opened his mouth and sucked the head of Arik's cock between his lips. Arik's head throbbed and his leg shook even as Reg took more and more of him. "Reg…." He gasped and wet his lips when Reg sucked all of him, swallowing around his cock, and then pulled away.

"You're a big man," Reg said. "But not as big as me."

Arik pulled him up in a kiss. "You going to prove that?"

"Soon," Reg said.

"Promises, promises," Arik teased, and he would have smiled had Reg not chosen that moment to repeat his earlier movement.

When Arik was working, his focus often narrowed to the point where he ignored the rest of the world. He experienced that same sensation as Reg cradled his cock in his mouth and throat. All other thought flew from him. He clutched the bedding, held on tight as the world spun away and he was left with only mind-blowing pleasure. Arik's mouth hung open and his eyes rolled into the back of his head. He was seconds from coming and unable to say a single word. When

Reg backed away and stepped off the bed, Arik used the distance to recapture his breath.

Reg watched him like a hawk, and after a few seconds, Arik latched his gaze onto Reg's, tearing it away only when he realized Reg was undoing his pants. Jeans fell to the floor in a rustle of fabric. Arik's mouth watered at the bulge in Reg's black briefs. He wanted to open the package, but it seemed Reg had other ideas as he shucked the last of his clothing, then approached the bed like a wall of flesh, muscles, and rippling artistic manhood.

"You tattooed your buttcheek?" Arik said, following the flower and vine design down Reg's side to his hips and buttcheek. "Damn that's hot... and stunning."

"I'll show you stunning." Reg stalked closer, stroking up Arik's belly to his chest. "You are stunning."

"No, I'm not. I'm small and skinny. Always have been." He'd never been strong, and he was never going to be. Arik ran his fingers over Reg's shoulder, feeling the power beneath the skin.

"You are you," Reg said, stating the obvious, but from the deep, swirling desire in his eyes, Arik let himself believe that Reg was telling the truth. "That's always enough."

"Not really. I've never been enough for anyone." Arik held Reg's hand to his chest, keeping it in place because he needed the contact. "I wasn't enough for my parents, and I was never enough for the other two guys I've been with." Arik sat up. "Do you know what it feels like to be a curiosity? I was with Parker when I was a freshman, just once. He had some sort of bet that everything on me was proportional... or something like that. I gave him quite a surprise," Arik giggled and then stopped abruptly when Reg ran his hand slowly over the ridge of his cock.

"I bet you did. And if I'd been around, I'd have given this Parker what for right between the eyes. How dare he...." Reg hissed. "That's so cruel."

"At the time I thought it was okay because... well... I'm a guy and it meant I got laid, but yeah, I wanted to kill him afterward." Arik giggled harder. "He was the one who wasn't proportional." Arik wagged his little finger, and Reg grinned.

"Well, you aren't that," Reg said, pouncing on him, hugging Arik, covering him with warm skin that sent Arik's entire body into overdrive. Reg rolled on the bed, and Arik found himself on top, looking down at Reg. "I didn't want to crush you." He held Arik's cheeks in his hands, guiding him down into a kiss.

Arik had no illusions: even though he was on top, Reg was in control. Arik liked it, straddling Reg, rolling his hips, sliding his cock on Reg's belly. Damn that felt good. He closed his eyes as Reg cupped his butt, teasing one finger along his cleft. "What...?"

"Making you feel good," Reg whispered, ghosting over his sensitive opening. "Hasn't anyone ever touched you here?"

Arik stopped. "No. I'm a top. The guys I was with, I... was in charge... well, sort of. See, Parker was this big guy, but he had more helium in his heels than a Macy's Thanksgiving Day Parade balloon." He smiled. "Especially once he got a look at what I was packing."

Reg laughed deeply, even as he continued teasing him. Arik groaned when Reg pressed to him without going too far, tapping his opening, and Arik rolled his hips faster. Reg gripped his butt, lifting him up and positioning him across his chest. Reg leaned forward, guiding Arik between his lips, stroking, lips and mouth sucking him. Arik resumed moving his hips, much more slowly, and good God, Reg took all of him once again.

Arik wasn't sure how much longer he could hold off. Just watching his cock slide between Reg's lips was enough to send him near the edge. "So hot."

Reg sucked him harder, and Arik threw his head back as his release built and built. He tried to pull away, but Reg held him in place, taking him all the way as Arik exploded, his release taking him with freight-train force.

Arik almost collapsed. He sat still, his cock slipping from Reg's lips. Reg tugged him down and held him tight, his warmth and care surrounding Arik. "I always liked big guys, but they scared me. I didn't expect you to be so gentle."

"I can be rougher if that's what you like. But you should know by now that I'm pretty aware of my own strength."

He couldn't argue with that. Once he could breathe and move again, Arik slid down Reg's body, coming face to face with his thick cock. He licked along the length, smiling when Reg's cock jumped to meet him. He could feel the excitement and anticipation in Reg's body and hear it in the hitch in his breath. He felt really powerful seeing that he could make Reg, as big as he was, act like this.

"Arik, no teasing."

"I'll be good, and you're gonna love this." Arik licked and sucked along his length before taking him in. He couldn't do what Reg had done and take all of him, but from the groans, he was doing just fine, and they only increased as Reg became more and more rigid and his body filled with tension.

Arik could tell Reg was getting close so he moved faster, sucking harder, loving the way Reg felt sliding on his tongue.

"Arik," Reg cried as a warning, but Arik sucked hard, pulling Reg's release from him.

They settled together on the bed afterward, kissing deeply, sharing the flavors that lingered on their tongues. Reg put an arm around him, holding them close as Arik slowly stroked Reg's chest.

"Jeepers," Arik sighed.

"Okay," Reg said with amusement. "I wasn't expecting this kind of afternoon."

Reg's blissful smile said he was more than content. Arik was grateful Reg wasn't ready for a huge postcoital conversation, and soon soft snores filled the room.

Arik smiled and lay close to Reg, closing his eyes to rest. But none came. Reg shifted slightly, and Arik carefully got out of bed and walked to the table in the other room. He grabbed a pencil and a pad, returned to the bedroom, and sat in the one chair in the corner where he could watch Reg.

There was nothing quick about his sketch. He had to be very careful with each hand movement, but what surprised him was the ease with which the small lines he drew created overlapping depth. He made as little sound as possible, drawing his sleeping lover just as he lay, arm thrown over his head, large, long body in beautiful repose. Arik spent time on the tattoos that adorned Reg's body. After working for an hour or so, he started a fresh page concentrating on Reg's face, relaxed and innocent looking. The lines that were usually present around his mouth had smoothed out, and his lips had a slight upturn.

"What are you doing?" Reg asked without moving.

"Drawing you," Arik answered. "It's much slower now."

"How come you aren't here in bed with me?" Reg shifted, rolling onto his back. "The bed is more than a little cold."

"I wasn't sleepy." Arik continued working to finish what he'd started. "And I didn't want to disturb you by tossing and turning. So as soon as I saw you, I knew I had to draw." His art had spoken to him. "I can stop." Arik set the pad aside and approached the bed. Reg reached out, took his hand, and gently drew him down onto the bed.

"You feel good just like this," Reg whispered, rolling onto his side, spooning Arik to his chest.

"So do you, but I'm not getting anything done like this, and my hands are itching for a brush."

"Do you think you can paint?"

"I don't know if I can produce anything that's decent, but the inspiration is there, and I have to give it a try."

"Then get dressed and go to work. I'll be right behind you." Reg tightened his hug, kissing his shoulder, then released him. "It's okay. Go on and work for a while."

"You aren't mad?" Arik asked.

"Of course not. Go paint and make the world a more beautiful place." Arik wasn't sure if Reg was serious. He sat at the edge of the bed, turning back to Reg just to check his expression once more. "I'm serious. It's okay." Reg stretched and then propped his head on his hand. "I'm taking a guess here, but someone told you that your work isn't important."

"My dad," Arik answered. "He always said that throwing paint on something wasn't a real job." Arik stood and pulled on his pants. A slew of insults and self-esteem-ripping comments always followed. "You don't want to hear about this." He smiled and slipped on his shirt.

"He was wrong. You're very talented. So go on and work for a while. I'll get dressed and be out with you in a few minutes."

Arik bent over the bed, kissed Reg, and then hurried to the other room. The skies had continued to cloud over, but Arik didn't mind. He opened the door and set up there, still looking out at the garden. For whatever reason, the low gray overcast sky struck a chord with him and provided interesting shadows, and wisps of low fog blew and floated through the garden.

Arik figured it was an exercise in futility, but he got his oil paints. He set the can of brushes nearby, choosing an extra small one and holding it the way he had the pencils.

"Staring at the canvas isn't going to help you," Reg said from behind him.

"I'm afraid of making another mess."

"People have been able to paint with their feet, mouths, or holding a brush between two fingers, because it's all they have. They painted masterpieces. So you need to stop letting your hand hold you back. That isn't important."

Arik dropped the brush he'd been holding. "It isn't important? Look at it. My hand hurts most of the time. I can't feel with parts of my fingers. I swear if George Lucas saw my hand, he'd use it as the inspiration for an alien melting creature in one of his movies." Arik waved it in the air. "I don't like to look at it, and—"

"That's the issue. It's all inside you. Your hand is just fine because it's your hand. So accept it, and let the images in your head come back out again. This whole artistic-constipation thing doesn't have anything to do with your hand." Reg took it, threading his perfect fingers between Arik's injured ones. "It's all up here." Reg tugged him close, gently rubbing his head. "So let it go."

Arik let himself be held even as he shook his head.

"Yes. You will create amazing things if you let yourself go." Reg stepped away, and Arik picked up his brush one more time, staring alternately at the canvas and then out at the garden.

Within minutes his mind had wandered to the drawings he'd done of Reg lying on the bed, eyes closed, relaxed after their lovemaking. Arik smiled and let his mind wander for a few seconds. Once he refocused on the garden again, the images in his mind mixed together, the flowers morphed into parts of Reg's body, the amazing tattoo on his hip integrating into the scene. Without thinking or looking, only going by feel, he dipped his brush in the paint and began working.

ARIK HAD no idea how much time had passed. He knew Reg was nearby, sitting in the chair, reading some book he'd found. The late afternoon had grown cold. Arik hadn't noticed, but Reg must have gotten a blanket and curled it around him. Arik's fingers ached, but the vision of what was on the canvas and where he was going was as clear and bright as the sunniest summer day, and the canvas looked like his image. Well, the bones of the image were there. He still had a lot of work, but it was there.

"I'm losing the light," Arik said with a strong sigh. He set down his brush and flexed his hand and fingers to work out the kinks that had crept in.

"Then you should stop." Reg was smiling, wide and strong. "Are you going to show Ken?"

"No. I need to make sure this is going to work before I do anything." Arik set the work to the side where it could dry. "I think some food is in order."

"I can get some and bring it back if you like. I need to go get the airbrushes for you."

"Give me a minute. I want to ride with you." Arik knew that was going to complicate logistics, but Reg jumped up and folded the blanket and set it aside as Arik quickly cleaned up and got a jacket. Once he was done and had locked the house, they went to the bike and rode to Reg's house as it started to mist. Not that Arik cared; he was happy and soaked up the energy from the speeding bike and the heat by pressing as close to Reg as he could.

"Have you ever thought of getting your own bike?" Reg asked when they pulled to a stop.

"Why? I like riding behind you." To accentuate his point, he made sure Reg knew just how excited he was. "That's half the fun."

"I see." Reg put the bike in gear, and they took off, making the turn to reach Reg's house. Reg put the bike in the garage, and they moved over to the truck. It wasn't nearly as much fun, but when the sky opened up on their way to the gas station, they were both happy to be out of the weather. "We'll get the airbrush supplies, and then we can have dinner." Arik agreed, and a minute later Reg pulled up to the station.

"What the—" he began. The entire area was full of bikes, most covered to protect them from the rain. The main bay doors were up, with bikes filling the inside. Reg parked on the street and got out. Arik stayed where he was when he saw the men gathered around in groups talking, many of them dressed in leathers. The only one he recognized other than Reg was Slasher, and he didn't look the same. Intimidating was the only word that came to mind.

Arik pulled out his phone and brought up the radar app, which showed solid green in their area, meaning the rain wouldn't be stopping anytime soon. Looked like the bikers might be settling in for a long visit.

Reg approached and pulled open the passenger door, then placed the airbrush kits behind the seat. "Come on out and meet the guys. They were on their way back from the camping trip and stopped on their way into town for some shelter from the rain."

"These are your friends?"

"Yeah. They're good guys, even if they look a little scary." Reg held the door open, and Arik reluctantly got out, closing the door behind him. He stayed close to Reg as they walked across the strip of lawn near the street and approached the milling crowd of men who'd taken cover from the rain.

"Reg," one of them called and reached out to shake his hand as soon as they got close enough. "Hope it's okay we barged in. It started to rain, and Slasher here said he had the keys and that we could take some shelter until it stopped."

"Of course," Reg said, standing next to the huge man, who seemed about Reg's age, dressed in all black, with a bushy beard that hid some sort of scar. At least that was what it looked like to Arik. His eyes seemed a little too close together, and his lip curled upward in a permanent snarl rather than a smile. Arik kept Reg between them. "How long you planning to stay?"

"Just until the rain stops. Most everyone has to get home."

"Gadrey, this is Arik, a friend."

Arik shook hands with Gadrey, who stared at him, sizing him up. A chill went down Arik's spine. He ignored it because this was a friend of Reg's and plastered a smile on his face.

"Good to meet you," Gadrey said rather flatly. "Guys, we're going to get going as soon as the rain stops." The power and authority in Gadrey's voice sent Arik's nerves fluttering.

"I'm going to use the bathroom," Arik told Reg quietly, and he stepped away, walking away from the group and around to the outside doors. As he approached, a sweet, tangy smell he knew way too well tickled his nose. He rounded the corner and saw one of the men leaned against the building, puffing and then snuffing out the joint between his gloved fingers. Arik ignored him and pulled open the bathroom door. He looked at the scene inside, shut the door once again, and turned, walking right back to Reg.

Bike engines revved as they came to life. Others were walked out of the bay as the guys got ready to leave. Arik looked around for a few more seconds at the stragglers coming around from the bathrooms. "Are they friends of yours?" Arik asked.

"Known them all my life. These are all really great guys," Reg said, and Arik felt his heart tear. "We've been through God knows what. These guys were the reason I was able to keep the station going through that first year or so."

Arik nodded and moved away from Reg, hurrying to the truck. He climbed in and closed the door, watching as the group of motorcycles took off in a roar and flashes of black, red, blue, and green. Reg waved as they left and then closed the garage doors. Arik settled in the seat, trying to make sense of what he'd seen and what Reg had said, and he could come to only one conclusion.

"Are you ready to go to dinner?" Reg asked, climbing in the truck.

"I'm not really hungry. Could you take me home? I'm not feeling well." Arik stared out the front window as he leaned against the locked door, rubbing his injured hand. He knew what he had to do, even if it hurt like someone was ripping at his heart. He'd come all this way and had left his parents behind in the hope that he could keep stuff like that out of his life. And what the hell had happened? He'd ignored his instincts and let someone work their way into his heart, someone who would only bring all that back to his doorstep. He couldn't let that happen. No way. He was not going to go through that pain all over again.

"Okay," Reg said and started the engine. Arik didn't talk during the ride. When Reg pulled up in Ken and Patrick's drive, Arik unlocked the door and got out as soon as the truck had pulled to a stop. "Thanks for the ride and the day." He closed the door and hurried around to the backyard without turning around, forgetting about the airbrush stuff in the truck. He fished out the key to the garden house as the rain started again.

Arik unlocked the door and raced inside, closing and then locking it behind him. The rain began in earnest again, pounding on the roof as Arik's heartbeat pounded in his ears. He'd opened himself up to someone, and he'd let his guard down only to have the devil that had plagued him his entire life show up again. "Shit sucks!" he yelled as he collapsed on the sofa, burying his face in the pillow that still smelled like Reg as the tears he didn't want to shed came anyway.

CHAPTER
Six

REG WAS confused. He'd called Arik and left messages over the past two days, but he'd gotten no response, including the call to tell him that the work on his car had been completed. Reg was working in the paint area putting finishing touches on some Celtic knot detailing on a fuel tank when his phone rang. He let it go and continued working to a good stopping point before standing to look who it had been.

It wasn't Arik, but he recognized the number and returned Ken's call. "What's going on?"

"I was going to ask you the same thing," Ken said. "Did something happen with Arik?"

"Not that I know of. He said he wasn't feeling well on Sunday, so I brought him home. He hasn't returned my calls, and I was worried he might still have been feeling bad. To tell you the truth, I was about to call and see if he was okay." Reg looked back to his work to make extra sure he could leave it before walking through the shop to the office.

"I don't know about him being ill. He never mentioned anything, but he's been locked in the garden house for the last two days. He says he's not hungry, there are lights on half the night, and I can tell he's been working, but he isn't talking to anyone." Ken sounded worried. "I understand a working jag where things are happening, but this isn't one of those."

"Did you ask him?"

"He says he's fine, working hard, and that he got himself something to eat."

Reg sighed with relief. That sounded like Arik was hard at work to him.

"He looked like hell when I saw him this morning. Bags under his eyes, hair ratty and plastered to his head. He isn't taking care of himself."

"Okay...."

"His clothes were painty, but dirty too, and he hasn't changed or shaved in a while. I haven't known him any longer than you, but that seems out of the ordinary. Patrick thinks something is wrong, and he has great instincts about things like this. We've both tried to get him to talk, but he won't." Ken sighed. "If I didn't know better I'd say he was suffering from a broken heart."

Reg lowered his rear into the old chair behind the desk Uncle Ron had used, swallowing hard. "That's news to me. We had fun at the children's home and then had some lunch here after some airbrush time. I have what he made, and it's incredible. We went back to his place so he could work." Reg didn't plan to go into any other details. "Then we ran an errand here to get the airbrushes for him, and he said he wasn't feeling well, so I took him home." Reg pulled the phone away from his mouth. "Slasher," he called.

"Yeah?" Slasher said, wiping his hands as he came in.

"Did you see anyone do anything to Arik on Sunday?"

He shook his head. "I know you said he was skittish around bigger guys, but he wasn't with the group for more than ten minutes, and I always saw him with you. He looked about ready to bolt at any second, with huge eyes watching everyone like he expected trouble."

"Thanks," Reg said and returned to his call as Slasher went back to work. "I'm at a loss," Reg said to Ken. "Do you think I should come by to see him?"

"Maybe tomorrow," Ken said. "I'm going to send Patrick over tonight to see him. He can't talk, but he has ways of touching people's hearts. So I'm hoping he'll learn something."

"Okay." Reg sat back, worried even more than he had been before about the silence. "Please let me know." He disconnected and began running through every detail of their day together. The smiles and laughter at the children's home, both during the art lessons and the tea party. Eating lunch together, their time alone, which played in Reg's head every night. Just thinking about it made him squirm and wish Arik were there with him.

They'd had a great day, talking and laughing it up until they got to the station. All that Reg could think was that something must have happened. But Arik was out of his sight for only a few minutes, and that had been to go to the bathroom. Arik had been gone less than two minutes…. The more he thought about it, the greater his underlying confusion became, especially as he came back to the broken-heart remark.

"Are you coming to the rally tonight?" Slasher asked.

He hadn't been planning on it because he'd been hoping to spend the time with Arik. "I could," he said, thinking out loud. "Where is it?"

"At Lake Park. It's supposed to be a picnic, but you know that means sitting around, drinking beer, and telling stories."

"I think I'll take a pass tonight. I have some work I need to finish, and I'm already behind. Go on and have a good time. Derrick will be here in a while, and he can watch things so I get a few hours of work."

"You sure?"

"Yeah." Reg smiled, and Slasher went back to what he was doing. Reg wandered around the office, wondering what in heck could have happened. Of course there was the possibility that Ken was incorrect in his assumptions and that Arik was busy working. He had seemed focused the last time Reg had been there.

He thought about trying to call again, but he didn't want to seem desperate. He was usually a man of action, and sitting by was not his normal response. He needed something to take his mind off this. So he got up and went back to the paint room, closed the door, and sank his attention back into his work… or at least he tried.

"WHAT'S WRONG with you lately?" Slasher asked him the following afternoon after yet another tool clanged onto the floor of the garage. "You've dropped tools and growled at everyone except the customers all day, and the only reason they've been spared is because I've run interference. So what gives?"

"I don't know." He placed the wrench back in the drawer where it belonged and gave the hell up. "I've been trying to get this damn bike back together, but it seems to hate me."

"It's not the bike and you know it. Your head has been somewhere else since yesterday. So fess up. Is it that Arik kid?" Slasher stood up from where he'd been bent over the hood of a '96 Chevy and stared at him. "It is."

"I've called but he hasn't called back. Ken said he wasn't sick but was either working himself to death or pining for something." He left out the broken-heart bit because he didn't know what the hell that could mean, not without talking to Arik. If anyone had a broken heart and a belly twisted with concern, it was Reg. He had spent the last day trying like heck to figure out what could be wrong.

"Then go see him and leave me in peace. I don't have any answers for you. Women are confusing enough for me, so don't expect any answers on boyfriends." Slasher rolled his eyes. "I can give advice on how to make women so crazy they bay like she-wolves, but guys? Nope... nothing."

"That's not what I heard from your last girlfriend," Reg retorted, closing his eyes and snoring loudly. "She was in here all the time."

Slasher actually bought it for a second and then threw a rag at him. "Fucker," Slasher groaned. "I'm just saying I don't the hell know what to tell you. If it was a girl I'd probably see if I could ask one of her friends or something. Maybe send flowers or something, they like that. But you're on your own with this one." Slasher grabbed a socket wrench and leaned back over the car. "And for God's sake, don't be looking at my ass."

Reg laughed. "Please. I've seen your ass. Remember last year when you and Georgie decided to go for a late-night swim in the lake, and one of the rangers investigated what was going on? He shone that floodlight on the water, and we all got a look at your lily-white ass, full moon." Reg turned away. "Wasn't interesting then, isn't now." He went back to work, determined to keep his head where it belonged. If nothing else, it gave him something to smile about for a few seconds.

When his phone rang a half hour later, he jumped and grabbed it. "Hello?"

"Reg, it's Ken."

"Is he all right?" Reg blurted right away. "He isn't sick, is he?" Jesus, his heart jumped slightly. He had it bad, and that only added to his worries.

"He's fine and doesn't seem sick, but Patrick said he didn't open up about what was bothering him. He is working a lot, and we made him come to dinner last night, but most of the time he kept looking back toward the garden house through the window and disappeared inside afterward."

"Was he rubbing his hand?" Reg asked. "The one that's hurt? Was he rubbing and cradling it a lot like it hurt?"

"Yes. But what does that have to do with anything?"

"Maybe nothing, maybe everything," Reg answered cryptically. He did know it meant Arik was stressed. "Once I'm done with work tonight, I'm going to stop by. I'll see if I can get him to talk to me." There had to be some way he could get Arik to open up. But he wasn't sure what that could be if the guru of confession and the most listening ear in town—Patrick—hadn't gotten anywhere.

"All right. We'll look for you." Ken hung up, and Reg went back to his work. At least with a plan in place, such as it was, he thought he could concentrate. He made some progress and kept Arik in the back of his mind for a few hours.

Good intentions and reality sometimes parted company, and that was certainly the case for Reg. He still worried and wondered, giving up and working on the books for the business because he was as fumbling and unproductive as he could ever remember being. And since the books were his least favorite chore, he figured he might as well add insult to injury and make a real evening of it. Slasher headed out, and Derrick was watching the pumps and the office, so he worked as long as he could stand it before turning out the office lights and checking that the garage was locked up. Then he said good night to Derrick and hurried home to shower and change.

The ride to Ken's had never made him nervous before, but the closer he got, the jumpier he became. Reg pulled his truck into the drive, and Ken came out of the house to meet him.

"Go on around back," was all Ken said.

Reg nodded, walking around the side of the house and out through the garden. He saw Arik through the windows, sitting in one of the chairs, the top of a sketchbook just visible. Arik's head was down as though he was concentrating. Reg hated to disturb him, but they had to talk. He knocked on the door and waited for Arik to open it.

"I've been really busy, so I haven't had time to call," Arik said. The chill coming off him made the lake breeze seem tropical. He turned, and Reg saw a pile of sketches and drawings on the table.

"I was worried about you. You always call me back." Reg saw what Ken had described. Some of the energy and spark that Arik had had the last time they met was definitely gone.

"The work has been coming." Arik rubbed his hand. Ken had been right. Arik's hair hung limply to his shoulders, and his eyes were red and puffy, with circles under them.

"Arik," Reg said softly. "I don't understand." He reached for one of the drawings on the table.

"What's there to understand? I've been working a lot and…." Arik swallowed. "Please don't look at them."

"What's this?" Reg asked, nearly taking a step back at the power in the drawing. It leaped out at him, along with hatred and pain. "Who is this?"

"No one. It's not important." Arik snatched the page from his hand, and Reg jumped, sucking his finger where the page cut him. It stung like hell, and he started bleeding. "Shoot."

"It'll be okay," Reg soothed, but the cut bled more.

"I'll get a bandage, and then you need to go." Arik grabbed a tissue, wiping the blood from the page. Then he placed it back on the table with the others and went into the bathroom. He returned with a box of bandages and got one out, then put it over the cut at the base of Reg's index finger. "I really need to go back to work."

"I think you need to tell me what's going on," Reg pressed. "You've been holed up in here for days, you're barely eating and you aren't sleeping, drawing pictures that look like some villain in horror movies."

"I'm fine. I draw things. It's what I do." Arik seemed to be trying to be flippant, but Reg heard the fear in his voice.

"No. It's how you process what you're feeling." Reg reached for the drawing again. "What I want to know is what got you so scared that you'd draw this?" Reg looked closer at the man's features, then shifted his gaze to Arik. "Is this your father?"

"Reg," Arik said, looking at him with eyes as cold as steel. "You need to go." His expression changed, and Reg dropped the page, sending it fluttering to the floor. He saw fear, from Arik, directed at him. This wasn't standoffishness, but real terror and pain.

"What the hell did I do to make you look at me like that?" Reg asked, a chill running through him.

"You...," Arik began and stopped. "I can't be around someone who allows things like that to happen. I'm sorry, I just can't. Now you have to leave." Arik sat down on one of the two wooden chairs around the tiny dining table that now held his drawings.

"Okay. I was on my way to see Bobbie Jo for a few minutes before she went to bed. I stopped because—"

Arik jumped to his feet, the chair toppling over. "You can't do that. How can you? That little girl deserves so much better than that. What if that stuff... they...?" Arik shook from head to toe. "For God's sake, leave them alone." Arik used his hands to prop himself up, still shaking. Reg was trying to make sense of what he was saying, but he couldn't get past how pale and drawn Arik looked. Ken had said that Arik had eaten dinner with them, but he wondered.... Sweat broke out on Arik's brow, and Reg hurried forward, catching him as he began to go down.

Reg gently cradled Arik in his arms and carried him to the sofa. "Calm down. You're okay," Reg said as Arik struggled. "I'm not going to hurt you, but I am really worried." He set him down gently and opened the small refrigerator, thankful to find some juice. Reg opened the plastic bottle and brought it to Arik. "Drink this and then tell me what's going on."

Arik grabbed the bottle and drank like he'd been crossing the desert for days.

"What have you been doing to yourself?" Reg whispered, taking the empty bottle and getting Arik a glass of water, then pressing it into his hands.

"I'm fine. I've been too busy...."

"I see that. You're too busy to eat, drink, even bathe." Reg fixed him with a stare. "Just tell me what's going on. I'm worried and I care about you."

"Do you?" Arik snapped.

"Of course I do."

"I thought you were...." Arik drank some of the water, the hurt returning, filling his eyes. "I thought you were someone I could grow to love, but I was wrong. I could never be with someone like you."

"What about me? I thought...."

"How can I be with you when you allow things like that?" Arik shook less and his eyes seemed clearer, but Reg was still worried.

"Like what?"

"Those men are your friends. You go camping with them and spend a lot of time with them, so you...."

Reg encouraged Arik to drink some more. "Did something happen with the guys? Did they say something to you?" Reg knew he was jumping to a conclusion of sorts, but he'd gone over their day together in detail, and the only time Arik had been away from him was when he'd gone to the restroom.

"No. They...."

"Arik, I really don't know what's going on. You have to tell me." He leaned over Arik and met his gaze. "Please."

Arik closed his eyes, most likely trying to pull away from him yet again.

"Okay." Reg said, standing up. "I can't make you talk to me, but I really wish you would." He kept his voice as gentle and quiet as he could. "If one of the guys hurt you, I really need to know."

"They didn't touch me or say anything."

"Then what happened?" Reg asked more firmly and waited to see how Arik would react.

"Fine. I went to the bathroom and smelled... marijuana. They were smoking it around the side."

"Are you sure?"

"I've smelled pot since I was a toddler. My mom and dad smoked it almost every single day." Arik sat up, his eyes steeling. "I didn't meet their eyes and continued on because I needed the bathroom, but there were men in there, and...."

"What happened?"

"They were.... One of the guys was selling... I think it was crystal meth."

"One of the guys in the club?" Reg's hands curled to fists. "Are you sure?" He wanted to scream. "What did he look like?"

"I don't know. He was wearing black leather like the other guys. All I saw was money and a packet change hands, but I've been around that shit enough to know a buy when I see one. You said that these were your friends, and they were doing this at your place... I can't be around that ever again. I won't. It took me too long to get away, and I paid a huge price to do it."

"And you thought I had something to do with that?" Reg asked. "That I'd allowed it?"

"I asked, and you said you knew all these people, that they were your friends." Arik drained the last of the water, and Reg took the glass.

"I would never.... I don't use drugs—never have—and I don't condone it."

"But they're your friends," Arik said. "You said you knew them... so...."

"Some of those guys are better friends than others." Reg curbed his anger. "I need you to try to describe the guys you saw smoking pot and the ones in the bathroom."

"I can't. Not really. I didn't want to look at them. They were young and talked a lot. One guy wore red pants. I remember that."

"Okay," Reg said. That gave him a pretty good idea of the contingent involved. "Thank you for telling me. But you should have said something right away."

"I can't be around that at all." Arik began shaking again.

"I won't have it either," Reg said. He was so angry he could spit, but at the moment, he had to calm Arik down. That was what counted. "I did plenty of stupid things when I was growing up, but my uncles would have skinned me alive if they even thought I might be involved with things like that." He took a deep breath and released it. "You should have told me rather than become so upset."

"They were your friends. I didn't know if you'd believe me or if you knew… or what…." The shaking began again, and Arik seemed ready to fly apart.

"I understand, but if you'd told me, I'd have called the police right then. We're a motorcycle club, not a drug gang." His anger rose once again. "Sometimes people think we're a bunch of hooligans because we like to ride. They expect us to be into drugs and cause trouble. And these guys are fulfilling that expectation. It really pisses me off."

Arik slowly sat up. "You really believe me?"

"Of course I do. But I'm a little mad at you too. You worried yourself sick for three days, and I kept wondering what I'd done wrong. Ken and Patrick were also worried about you." Reg stared firmly at Arik. "If you're upset, keeping it in won't help. You've rubbed your hand raw these past few days." Reg took Arik's injured hand. "You need to go get cleaned up and then let me take care of you."

Arik's hand was red and slightly swollen. It was obvious that Arik had taken his nerves and uncertainty out on his poor hand. Reg wasn't even sure Arik had realized he'd done it.

"Reg," Arik whimpered.

"It's okay. Go wash your face. You'll feel better, I promise." Reg gently guided Arik to his feet. "I won't go anywhere until you come back." How could he? Arik acted like he was ill, but Reg figured there was nothing physically wrong. He'd worked himself into a state in the last few days.

Arik went into the bathroom and closed the door. As soon as Reg heard water running, he pulled his phone from his pocket and called Slasher.

"Hey, man," Slasher said, answering the phone. "Is everything okay?"

"No. I think there's a problem. Arik talked to me."

"So things are good between you."

"I don't know about that," he said, treading carefully. "But I know what upset him, and I'm angry enough to spit quarters." Reg took a deep breath, hoping like hell his friend wasn't involved in all this. "Karl Hastings wears red leather bike pants. Right?"

"Yeah. The ostentatious twerp has this thing for them. Why?"

That was encouraging. "He and his friends were smoking pot around the side of the station. Stupid assholes. They could have sent the entire station up like a rocket."

"They're stupid asses," Slasher groaned. "I'm sorry I suggested they go there to get out of the rain. I won't do it again."

"It's worse than that. I think they're dealing. Arik saw a buy going down in the bathroom. That's why he freaked. At least that's what he's saying. I know just enough about his past to know that would do it."

"Fucking hell...," Slasher breathed.

"Did you see or hear anything over the weekend? If they were doing business then, they must have been doing it at camp."

The line went quiet for a few seconds. "Not that I saw. But it wasn't like I was on the same side of the camp as they were. The younger guys are always up half the night—you know how it is."

"Yeah, I do. But the problem is that these guys have brought drugs and drug money into our group." Reg was seeing red again.

"You want me to ask Gadrey about it?" Slasher volunteered. "I can say that I saw some things at camp that made me wonder. I'll see what he says."

"What if he knows? You know him and Karl joined together. Be careful. Don't let on that it was Karl specifically. Just be general to check his attitude, and let me know what he says." Reg thought a minute. "If he challenges you, back off and say you think you could be mistaken. You don't need to put yourself in a difficult position for me."

"We've been friends for years, and you're the best boss I've ever had, so if you don't think this sort of thing going on at the station doesn't piss me off as much as it does you...." Slasher's vehemence was comforting in a way. "I don't want to be part of an organization that condones that. I'll quit first."

"Thanks," Reg said, and Slasher hung up, most likely to go make his calls.

Reg sat and stewed, getting angrier, pounding his hand with his fist. He should have made the call himself instead of asking Slasher, but if he did, he'd yell and lose his temper. All that changed when

Arik stepped out of the bathroom. "Feel better?" Reg asked, getting to his feet.

"I heard you on the phone."

"I can't just let this happen," Reg said. "Slasher is going to make a few calls and see what we can find out." He had a very deep suspicion that the club he'd belonged to for years had been undergoing a change and he was only seeing it now. New people had stepped into leadership roles, and the old guard was now sitting on the sidelines. "We can talk about it later if you like."

"I'm okay," Arik said.

"No, you're not. You're still pale. I'm going to get you something to eat."

"I'm not hungry."

"Yeah, right. You need to eat, and I need to take care of you, so just let me." Reg fixed him with a stare, and Arik backed down. Reg checked the bathroom and found the lotion. He put it on the table and opened the small refrigerator. There wasn't much. He did find some popcorn in the cupboard and made a batch in the microwave, buttered it, and placed the bowl on the table.

Arik joined him, and Reg added drinks and got Arik to settle. Reg took his hand and began rubbing lotion into it to try to soothe the roughened skin while Arik absently ate handful after handful of popcorn, emptying most of the bowl. For someone who wasn't hungry, he ate nearly the whole lot.

"Do you want to tell me everything?"

"You know what happened," Arik said.

"I'm not talking about Sunday. I understand not wanting to be around drugs and the people who use them. I can also understand being upset when you encounter things you shouldn't. But your reaction was extreme by anyone's standards. You refused to talk to me and ask me about it. People who you admire tried to help you, but you pushed them away." Reg continued rubbing Arik's fingers. "So there has to be more to it."

Arik tried to pull his hand away, and Reg released it. "I don't want to talk about it."

"Why? What is it you're afraid of?"

"It hurts to talk about it."

"No," Reg countered. "What hurts is holding in the pain. It eats away at you." Reg once again took Arik's hand to keep him from rubbing it. "You're hurting yourself because you're so freaked out. Is actually telling me whatever is bothering you that hard?" Reg began stroking again, working more cream into the now softening skin.

"I don't know. I feel so stupid."

"Okay. This whole 'guilt and feeling bad' thing has to end. Let out what you're afraid of and be done with it."

Arik turned, looking down at the floor. "It's because of my hand."

"What is?"

"My parents, actually my father, I guess, got deeper and deeper." Arik sighed. "You know my mom and dad were useless as parents. They smoked a lot. They considered themselves hippies and thought drugs freed their minds. All it did was fry them. That's why I spent so much time with Gran. I had to get away from them. Well, my mom called because she said Dad was in trouble. I wasn't sure what she meant, but I came to see them." Arik grew tenser by the second.

"Okay. Just take it easy."

"I found my dad cooking meth. He got in to some men for a bunch of money and figured he could mix his way out of it. The moron. Mom was worried, and she sent me to try to help him. He and I fought and, well, things got out of control." Arik looked down at his hand. "Dad wasn't paying attention, and stuff caught fire. The accelerant he was using got on my hand and...." Arik swallowed. "Drugs ruined my life, and I didn't want to go anywhere near them again. Mom begged me to come, and my father was so stoned out of his mind that he burned my hand." Arik looked down at his hand and began to cry. "My own father did this to me, and my mother expected me to deal with the trauma on my own rather than calling in professional help." Arik sniffled as tears ran down his cheeks. "What the hell was I supposed to do?"

"My God," Reg whispered under his breath.

"Yeah. My whole life, my parents cared more about drugs and having a good time than they did about me." Arik pounded his fist on the coffee table.

"Where is your father now?"

"He's in prison. When the EMTs asked me what happened, I told them everything. They said I was lucky, that the burns could have been worse if I hadn't gotten my hand in water right away. But I went through months of pain, rehab, therapy, and still my hand is only partially useful." Arik turned to him. "Do you see now?"

"Yeah, I do." Reg took both of Arik's hands in his. "And I'm glad you told me. But…." Reg leaned back on the sofa and waited for Arik to do the same. "What I don't understand is why you were so reluctant to tell me."

"It's easy to say that this was my dad's fault."

"He was cooking meth. Of course it was his fault."

"I knew how dangerous it was. I've told myself a million times that I should have told my mother no, stayed away, and let them deal with their own crap themselves. I'm their son. I shouldn't have to solve their problems for them, especially as messed up as they are and have been for decades." Arik wiped his eyes.

"Maybe because you have a good heart. You wanted to try to help because you could see the mess they'd made."

"Yeah." Arik inhaled and sighed. "They made the mess, and they have to deal with the fallout and cleanup. I can't do it, but I also won't have any of that in my life." Arik steeled his gaze, lips firming. "Not from you, my dad, my mom, or anyone. That's why I took off. I've been through too much." He swallowed, and Reg watched as Arik's Adam's apple bounced slightly. He wanted to lean forward, kiss it, push Arik back onto the cushions, and somehow take all this away.

"I think I understand. Your mom and dad put getting high ahead of you. Just like mine put each other and Marianne's memory ahead of me. You had your gran, I had my uncles… and for the record, I will not condone anything that takes away the only legacy of their care and concern I have left." Reg clenched his hands to fists once again. "If those bastards had been caught, the police could have closed my garage, and hell, if they thought I had anything to do with what those guys were doing, they could seize and sell it. I could lose everything because those bastards were stupid. So don't think for a second I want anything to do with that shit."

Arik lowered his gaze. "I believe you."

Reg touched his chin. "Hey. Don't feel bad."

"But I overreacted."

"Yeah, maybe you did a little," Reg admitted. "But the biggest thing you did was not talk. You clammed up and got all nervous." He lifted Arik's injured hand. "And you were hurting yourself."

"I was working," Arik protested.

"We all have our limits, and you're just learning what they are for your hand." Reg rubbed the back of the injured hand with his thumb. "And your hand has limits. You can't do what you did before."

Arik looked over at the table. "I guess, but I got a lot done anyway."

"Maybe, but at what price, and is it the kind of work you're proud of? The kind you'd want to frame, hang on a wall, and have the rest of the world see? Because that's what you deserve. You have the talent for that." Reg picked up the drawing he'd seen before and then some of the others. "These are really good, powerful, but there's so much pain in them. Especially the one of your father." Reg continued looking until he saw one of himself.

"Don't look at that one," Arik said and reached for the sketch, but Reg held it out of his grasp. "Is this how you see me?" The stance, posture, and expression were animalistic and cold.

"No. When I did that I thought…." Arik sighed and reached for a pad, handing it to him. Reg set down the sketch and opened the pad. His face stared out at him from page after page. Some were just his head, others his torso, a few showed all of him with nothing left to the imagination. "Most of those are from before I… well, before we… you know." Arik blushed so cutely.

"I'd swear you had X-ray glasses, then."

"I hadn't seen your tattoos, at least not all of them, so I left those out." Arik reached for the pad and flipped to the last pages. "These are the ones I did when you were sleeping. See, when I first met you I thought you were scary, but now I see you differently."

Reg leafed through more than a dozen sketches and drawings of himself.

"These aren't what I'd want to put in a show either. These are mine, and I don't plan to let them go." Arik closed the pad and crossed his arms in front of it, holding it to his chest. "I am working on something, or at least I was until all this happened."

"Can I see it?"

"Not yet. It isn't nearly finished, and I want it to be a surprise." Arik set down the pad. "I hope I can finish it."

"You will."

Arik sat back down and Reg did the same, letting Arik curl against him.

"I don't know what I'm going to do after my time here is over. I have the money to pay for my car and all, but I think I'll need to find a job of some sort for money."

"How did you work before the accident?"

"I sold some works and things were starting to happen. I also did some graphic design and things, but those people have moved on because I wasn't able to work for a long time. Thankfully my needs are small, and I had some money Gran left me for a rainy day. But all that is gone now."

"Just take things a little at a time," Reg suggested, gently holding him around the shoulders. "Have you seen your mother again?"

"No. I hope she left."

Reg hesitated. "I thought I saw her the other day at the station, getting gas, but I'm not sure because she was gone before I could get close enough to see."

"Why would she still be here?"

"If you want my guess, she wants to talk to you and is looking for a way to approach you again. You don't have to do anything you don't want to do, sweetheart, but you might want to think about talking to her." He felt Arik tense in his arms, but he didn't pull away. Reg counted that as a victory.

"Would you go see your mom if she called?" Arik asked after a while. "I know she's sick and all, but what if something changed and she got better? Would you see her?" Arik wound his arms around Reg's waist, and damn, he wanted things to stay like this forever— warm, quiet, just the two of them.

"Honestly, yes. If my mother were to get better, I'd go see her and my dad, and I'd offer to take you with me if you wanted to go."

"Me?" He sounded surprised.

"Yeah. This isn't likely to happen, but if my mom were lucid enough to remember that I exist, and if she wanted to see me, then I'd go and take you. I'd want both my mom and dad to meet the special someone in my life." As soon as he said it, he knew he might have been rushing things and taking a step down a very slippery slope that would only lead to heartache. Arik was wonderful, and problems or not, he was falling for the smaller man with the huge eyes and gentle heart. But he didn't want to scare him off.

"You would?"

"Yes. See, if such a thing would happen, it would be temporary, and I'd want both my parents to know me and my life. My uncles taught me that hiding sucks, and that you can't be true to yourself unless you're honest."

Arik sighed and sank a little closer to him. "I don't know if I can see her without wanting to hurt her. When she was at my door, I slammed it closed because the alternative was to hit her. I know that sounds terrible, but...."

"Such rage isn't healthy, and it isn't good for your creativity. I know—I dealt with it when I first came here. I mean, my parents barely saw me, and I kept wondering what I'd done wrong, why I wasn't good enough." Arik nodded against his chest. "It's what kids feel when they're rejected or not important enough to the people who should be the ones who care most for them in the entire world."

Arik's shoulders began to shake, and Reg held him closer, letting him get out whatever he was holding inside. Reg wondered how long all of this had been building up.

"Everything was more important than me."

The sheer volume of pain in those simple words wrenched at Reg's heart. He knew them; that pain was an old enemy. He knew how it felt, and he'd been able to look it in the eye and beat it. At least he thought he had, but feeling that old son of a bitch again opened wounds he'd thought long closed.

"It's all right, sweetheart. I'm here and you aren't alone," Reg whispered, trying to keep hold of himself before he burst apart. He was just as close to the swirling mass of pain as Arik seemed to be, and he needed to be strong and try to pull them both back. "The past is only that. We can't change it, but we also can't let it color and define the future. I know it sounds corny, but it's true."

Reg lightly stroked Arik's blond locks, then leaned forward, cradling him.

Arik didn't say anything more. Reg wanted to help him and let him get out what he needed to. He almost wished Arik would yell and let loose the rage. The grief was near the surface, but Reg had a feeling the rage was still inside, bottled up deep.

"You really forgive me for... this whole mess with my family?"

"There's nothing to forgive, but of course I do." Reg was relieved, most of all. He and Arik sat quietly for a good half hour, just breathing and being still together. It was funny what could trigger a memory, but an image of his uncles sitting together on the sofa when he got home from a school function came to mind. Not watching television, no music, the house had been quiet, and they'd sat together quietly, just happy being together. Reg hadn't understood at the time, but he thought he was starting to now. His uncles were happy in each other's company, and they didn't need anything more. "Come on, let's get you ready for bed."

"Will you stay?" Arik asked, and Reg nodded. He waited for Arik to get up, and then Reg got to his feet as his phone rang. Reg pulled it out and realized how quickly the time had gotten away from him.

"Slasher, what happened?"

"Jesus Christ," Slasher began and then launched into a stream of profanity that left no doubt about how his phone call had gone.

"Calm down and tell me what happened."

"Gadrey's in on it. The fucker didn't bother to try to cover it. At first he said boys would be boys and that he'd talk to Karl and tell him he needed to be more careful. He didn't get outraged or upset. I think he's probably the one behind it all."

Reg sat, mouth open, trying to breathe as he saw the group he'd been part of for years beginning to disintegrate in front of his eyes. "Did you give him any details?"

"I didn't have to. He knew everything. I never mentioned who I saw, and he said he'd talk to Karl. So either Gadrey is completely stupid, or he thinks he's untouchable or something." Something scraped behind Slasher, probably a chair on tile. "What the hell should we do? I don't want to be involved with anything like this."

"Leave and set up our own club, for starters," Reg said. "I do know that the club won't be meeting at the station any longer." Reg looked at Arik, who had returned to rubbing his hand. Reg reached out, shaking his head and moving closer to him. "I'm not going to have someone smoking there and set the place on fire. And what would we do if someone were busted on the property? It would kill the business because we'd be guilty by association."

"I never thought about that. Okay. I guess we bow out and figure what we want to do. I'll see you at work." Slasher hung up.

"You don't have to quit because of me," Arik said.

Reg shook his head. "I'm quitting and distancing myself from the club because I don't want to be a party to that. It has nothing to do with you. So stop getting nervous and feeling guilty."

"But you're going to give up your bike club," Arik said.

"If the group is willing to shelter drug dealing, then it isn't my club." Reg guided Arik back down onto the sofa. "There were images published in news articles in the sixties of guys on bikes, leaning back like they were stoned, surrounded by empty beer cans. Those images came to define guys who ride Harleys and other bikes. Then, to make matters worse, *Easy Rider* and all those other gangland bike movies came out, and we got a worse reputation, not to mention the Hell's Angels and other clubs. But that isn't us. We get together because we love to ride and be around other guys who like the same things. That's all."

"So what are you going to do?"

"Probably talk to Slasher in the morning and call the police. Let them deal with Gadrey and his bunch. They may even suspect them already, I don't know." He also thought he needed to check that side of the building very carefully to make sure they hadn't left anything behind.

"I'm sorry."

Reg drew Arik to him and with a grunt shifted him onto his lap and then stood, carrying him toward the bedroom.

"I can walk, you know."

"Yeah, but this is fun." Reg angled him through the door and set Arik on the bed. "You're cute when you don't quite know what to do with me."

"I'm not a child."

"No. That's for sure." Reg leaned over the bed. "You're anything but a child." He nuzzled Arik's ear. "Let's go to bed and get some sleep. I'd like to get up early so I can go see Bobbie Jo before I get to the station. Slasher will open. Will you go with me?"

"Sure." He smiled and slid to the far side of the bed.

Reg tried not to stare, but gave up after two seconds. There was no way he wasn't going to watch Arik undress.

"Sometimes the way you look at me makes me want to hide," Arik said.

"Why? You're a beautiful man and should be looked at." Reg pulled off his shirt and sat down on the edge of the bed to take off his shoes and socks. The bed shook, and Arik pressed up against him, wrapping his legs around him. Reg settled Arik's feet in his lap and leaned back into the embrace.

"I don't want to be. I want to turn out the light so you can't...."

"See your hand?"

"Yeah. I know it's dumb, but I wonder if it will turn you off. It didn't last time, but I keep wondering if you were just being nice."

Reg guided Arik's hands to his belly, holding both of them there. "I'm never that nice, and I know what your hand looks like and feels like. I've rubbed it, and in case you've forgotten, it's touching me right now." Reg turned slowly, Arik's legs falling to his sides. "I like having you touch me, with both your hands." Reg leaned back toward Arik, kissing him, tugging on his lower lip with his.

"I guess."

Reg growled and deepened the kiss before pulling away. "I think you better go get cleaned up and ready for bed." He breathed heavily, his head spinning. "If you don't give me a breather, I'm not going to be able to stop."

"Maybe I don't want you to stop." Arik sighed but still got off the bed. He shed the rest of his clothes and went into the bathroom. Reg blew out a deep breath, wiping his forehead with the back of his hand. The shower started, and Reg watched where Arik had turned out of the doorway. He thought about what he wanted to do and then stood, stripped off the rest of his clothes, and walked to the closed bathroom door. He hesitated and then knocked before opening the door.

Arik was humming softly. Reg closed the door and the humming stopped. He pulled the shower curtain aside and stepped into the small shower right behind Arik, his chest sliding along Arik's back, hips pressing to Arik's butt.

"There isn't room," Arik said, chuckling.

"Just lean back and let me hold you." Arik complied and Reg held him. "See? There's plenty of room." He reached for the soap and rubbed it between his hands, then stroked slowly up and down Arik's chest.

"Why did you come in here?"

Reg chuckled deeply. "You always ask why. Can't you just accept that something good and wonderful has happened?" He ran his hands over Arik's shoulders, the water rinsing away the soap. Reg bent slightly, kissing and licking the skin he'd just cleaned. His excitement rose by the second, along with his dick. He shifted and pressed his cock to the cleft of Arik's butt.

Arik moaned softly, and Reg flexed his hips slightly. He ran his hand up Arik's neck, moving his wet hair to the side, sucking lightly at the smooth pale skin at the base of his neck.

"I'll try to do better. Especially if I have the right incentive," Arik groaned.

Arik wriggled against him, and Reg clamped his eyes closed, groaning softly. This felt so right—Arik against him in his arms, the salty taste of his skin on his tongue. "Is this enough incentive?" Reg pressed his groin right to Arik's butt. It was crass, crude, and felt perfect.

Arik reached forward and turned off the water. "It's perfect." He pulled the curtain to the side and stepped out, cock bobbing like a metronome with each movement. Reg's gaze followed it shamelessly, and he noticed Arik doing the same to him. "I think we need a bed."

Reg grabbed a towel. If there were a timed Olympic sport for drying off, Reg would have won. Arik seemed to be taking his time, bending over to dry each leg. Reg chuckled and knelt behind him, turning Arik around until his cock pointed at Reg's lips. He leaned forward, sucking him deep, musk, salt, and the touch of sweetness he'd forever associate with Arik bursting on his tongue.

"Reg... oh God," Arik gasped.

He hummed and ran his tongue along Arik's length, sliding his hands up his leg to cup the most perfect ass he'd ever seen or felt in his life: small, firm, tight, and with the perfect curve. Arik's leg vibrated and Reg backed away, Arik's perfect cock, just the way he was made, slipping from his lips. "Come with me," he whispered. Getting to his feet, he opened the bathroom door. Needing to hold Arik right now, he enfolded him in his arms and guided him out to the bed. He released Arik long enough for him to get under the covers and then joined him, tugging Arik to him, sliding his leg between Arik's, soaking in the rub of male legs, the slide of Arik's hand along his hip, the scent of Arik's hair as it tickled his nose, the taste of him when Reg sucked a nipple.

Within minutes Reg had forgotten everything outside the small bedroom in the tiny garden house. None of it mattered at that moment. Arik wrapped his legs around his waist, nibbling on Reg's ear. "I need you to fuck me," Arik whispered.

"Are you sure?"

"Yes. Slow and long. Take it all away. Let me know you truly forgive me." The pleading in Arik's eyes was too much for Reg to take.

"I already forgave you." Reg's whisper turned to a groan when Arik sucked harder.

"I need to feel it." Arik turned his head toward the nightstand, and Reg took the hint. He didn't want to pull away, so he made the preparations as smooth as he could, opening Arik for him with fingers and tongue, listening to his lover, gauging what was too much and what was just right by the moans and whimpers that filled the small space, threatening to burst outward. Arik groaned loud and long as Reg entered him as slowly as his overheated brain would allow.

"Is this okay?" Reg gazed at eyes clamped closed and Arik's thin mouth and tense cheeks. Slowly the lines smoothed away and the tension eased. Arik slid his incredible eyes open, lips curling into a smile. Only then did he begin to move, taking what Reg had to give.

"Yes. What do I feel like?" Arik asked.

Reg kissed him hard. Words seemed too static for what he felt, so he let his kiss and his touch convey his meaning. He held Arik in his arms, surrounding him, mimicking the way Arik encased him. "Heaven," he finally whispered. "You are sheer heaven to me," Reg repeated and proceeded to do his best to take Arik along with him.

CHAPTER *Seven*

WHEN ARIK woke, Reg was gone, the bed next to him cold. He sat up and looked around, needing to know if Reg had left him in the middle of the night or if he was only somewhere else in the small house. Listening intently, he heard no one else, so he checked for Reg's clothes, which were gone. "I should have known," he groaned to himself, running his fingers through his hair. He pushed away the covers and got out of bed, padded to the bathroom, and closed the door with more force than was necessary.

He used the bathroom and figured he might as well get up, even if it was some ungodly hour of the morning. His painting sat where he'd left it, so he should just go back to work and try to figure all this out with Reg later. After cleaning up and running a comb through his hair, he stepped out of the bathroom, squeaking like a little girl when he nearly ran into Reg. "Jesus, you scared the hell out of me," he snapped.

"I couldn't sleep, so I got you some breakfast." Reg held up a bag from McDonald's. "I know it isn't fancy, but after last night I thought I might have worn you out." Arik's stomach rumbled loudly, and Reg set down the bag, watching him as he hurried to pull on his clothes. "Don't be embarrassed."

"I'm not. It's a little cold in here," Arik said, coming up with the excuse because he felt foolish with Reg dressed and him stark naked.

"Are those marks from the accident?" Reg asked, bending down to take a closer look at his side.

"Yeah. They healed pretty quickly and only left the light scars, not like my hand…." Arik pulled on his faded jeans. He knew Reg had seen them, and it was stupid, but….

"You don't have to hide."

"Yes, I do," Arik argued.

"Do you think they're ugly?" Reg asked, grabbing the bag and going into the other room.

Arik swallowed hard. "Of course they are." He pulled on his cobalt T-shirt and straightened the fabric. He joined Reg at the table.

"They aren't. No matter what you think, they are not ugly. I know it's easier to believe the bad stuff in our heads, but your scars aren't ugly. I have them. I got one on my leg in a fall about three years ago, and look at this face…." Reg smiled. "I'm never going to win any beauty contests."

"You would for me," Arik said quietly, lifting his gaze. "I think you're hot, and I like how strong and badass you look." Even if those same traits had warned him off at first.

"See, you just made my point." Reg smiled, and Arik stifled a groan. He'd stepped into that one full force. "Go on and eat. I called over to the children's home, and they said that they'd have Bobbie Jo dressed so we can visit with her."

Arik nodded, appreciating that after Reg made his point, he didn't belabor it. That alone was special. He reached for his share of the food and tucked in, his appetite driving him. Reg had been right last night—he hadn't been eating well, and he was starving. The muffin sandwiches disappeared faster than he intended, but he felt better as he drank his juice, waiting for Reg, who seemed intent on smiling and chuckling through his breakfast.

"I like seeing you happy, sweetheart."

Arik liked seeing Reg happy too, and he found himself smiling as he gathered the trash to put away. "I think we better go," Arik said when Reg had finished. They got up to leave, and Arik grabbed a jacket.

"I thought that once we were done, I'd give you a ride to the station so you could pick up your car."

Arik grabbed his checkbook and shoved it into his pocket. Then they left, Arik locking the door behind him, and walked hand in hand around the side of the house. He stopped as soon as he saw the old green Toyota parked out front. He knew that car and what it meant. He released Reg's hand, wishing he'd never set sights on that thing again. "My mother," he groaned, looking over at Reg. The car door opened, and Arik watched his mother get out and walk slowly, almost carefully, toward him.

"I just want to talk to you," she said with an earnestness that almost touched Arik's heart. "Only talk, I promise. I don't want anything from you, and after we talk, I'll go away forever if that's what you want."

Arik watched her expression for any signs of guile but saw none. He glanced at Reg, who nodded and took his hand once again. "I'll stay with you if you like," he offered in a whisper.

Arik wanted to shrink away and go right back to the garden house and lock the door. Behind him he heard the front door of the main house open.

"Is everything all right?" Ken asked.

"Yes," Arik said without looking away. "Okay. I'll meet you. But at the diner in town, Faye's, for coffee at four."

"Okay. Thank you," she said, and to Arik's surprise she got right back in her car and drove away. Arik turned to Ken and waved to let him know he was okay. Ken nodded and went back inside, and Arik got in Reg's truck, thankful that on the drive to the children's home, Reg didn't say anything, allowing Arik time to be alone with his roiling thoughts.

"I should have asked her to come to the gas station," Arik said as he got out of the truck once Reg had parked outside the children's home.

"Someplace public is best. That way you can easily leave without feeling pressured." The front door opened, showing Bobbie Jo standing in the doorway, bouncing from one foot to the other. Reg sighed and got down on one knee on the sidewalk. Bobbie Jo hurried down the steps and into his arms.

"You came!" she squealed. Arik realized it was the same thing she'd said the last time they visited.

"Yes, we did," Arik said with a smile, and once Bobbie Jo had soaked up Reg's hugs, she came over for one from him. As he wound his arms around the tiny girl, he closed his eyes to keep the tears from spilling down his face. When he ended the hug, she turned to Reg, and Arik wiped his eyes, hoping no one saw.

"We can have tea. Miss Maggie said so." She took Reg's hand and led him inside. "Real tea," she said with enthusiasm.

Maggie met them with a grin. "She's been up and watching for you since I told her you were coming." She led them to the corner of the activity room, where Bobbie Jo's tea set had been set up. "The tea is apple juice," Maggie told Arik in a whisper before she left the room.

Bobbie Jo took her seat, and he and Reg took theirs. Then she poured their cups of "tea" with careful intensity, her tongue between her teeth, using both hands. The pot didn't hold much, in case she spilled, and Arik saw the stack of napkins on the next table. Maggie had thought of everything.

"Does your hand hurt?" Arik asked when he saw Bobbie Jo favoring it.

She nodded. "I have to go to the hospital again," she said as though it were an answer that every child gave. That alone made Arik turn away to brush his eyes. "Miss Maggie says it will be soon."

"They're going to fix her last two fingers," Reg explained. "We'll visit you when you're there," Reg promised her, and Arik nodded his agreement. "We may not be able to have tea, but I'll sit with you and read you some stories." The hitch in Reg's voice was something Arik had never heard before.

Bobbie Jo smiled for a second and nibbled at one of the crackers, crumbs falling to the table. She seemed to be thinking about something pretty hard. "When they fix my hand, will I get adopted?"

Arik blinked and looked to Reg. He wasn't sure how to answer that question.

"I don't know. But you'll be able to use your hand more," Reg said, glancing back at him with equal confusion.

Bobbie Jo began to whimper softly, and Reg got off his seat and hugged her. As soon as he had her in his arms, Bobbie Jo began to cry, tears running down her cheeks. Arik turned away, seconds from joining her. Reg looked at him over her shoulder, looking dazed. Arik rolled his eyes, understanding exactly what was going on. Bobbie Jo had either been told by someone well-meaning, or she'd come up with the idea on her own, that once her hand was fixed, someone would adopt her.

"Honey, I'm sure someone will want to adopt a little girl as special as you," Reg soothed, rubbing her back. "You're going to have a family who will love you so much." Reg was barely keeping it together, and Arik sat down next to them. Bobbie Jo turned away from Reg and moved into Arik's arms. He had no idea why, but she wanted him to hold her.

"I want a mommy," she whispered.

"I want you to have one too," Arik said, sniffing, and it was his turn to look at Reg. "It's going to be okay. I know it. You're going to get your little hand fixed, and Mr. Reg will be there with you."

"You too?" she asked, holding him tighter.

"Yes. I'll be there too." Arik hoped he wasn't promising something he couldn't deliver. He and Ken had agreed that he would stay for a few more weeks, but then he was supposed to go home. Not that he had roots there, so if he was lucky, he'd be able to find work and a place to stay here. But that was more than he could deal with at the moment.

"Bobbie Jo," Maggie said from the doorway. "It's time for you to get ready for school." Arik wondered if they had made her late.

"Afternoon kindergarten," Reg explained. "We need to go because I have to help Mr. Slasher at the garage. So say good-bye to Mr. Arik and me." Bobbie Jo hugged him again and did the same with Reg. Maggie took her by the hand, leading her away. Arik watched her go and managed to last until the door to the room closed before putting his hands over his face.

"Sweetheart," Reg said, hugging him. "What is it?"

"She wants a mother so bad, and I don't even want to talk to mine." Arik lifted his face from Reg's shoulder. He clenched his fists and released them. "I'm so damned confused right now."

"Take it one thing at a time. That's what I'm trying to do."

Reg's phone rang, and Arik moved away so he could answer it. "Yeah, Slasher," Reg said, and as Arik watched, Reg turned white, and then his cheeks got red, eyes bulging. "I'm on my way. Call the police and explain what's going on. I'm not having any of it." He hung up. "We gotta go."

Arik wiped his eyes. "What happened?"

"There's a problem at the garage."

"Let me clean this up for Bobbie Jo, and then we can go." Arik was already carrying the dishes to the sink. In a matter of minutes, he had the set cleaned, dried, and stacked neatly on the table. When he was done, he and Reg left after telling Maggie where everything was on their way out.

"I'll take care of everything from here," Maggie said. Arik wanted to ask her if Bobbie Jo was okay, but Reg got antsier by the second, and as soon as they were outside and in the truck, he drove as fast as he could to the gas station.

Police cars were parked on the street, and when Reg drove in, an officer approached them. "Sir, I'm Officer Ravenwood. We received a call from William Sashinski about a problem." It took a second for it to click that was Slasher's real name.

Slasher walked up to them. "Our friends from the club showed up with some other guys and said they needed the bathroom. I was about to give the officers their names," Slasher said. "I called the police, but as soon as they heard the sirens, they took off."

"Do we have your permission to search the restrooms?" Officer Ravenwood asked.

"Yes," Reg said.

Arik stayed close to him. "I can give you descriptions of what I saw this past weekend," Arik said. "I don't know their names, but I can describe them, and Reg can help you with identification."

"Are you part of this club?" Officer Ravenwood asked Reg and then turned to Slasher. Both of them nodded. "We've suspected that the group has been involved with trafficking for a while."

Arik saw Reg's expression fall. "We have never had any part in that, and neither have a lot of the members. We went through a membership boost a few years ago, and those members have taken over." Reg looked over at Slasher, then said, "We've talked of leaving and forming a new group of our own." Reg looked the officer straight in the eye. "All I'm asking is that you don't paint us all with the same brush."

Office Ravenwood grinned. "I won't. I have a bike myself and have been looking for a club." He turned to the other officers, and they walked around to the bathrooms and were gone for a little while before coming back with very serious expressions.

"We found where someone tried to flush pills and other things down the toilet. They didn't all go. There are also the remnants of joints. We're bagging everything and will take pictures, but we're going to have to seal off the bathrooms as a crime scene for a few days."

Reg groaned but nodded. "Go ahead. I want this cleaned up."

Arik turned and walked back to Reg's truck. He opened the door and got in the passenger seat. Leaving the door open, he placed his head on the dash and tried to tell his stomach not to throw up what he'd had for breakfast. He wasn't sure where Reg was and knew he had important things he had to do. So he jumped when a large hand rested gently on his shoulder.

"I'm sorry," Arik rasped, keeping his eyes closed. "Lately everything seems to turn to crap for me."

"Why are you sorry? For the police? Because some people I know decided to take advantage of my business and friendship? None of that is your fault."

"But I saw it and...." Arik lifted his head, hoping everything would stop spinning.

"You did what was right. You said something." Reg tugged him into a hug. "You've spent all your life around drugs. Your parents taught you to keep your mouth shut and to say nothing." Arik nodded. "So you did. I bet you went to school hungry because there was no food in the house, Mom and Dad were stoned, and you covered for them at school." Arik nodded once again. "Drugs don't just hurt the user, they affect everyone, and they affected you."

"Is everything all right?" a gruff voice asked.

"Yes," Reg answered.

"He looks a little out of it." Suspicion was clear in the tone.

Arik turned to see the officer. "I'm okay." He sat up, wiping his eyes as he'd done so many times over the last few hours. "I promised I'd help you identify the people I saw." Arik got out of the truck, staying close to Reg. He spent time recalling what he'd seen and describing the men. Slasher and Reg supplied the corresponding names.

"How did you know what was happening when you went into the bathroom?" Officer Ravenwood asked.

"I grew up in a drug house. My parents were users. Dad's in prison for cooking." Arik held up his hand. "Their activity came at a dear cost. So yeah, I know what a buy looks like, and that definitely was one. I also know what a user looks like, and these guys are most definitely that. They were stoned enough that they didn't think to try to stop me. Either that or they thought I was the next customer."

"Would you be able to positively identify the men?"

"As long as they were wearing the same clothes. That's what I remember most."

"Leathers are distinctive," Reg said. "As a biker you know that."

"They are. And your descriptions were helpful." He continued taking notes, pausing after a few seconds. "You do know that this could make you targets."

"Not if you catch them and get them off the streets," Reg challenged. "We've handed you this one on a silver platter."

"I only wanted to caution you to be careful." He closed his notebook and returned to where the other officers were working.

"It looks like my business day is shot to hell," Reg groused as they watched cars drive past the station. No one was going to stop in with police cars around. "Slasher, can you work on finishing up the Caddy?" At least the service work could get done.

"I need to pay you for my car," Arik said, getting out his checkbook, watching as Reg went into the office. When he came back out with the invoice, Arik looked at it twice. "What's this?"

"It took longer because Slasher and I did the work over a few days, so this is just for the parts." Reg put his arms over his chest. He didn't say another word, but he was daring Arik to argue.

Arik knew what Reg was up to, and part of him wanted to argue but another was so grateful he could hardly speak. Arik pulled out his checkbook and wrote the check, then handed it to Reg. "Thank you. I don't know what I did to deserve… this."

Reg took the check, smiling. "You're welcome." He leaned in and Arik kissed him. "That's more than payment enough." Arik loved how Reg looked when he smiled like that. The care lines fell away and his entire face lit up. When he was angry there was no hiding it, but when Reg grinned, he could outshine the sun.

"Can I get your full name for my report?" Officer Ravenwood said to Reg.

"Beauregard Thompson," Reg answered, and Arik placed his hand over his mouth. He had assumed his full name was Reginald. "Don't you dare laugh—it was my grandfather's name."

"Your poor grandfather," Arik quipped and began giggling.

Reg glared at him, shaking his head. "There was a reason I never told you." Reg gave the officer the rest of his information, and the police personnel began packing up to leave.

"Give us a few days in case we need to come back. I'll call you when you can open the restrooms again."

"Thanks," Reg said, and Officer Ravenwood nodded to Arik before gathering the rest of the men. Then they got in their cars and left. At least it was quiet.

"Do you need me to stay?" Arik asked.

"No. I need to get work done, and hopefully I can make the station seem as normal as possible. You should go and see if you can get some work done. I'll meet you at Faye's a little before four."

"You don't have to," Arik said, once again becoming nervous about what his mother wanted.

"I'll be there unless you tell me not to," Reg said.

"Thank you for that."

"What?" Reg asked.

"Just being there." Arik moved closer for a kiss.

"This is a place of business, you know, not a make-out hot spot, and it's not nice to see all this lovey-dovey stuff when some of us go home to an empty house every night." Slasher turned away and went back into the garage.

"I'll see you later," Reg told him, and Arik walked toward his car before racing back into the office and giving Reg a kiss. Slasher saw them, and Arik stuck his tongue out at him before hurrying back to his car.

PATRICK AND Ken saw Arik return and invited him to lunch. They were pleased that he seemed happier, and Arik brought the two of them up to date on everything that had happened. He hesitated but decided to tell them about his mother as well.

Patrick nudged his shoulder from his place, signing quickly. "Patrick says that if he's not too busy with everything that's going on, he'll go with you."

"Thanks," Arik said, putting down his fork so he could hold Patrick's hands in his. "I really appreciate that. But Reg said he would go with me, so I won't be alone." He pulled his fingers away and intended to pick up his fork, but stopped, looking at Patrick and then at Ken. They watched him in return but seemed to be waiting. "Everyone here has been so nice… and there's nothing for me back in Pontiac. I was wondering if you could help me find a place to live here."

Patrick and Ken shared one of those looks that Arik had seen before. He assumed it was their silent communication. Ken nodded, and Patrick smiled. Whatever had gone on between them seemed to be settled.

"You can rent the garden house for a while if you like. It's insulated and can be heated in the winter. It's small, but it will give you a place to stay until you decide on something more permanent." Ken seemed extraordinarily happy. "That would also give us more of a chance to work on our exhibition together."

"Are you sure? I won't get in your way or anything," Arik said. "I really like it here."

There was another of those shared looks, like a current passing between them. "We can tell." Ken raised his eyebrows expressively, and heat rose in Arik's cheeks. "A certain service station owner has really grabbed your attention."

Arik looked down at his plate of chicken salad and home-baked bread. "Yeah. But that isn't why I'd move here. I like Reg…." He more than liked him, but Reg needed to be the one he said the words to. "But I'd like to move here because it's so different from… there. I can breathe here, and my mind seems freer here without… the weight of the past. I can make a fresh start, and I think I need to." He was still blushing, and Ken didn't look as though he was buying it, but Patrick simply smiled and nodded before returning to his lunch.

After eating and helping Ken clean up, since Patrick had to go back to his shop across the street, Arik walked to the garden house, now his home, at least for the time being, and returned to the garden and the painting he'd started before he'd let everything go to hell with Reg. He still felt bad about all the conclusions he'd jumped to, but Reg had forgiven him, so he thought he could forgive himself.

The image of what he'd intended to do came back to him almost immediately, only now it had morphed slightly into something even better: his grandmother's garden, the one in front of him, and Reg all mixed together. If he tried to describe what was in his head, it would come out jumbled and unexplainable, so instead Arik simply got to work to put his vision onto canvas.

Progress was slow, but the techniques he'd worked through with pencils and other media seemed to be working for him as long as he was careful with each brush stroke. The work didn't flow easily, like it had before the accident, but it was coming and would only take more time. Arik wasn't patient by nature, but he would need to learn to be if he wanted make a go of his art. Things had changed since his accident—not just because of his injury, but inside him as well.

He worked for hours, until his hand ached. Then he set aside his tools and checked the clock. He needed to hurry or he was going to be late for his meeting with his mother.

As soon as he thought about that, the nerves and butterflies began in force. He carried his things inside, swearing under his breath the whole time. He hated that she could upset him like this. His mom and dad had been the reason he'd been injured. They had given him the crappiest of crappy childhoods and only thought about themselves. Now his mother wanted to speak to him, and he was upset and nervous about it. Shit, he wasn't going to give her anything or help her out. As far as he was concerned, his parents were on their own. He wasn't covering for or helping either of them. So what the hell was he nervous about? She couldn't hurt him any longer.

Arik steeled himself as he washed out his brushes, then stormed out of the garden house to his car and drove to Faye's to get this whole thing over with.

He parked out front, right behind Reg's truck. Arik didn't see his mother's car, but that didn't mean much. He went inside and sat next to Reg in the red booth. The diner looked as though the Coca-Cola advertising department had exploded inside. Everything was Coke-themed. Even the colors and chairs fit. It was cool, in a way, but definitely a little over the top. He might have had time to enjoy the kitschiness if his mother hadn't walked through the door. She was tired looking, but her clothes were clean and neat, which Arik thought was a decent sign.

Arik stood to get her attention and waited for her to join them. Then he sat back down as the waitress, in an apron of Coca-Cola fabric, approached to take their orders. They each ordered coffee, and then she left. "What did you want to talk about?" Arik asked, getting right to the point.

She fidgeted in her seat. "I've left your father for good." The waitress returned with a pot, filled their mugs, and then left again. "I honestly didn't know what he was doing, and I needed help." She grabbed a napkin from the holder and wiped her eyes. Arik stared at her, barely seeing what she was doing, finding it hard to care.

"So you called me," Arik said, lifting his mug with his injured hand, careful of the hot portion of the mug. "Mom, I can't be in the sun very long. The heat bothers my hand. It took months of therapy before I came here for me to be able to use my hand again. I'm only now able to start trying to paint again, and my hand hurts a lot of the time. Thanks to Reg here, and Ken and Patrick, the people who own the place where I live, I'm able to work, but it's slow and frustrating." He sipped and put down the mug, not really interested in the coffee. It only gave him something to have in front of him. "I was trying to build a life for myself, and you and Dad ripped that away, just like you've done my entire life."

"I did the best I could," she said.

Arik leaned over the table, anger rising by the second. "That was your best? How pathetic. I got up, got myself dressed, and went to school, leaving behind two stoned parents who had no idea I was gone… and I was eight. That was my life a lot of the time, and… and you did your *best*."

Reg took his hand and held it under the table, caressing it. That touch was all that kept him in control. Arik's head throbbed as his anger continued to rise. "Mrs. Bosler," Reg said softly. "Arik has been through a lot."

"I know," she whimpered, still holding the napkin.

"Why did you come here?" Reg asked. "You have to know that Arik isn't going to be able to forgive you and your husband—former husband, whatever—for everything. It's too much for you or anyone to ask or expect. He's building a life here, and he has people who care about and love him. That's what he needs right now."

"I understand...," she said and looked at Arik. "You are my son, and I'm sorry you are." Arik stiffened and was seconds from getting up to leave. "I mean that you deserved better parents than your father and me." She wiped her eyes and then sat a little straighter. "I don't expect you to forgive me, but I do want you to know that after your injury, I checked into rehab. I haven't had anything stronger than an aspirin in months."

Arik took a deep breath. He was happy for her if she was getting her life together, but that didn't change anything as far as he was concerned. Years of neglect and bad parenting couldn't be atoned for in a few minutes. "That's good." It was all he could muster at the moment.

"As part of my recovery, I need to visit the people I've hurt most, and I know that's you." She wiped her eyes again.

Arik nodded but gave her nothing. He wasn't going to let her off the hook. "What do you want me to do? Say that I forgive you? Maybe it makes me a small person, but I can't. Not right now. The pain is too real and too fresh." Hell, it was so deep Arik doubted he would ever be able to let it go.

"It's all right," Reg whispered as he leaned close.

Arik turned to him, filling with anger once again. "No, it's not. She has to know that she can't waltz in here and expect me to forgive years of pain and neglect." He turned to his mother. "I turned out to be a decent, hard-working guy despite you. I have a talent that I thought was gone forever because of you and Dad. Thankfully, it isn't. I can work, and Reg and my other friends here have taught me that my gift wasn't in my hand, but in my head and my heart." He turned to Reg, because his brain took that second to register what Reg had said earlier and the word he'd used. He leaned against Reg's shoulder and closed his eyes for a second. "Is there anything else you want to say? If not, I have a life here that I hope is going to make me happy." He was about to add that she wasn't part of it, but he kept that to himself. He gave himself a mental pat on the back for his restraint.

When his mother said nothing, Arik pulled out his wallet and got ready to place some bills on the table. He'd said his piece, stared down his mother, and now he felt a lot better, like he'd exorcised a demon that had been plaguing him, sitting on his shoulder for most of his life.

"Arik," she said in a tone that stopped him in his tracks. When he turned to look at her, he saw not the mother he'd come to know, stoned out of her mind or off to another party, but the mother who had once read him *Winnie the Pooh*. "When I was in rehab, they sent me to have a physical, and I found out I have cancer." She seemed more composed than she had at any time in the last few minutes. "It started in my liver and has spread to my lungs. There isn't anything they can do for me. The doctors said I should make plans and do my best to make peace with my life."

Jesus Christ. He blinked and sat back down. Why in the hell was it that nothing good ever happened without being followed by a truckload of shit?

"Once I sobered up, I learned that there was going to be a price to pay for the life I've led. I don't have any real friendships left. Your father and I have separated, and I already knew you were lost to me. But once the drugs were gone, I hoped I'd have time to try to repair some of the damage I've done."

"How long?" Arik asked. He knew he sounded cold, but there was only so much of this he could take.

"They gave me six months. I'll be functional for maybe three, and arrangements have been made for care after that." She reached out, touching Arik's hand. "I don't want anything, and I'm not asking you to forgive me, because what I've done is unforgiveable." She pulled back her hand and stood up. "I only wanted to tell you and to have a chance to say good-bye." She looked at Arik, her eyes glistening with unshed tears. Then she turned and quietly left the diner.

Arik was stunned. He sat in place, watching his mother leave, torn. Part of him willed his legs to move, but they didn't. "What in heck…?"

"I'm sorry. But you got what you wanted," Reg said.

Arik's mouth hung open. "You son of a bitch. What kind of man do you think I am that I would want my mother dead?" He shook, and Reg put his hands up in surrender. "I wanted her to leave me alone."

"No. You wanted to be able to hate your mother and your father. That way you'd have someone to blame for everything in your life." Reg's voice was so damn level and matter-of-fact that Arik got even angrier.

"Gee, thanks a lot." He stood, getting his legs to work, and threw some bills on the table.

"No," Reg said, holding his good hand tightly. "You aren't going to run from this. You're stronger than you give yourself credit for, and you can take what I have to say." Fire burned in Reg's eyes. Arik took a step back to the table and sat across from Reg, arms folded over his chest.

"You wanted your mother and dad to be there. See, as long as they were, you could hate them, and then everything that didn't go right was their fault. Yes, because of them you hurt your hand, and I'd do anything to have prevented that. But this is deeper than that. You could blame them for your artistic block, for being afraid of people who look like me. You could blame them for a crappy childhood. God, you could even blame them because you're small and short. Though I think that's part of your cuteness." He smiled, probably to try to lighten his message.

"So now you're a psychologist?" Arik asked, not liking this at all.

"Don't have to be. I blamed my parents for everything in my life too. They forgot about me after Marianne died… and so on. The thing is, the station, my business, the home I live in—I earned those. I did that. Those are mine. I worked hard for them. My parents didn't help me. Yes, my uncles did, but they stopped a while ago."

Reg took his hands. "Your life is your own now and has been for a long time."

"But...."

"This is going to be hard for you to hear, but you went to help your parents on your own. Your mother asked for your help, you went, and you got burned. Yes, your father should never have been cooking meth, but you could have walked away and called the police. You didn't. You tried to help because that's the kind of person you are." Reg took his injured hand. "This, these injuries, are a part of you. We all have scars, because life is a war. You have them on the inside and on the outside."

"What do you expect me to do? Just forgive her and sing 'Kumbaya' or something?" He glared at Reg and noticed others starting to turn to look at them. Overall the diner was fairly noisy, so most of their conversation had gone unnoticed, but they were starting to garner attention.

"No. I hope you can let the past go. It'll only eat at you until you do," Reg said more softly. "There's nothing you can do about what happened. Your parents, the accident, all of it. The past is the past. What you can do is make the best present and future possible." Reg stopped and just looked at him.

"How?" Arik finally asked. "All of that touched every aspect of my life. How can I just let it go?"

"It doesn't touch me, and none of it matters to me. You are the person I care about, as you are." Reg stood. "So think about whether you want to try to build a life on that instead of the quicksand of the past that you're so desperately trying to keep hold of." Reg squeezed his shoulder and then walked toward the door of the diner, leaving Arik all alone.

He should have known it would come to this. It always did. Him alone and everyone else walking away from him. That was what always happened. Arik made sure he had left enough money and hurried out of the diner.

"You don't get to leave on some fucking proclamation like that," Arik called as he hurried after Reg, reaching his truck at the same time.

"You think I'm wrong?" Reg whirled around. "Come on, protest or tell me that I'm full of crap." Reg stood there, arms over his chest, looking so sanctimonious Arik wanted to hit him... or kiss that look off his damn face. He wasn't sure which. "You can't. Because it isn't in you to lie." Reg let his arms fall to his sides, and his shoulders lost some of their rigidity. "There's nothing more I can do. Whatever happens from here is up to you. If you want to build a future, then you have to decide to do it. I can't do it for you. Whether you call your mom or ever talk to her is immaterial. What counts is what's in your heart and what you want to do going forward. If you want to live with the past as a millstone around your neck, you're free to do that. But if you want to try to build one with better tomorrows and a family of your very own, you know where to find me."

"I can't believe you're doing this," Arik said.

"I'm not doing anything other than asking you to decide what you want. I'm still here. I'm not turning my back on you. But I think you need to figure some things out."

Arik had no idea what that meant. Did Reg not want to see him unless he met Reg's standards? "Okay." He turned away and walked to his car. "I don't get you," he said before getting into his car, and Reg closed his truck door and walked over. "I thought when we were in there, you said that you loved me, and now you want me to make all these decisions so I'll be good enough for you."

"That's not it at all. I just want you to think about things. You'll be a lot happier, and that's all I want. Staying bogged down in the past sucks. I saw how you relaxed when your mother said that she'd cleaned up and was drug free. All I want is for you to be like that all the time. I'm not going anywhere except back to the garage. Why don't you go back to the garden house and work, let your mind free up and do what you do best."

"What's that, worry about the past?" He had to get a little dig in there.

"No," Reg said flatly. "You make the world a little more beautiful." Reg smiled, though he didn't kiss him because they were on the street. Arik watched Reg go back to his truck, and once he'd pulled out, he drove to Ken's. He parked and went back to the garden house, setting up his work again in the garden shade.

Of course, nothing came. He still had the image of what he wanted to do, but his mind wasn't clear. He sat on the stool, watching the flowers and his partially completed canvas, but never lifted his brush. His mother had told him she was dying. Footsteps on the lawn caught his attention, and he lifted his gaze to where Patrick walked toward him. He pulled out a pad.

What's wrong?

"I saw my mother today, and she said she's dying. Cancer."

Patrick shook his head and wrote something down, then handed him the pad. *Is that truly what's bothering you? I know you've had troubles with her.* Arik handed the pad back once he'd read the message.

"Yes… no… I…. Reg said a lot of things after she left."

What did he say?

"That he wants me to stop living in the past. I'm not sure if he gave me an ultimatum or not." He was so fucking confused he wanted to scream.

Patrick sighed and pointed toward the door of the garden house. Arik led the way inside, and Patrick went to Arik's old laptop and lifted the lid. Arik signed in and Patrick began typing.

I had to let go of my past. I was an opera singer, and until I could do that, I wasn't ready for what I have with Ken and to be there for him and Hanna, who is now cancer free, but we thought we were going to lose her. Patrick turned to him earnestly.

"But how do I do that?"

Patrick typed, *All you can do is be willing to let what you feel for Reg be more important than holding on to the pain. We all have it, but I'm not an opera singer any longer. I'm a woodworker with the most amazing family I could ever hope to have. You aren't a child any longer.*

"I know that."

So let your childhood be just that. Use it because it made you who you are, but don't let it decide your future.

"Should I forgive my family? Is that what I have to do?" Arik asked. He felt a little awkward, but Patrick had an amazing insight.

Okay. Close your eyes and think. Visualize your life in five years. Patrick pulled his hands from the keyboard and stood, placing his hands on Arik's shoulders. Arik did as Patrick asked and let his breathing even out. He was used to visualizing, so he thought of himself in five years. He was twenty-nine, standing in the yard of a nice home. It looked a lot like the one his grandmother had, except it was larger, with more color in the garden. He sat on the grass, letting its silkiness run though his fingers. The breeze rustled through his hair.

Patrick squeezed his shoulders.

"I'm there. We have a house with a yard like yours. Lots of color. The wind is blowing around me...." Arik smiled. "I have shorter hair."

Patrick chuckled, and as the image continued, Arik caught his breath and began to shake. For whatever reason his mother was there, standing at the edge of the lawn in a party dress, smiling in a way he'd never seen before. Arik sniffed, and Patrick pulled him forward into a hug. The last of Arik's emotional control broke, and he sobbed into Patrick's shirt like a child. "My mother is dying," he whispered, and Patrick held him tighter. "I know this is stupid after everything."

Patrick rocked him back and forth.

It took Arik a few minutes to get himself back together, and when he did, he stepped back, sniffling. "I'm sorry." At least his legs no longer quivered and he wasn't in danger of falling.

Patrick shook his head slowly and then shrugged, motioning gently with his hand. He was so expressive a single lift of his eyebrow conveyed what others did in paragraphs.

"Nothing is as easy as we'd like it to be."

That got Arik another nod. Patrick motioned once again, this time to where Arik had been working.

"Yes. I think I need to go back to work now."

Patrick sat back down at the computer. *You can have everything you want as long as you remember the past so you don't repeat it. But don't let it determine your future.* He turned and grinned at Arik. *Doesn't that sound like a Hallmark card?* Patrick got up and patted

Arik on the shoulder as if to say, my work is done here. At least that was how Arik understood it.

Now he understood what he wanted. Just like that, with a vision exercise, his priorities had fallen into place. Now to figure out how to make it happen.

Arik returned to the garden and picked up his palette and paint, sinking into his work with a peace of mind he hadn't known could be possible. His dreams, his hopes, could all come true if he wanted them badly enough and was willing to let go of what was holding him back.

He worked until the light faded and the angles changed so much that he wasn't going to get anything from the view in front of him. Not that he'd actually been painting it. His creative consciousness had sunk into itself hours ago, and when he blinked and stepped back, he smiled. The brushwork wasn't as precise as what he used to do, but he had used that to his advantage, creating a garden scene with illusions built into it. When he stepped to the left, he smiled as part of the flowers transformed slightly, creating the outline of a man, with a specific group of flowers forming his butt.

He shifted right and the figure receded, the scene in front of him becoming a garden once again. Gran's garden—well, after a sort. Arik was more than pleased his vision, the one he'd started with, had come to fruition.

"You look happy," Ken said through the open window from inside the house.

"What do you think?" Arik asked.

Ken left the window and came outside, joining him on the lawn. "It's beautiful. The style is different, but the same intensity of emotion is there," he said.

Arik shifted the painting. Ken stared, mouth open, speechless. "I'm calling it past and future, because they're both there."

"Those are poppies," Ken said, stepping closer. "Opium poppies. I doubt those were in any of the gardens you knew growing up."

"No. But they're part of my past, or at least the results from them are."

"Beauty from the flowers, the threatening clouds just peeking onto the canvas, poppies, and darkness and death hidden among the beauty. Then stepping to the side, a whole new image emerges...."

"The future—or what I hope is my future—springing from my past. When I envisioned the image and didn't know what it meant, Patrick helped show me in his own way." Arik wiped his hands on the cloth and began cleaning up, leaving the painting because Ken was still staring at it.

"You know what makes it so powerful is that the image is familiar to everyone. It's a garden, but it holds so much." Ken leaned forward, and Arik smiled. "Is that a snake?"

"Yes. The threat under the surface. That's what drugs and all I dealt with were. They promise happiness and light, but they're really insidious, hiding under the pretty veneer, getting ready to bite and eventually kill. But it's hidden and stays that way until the worst possible moment."

"This is very good," Ken said even as he continued looking, moving the painting back and forth. "Sometimes I'm not sure the man is really there. It's like a trick of the light. How did you do it?"

"The paint is built up slightly, so when you look at it from that direction, parts of the image catch the light differently. It's very subtle, and your eye does the rest of the work," Arik explained, and Ken nodded slowly, still examining the image.

"Knowing you, it's obvious who the man is and the way he's lying as though asleep and without care or concern. It's a great contrast."

"I was hoping for that. Sort of the treat—the real beauty hidden among the threats." Arik left to finish cleaning everything up and then put the painting inside to dry fully, careful not to touch anything.

Night fell fast, and by the time he was done, the shadows in the garden had lengthened to cover most of the grass. He loved this time of day and watched the shadows as they did their final dance until the sun dipped and the realm of night took over.

"Come join us for dinner. Hanna already ate, but I'm guessing you haven't stopped in hours," Ken said from the doorway.

"You're right." Arik did his best to keep from rubbing his aching hand. He wished Reg were here with his magic touch to soothe away the aches. Still, he was happy. His work was coming alive again, and his head and heart were light.

"Then come right in as soon as you're ready." Ken lightly knocked the doorframe and then closed it. Arik finished cleaning up and putting all his supplies away before joining them.

AFTER DINNER, Patrick and Ken had things they needed to do, and Arik was antsy anyway. Instead of going back to the garden house, he went right out to his car. He wished he could show Reg the painting, but he'd see it in time. Arik had other news he wanted to share.

The garage portion of Reg's business was closed, but the gas station was still open. As he pulled up, he saw the lights shining through the glass that curved around the cash register area. Arik pulled to a stop at the pumps and put some gas in his tank. Then he pulled ahead and went in to pay.

"I thought that was you," Reg said with a huge smile, standing up from where he'd been working.

"Are you here alone?"

"Yeah. It's been slow the past few hours, so I sent Derrick home. There was no need for him to stick around." Reg looked at the clock. "We close in half an hour." He motioned behind the counter and Arik came around, lowering himself into one of the battered desk chairs.

"I finished a painting this afternoon. Ken really likes it, and I'm pretty proud of it. I hope it helps exorcise some of the demons of my past." He didn't have any illusions that things would change so quickly, but he hoped he was on a path to deal with what happened and begin to let it go. "I really want you to see it."

A roar began at the edge of his hearing and grew louder. Soon a group of ten or twelve bikes approached the station, slowed, and roared through the drive, rounded the pumps, and took off again.

"What the hell?"

"Gadrey and his guys. They've been doing that for the last few hours. It's their way of trying to intimidate me. I pay no attention, and they'll get tired and go away."

Arik wasn't so sure, but he kept quiet, grateful when the engines faded into the distance.

"I called the police a while ago and let them know what was happening," Reg said. "Of course, Gadrey's not stupid enough to pull anything while anyone is here, so they waited until the customers left."

Arik groaned. "This is really hurting business, isn't it?"

"A little," Reg answered, but Arik figured he was understating. "The police arrested two of the guys from the club. They have them in jail now. Apparently the judge got a good look at their records and set bail sky-high. So now they're trying this crap. To what end, I don't know. They're only drawing attention to themselves, and that's going to bring more trouble down on them." Reg sat back down, but he didn't seem interested in what he'd been doing.

"So tell me about your afternoon," Reg said, and Arik found him looking at his hand. "It aches, doesn't it?"

"Yeah. I used it a lot, and now it's hurting." He probably should have taken something to ease the pain, but he hoped it would pass. "I have something I want to tell you. I was with Patrick this afternoon, and he said the same thing you did, in a different way." Arik began talking faster as Reg closed his books. "He asked me to visualize where I saw myself in five years."

Reg leaned closer. "What did you see?"

Arik grinned as he reveled in Reg's attention. He was about to explain when the thrumming he'd heard earlier started again, coming from the other direction. Reg stood, turning to look out the windows as the engine noise got louder and the bikes turned in once again. They wound around the pumps the way they had before.

"Get down," Reg yelled, turning as the glass window shattered. Reg fell to the floor, and the engine noise, louder now without the pane of glass, continued and then faded away. Arik stayed on the floor, shards of glass on his back, the floor littered with them. Carefully, once it was quiet, he lifted his head, looked around, and slowly got to his feet.

"Reg," Arik called and carefully went over to where Reg lay on his side, unmoving. Arik leaned over and saw red on Reg's shirt. "Oh God," he croaked, putting his hand over his mouth. Without thinking he reached for the phone on the desk and called 911. "I need an ambulance and the police at Thompson's Gas Station. Someone has been shot."

"Sir, please stay on the line. I'm sending help right away," the woman on the other end of the line said.

Arik shook, watching Reg. He was breathing—his chest moved—but Arik wasn't sure about anything else. "Should I do something to try to help?" He felt paralyzed.

"The ambulance is on its way now. It should be only a few minutes," the operator said, and sure enough sirens sounded, getting louder fast.

"I hear them."

"The ambulance garage is only a few blocks away from you. Just hold tight."

Within a minute a sea of cars with flashing lights of all colors filled the gas station parking area. Arik motioned to them and hung up the phone as groups of men rushed in, the EMTs approaching Reg.

"Are you all right?" one of them asked.

"Yes. I'm not hurt. It's him I'm worried about." Arik stepped back, leaning against the far wall to keep on his feet as the emergency personnel worked on Reg.

"Officer Ravenwood?" Arik asked when he thought he saw a familiar face.

"Did you see who did this?"

"The bikers have been driving through, and the last time, I think one of them took a shot at Reg. I didn't see which one, but I think Reg did. He told me to get down, and then the window shattered and...." Arik put his hands over his face. "Is he going to be okay?" The notion that bad always seemed to follow good for him crept back into his mind. Just like this afternoon, the pattern repeated once again. Only this time the price could be more than Arik ever imagined.

"They have things well under control."

"Is he going to be all right?" Arik repeated, his voice cracking, even though he knew it was too early for anyone to know anything. All he wanted was reassurance of some kind.

"We don't know," one of the EMTs said. "We're going to transport him."

"Can I ride with you?"

"It would be best if you took your own car."

"I need his keys so I can lock up the station for him," Arik said and then bent down to where Reg's phone lay on the floor. It must have fallen out of his pocket. Arik found Slasher's number and called.

"Whatcha need?" Slasher asked.

"It's Arik. Reg was shot," he muttered and then broke down. "Right in the station. Can you come here and lock up? The glass will need to be replaced in one of the windows." Arik shook like a leaf in the wind. "I'm going to follow the ambulance to the hospital."

"How bad is it?" Slasher asked. "I'll be there in ten minutes, sooner if I can."

"Thanks. He's not good." Arik hung up and managed to sit down before he fell.

"Is there anything you can tell us that might help?" Officer Ravenwood asked.

"I wish. This has to be connected to the guys who were selling drugs. But I don't know them nearly as well as Reg does." He looked to where the EMTs were loading Reg onto a gurney. An IV had been placed in his arm, and bandages covered his chest. "Slasher is coming in. He works here and is Reg's best friend. He can make sure the window is taken care of and that the station is locked."

"We're going to need to talk to you some more," Officer Ravenwood said, and Arik nodded. "Once they're ready, you can follow." He verified that he had all of Arik's personal information, and then Arik followed the EMTs out to the ambulance, watching as Reg was loaded in. He turned away as they closed the doors and saw Slasher approaching at a run.

"You aren't hurt, are you?" Slasher asked.

Arik shook his head, ready to fall apart, but he knew he couldn't. "No. I'm going with him." The ambulance pulled out, and Arik asked where the hospital was located. Slasher gave him directions, and after checking with the police and making sure they knew Slasher was there, Arik left and drove as quickly as he could. The town of Pleasanton wasn't very large, and he'd really come to love it. The downside was that the largest hospital was in Marquette, and he had to drive all the way there, worrying the entire time if Reg was okay.

Once he pulled in and parked, Arik raced into the emergency room and asked about Reg. He was told to sit and wait, which was incredibly frustrating. Even more so when, once someone did come to see him, they could tell him nothing other than that Reg was already being prepped for emergency surgery.

"Is there a way I can see him?" Arik asked.

"We're going to be taking him to surgery in a few minutes," the doctor said. "I wish I could say more, but there's nothing I can do. I'm bound by privacy rules."

Arik nodded and remembered he still had Reg's phone. He called Slasher and waited for him to answer. "Should I call Reg's parents?"

"I already did. Their numbers were in some of the papers here at the station. His dad said that they were going to get tickets and will fly up as soon as they can. Do you know anything?"

"Only that he's going into surgery." He knew nothing more than that Reg was still alive. "Can you get here?"

"I will as soon as everything is set here. I called an old friend, Hank Olsen, who I know from school. He's on his way to replace the glass. The police are still gathering what they need, but I expect them to leave soon, and then I'll be there. I called your friends Ken and Patrick, as well. They said they were going to come sit with you."

"Thanks." Arik didn't know what else to do, so he hung up, settling into an uncomfortable chair to wait for some sort of news.

Patrick arrived and sat next to him. He took Arik's hand and held it, and they just sat together. There was nothing either of them could do but keep the other company as Patrick worried for his friend and Arik sat in mortal fear that the man he'd come to realize that he loved might not make it through the night. "Part of the time I want to scream, and the rest I want to cry."

Patrick nodded and squeezed his hand.

After an almost interminable amount of time, Slasher came in and sat next to them. "Have you heard anything?"

"No."

Slasher immediately got up and talked with someone. Then he pulled some papers out of his pocket and handed them to the receptionist, who nodded. When Slasher returned, he was smiling. "Since he and I have been friends for years and neither of us has local family, we put each other on as medical emergency contacts. So they should be able to tell me what's going on."

"Oh, thank God," Arik breathed. Though if there was no news, it wasn't going to do any good.

"Mr. Thompson is still in surgery," a nurse said when she approached their little group. "The last update we have is that the bullet has been removed and the damage is being repaired."

"Is there any prognosis?" Arik asked.

"At this point, no. He is critical and the surgery is going as well as anyone can expect. All we can all do is wait. I suggest you get some coffee, because it's going to take some time yet." She nodded and left the area.

"I'll get coffee," Slasher said, and then he left as well. Arik stared at the walls and the clock, watching the second hand make its regulated circles. How many times it made its circle, Arik didn't count, losing focus as he slipped into his own thoughts.

"Arik," Slasher said, tapping his shoulder. He handed him a cup, which Arik took and held without looking or caring. It was only something to hold, and he ended up setting it aside untouched before sinking back into his thoughts. He'd only met Reg a few weeks earlier. How could all this have happened? He'd actually fallen for the guy. Just like that, Reg had worked his way into Arik's heart, filling the emptiness until the space was no longer hollow.

"The doctor is here," Slasher said, and Arik pushed aside his worries and stood, wobbling slightly until he saw the doctor smile.

"We repaired the damage as best we could. The bullet is out, and I'm cautiously optimistic. As long as we can control infection, he should recover."

Arik's legs almost collapsed under him. He found the chair and sat down. The tension and worry had been the only things keeping him upright, and now that they'd slipped away, he had nothing left at the moment. "Can we see him?"

"One at a time. He's in Recovery, and he'll be taken to Intensive Care for the night. Hopefully, if all is well, he'll be able to be moved to a room tomorrow. He isn't out of the woods yet, but it's much better than any of us hoped. That shot could have done more damage."

"Thank you," Arik breathed.

"I'll have a nurse come get you and escort you back when he's settled."

"We appreciate it," Slasher said. The doctor left, and they all breathed a sigh of relief, Arik most of all. It took longer than Arik expected, but a nurse came out half an hour later and escorted him back to see Reg.

He lay on a bed with tubes and sensors on him, wires running toward machines by the side of the bed, hooked to little screens. Arik ignored them and walked to the side of Reg's bed.

Reg was pale, ashen, and unmoving except for the slow rise and fall of his chest. He looked so much smaller than he was in real life, and it frightened Arik no end. He took Reg's hand, holding it gently, caressing his rough fingers. "What am I going to do? I just found you and now… this.…"

Reg's eyes were closed, and Arik was pretty sure he couldn't hear him, but it didn't matter. He had something he wanted to say. All that kept running through his mind was if something happened, this could be his only chance to tell Reg how he felt.

"I know you told me earlier that you loved me. You did it in this weird, backhanded way, but that's what you said, and I never told you that I love you too. That you're more important to me than my past because my past is dark, but you're in the light, standing in the sun, no matter where you are or what you're doing." He paused and blinked away threatening tears. He was not going to cry, at least not now. He could do that when he was alone at home.

Arik swallowed and steeled himself. "In art, we always work with the light, and you're the one person I want to work with for a very long time. You are my light, the sun in my soul." He stopped and grew quiet, watching Reg and wishing he'd wake up, but he knew Reg was probably being kept drugged so he would have a chance to start to heal.

"He needs to rest, and it looks like you do too," the nurse said gently. "Go on home, honey. You can come back in the morning."

Arik nodded and held Reg's hand for a few more seconds before releasing it. He followed the nurse back out to the waiting room, and after hugging Patrick and Slasher, he left the hospital.

The ride back to Ken's seemed to take mere seconds. With the panic and major worry gone, the trip that had gone by inches going to the hospital passed in a blur, and he parked and went right to the garden house, where he crawled into bed.

He was exhausted, but his mind had other ideas. It refused to turn off, so when he woke at four in the morning, Arik got up and went to work. His mind had been creating and rearranging images for hours, and it was time for him to get them down onto paper. He turned on the light and grabbed a sketchpad and pencil. Using his knees as a prop, he got to work.

"HOW LONG have you been up?" Ken asked after Arik had showered and answered the phone call that resulted in a breakfast invitation.

Arik shook his head. "I couldn't sleep after a few hours, so I sketched out and then started a new work." He sipped his coffee and looked out over the wet garden. It had started drizzling a few hours earlier and was now raining steadily. "I thought I'd go to the hospital this morning, and then this afternoon, I want to talk about our project. I know what I want to do."

"You're sure?"

"Yeah, I see them all—every work laid out in my mind's eye."

"Does this have anything to do with what happened to Reg?" Ken asked with a wry smile.

"Yes and no. Last night clarified what I want to do. We wanted to illustrate our journeys, and I think I have mine." He sipped from his mug and set it down. He didn't need the caffeine; he was wired enough already. He worked on the bacon and eggs on his plate.

"Do you have something special going on today?" Arik asked Hanna, who seemed on the edge of her chair.

"I'm going to visit my friend Sophia for the day. Uncle Gordy and Uncle Howard are going to take us to Pictured Rocks. She already called, and the tours are running. This is like the fifth time we've tried to go."

"Are you going to come with us to visit Uncle Reg first?" Ken asked.

"Is he awake?" Hanna asked.

"I don't know." Ken was quiet for a second, and he and Patrick shared another of those moments. He'd swear the two of them were telepathic. "We'll take you up to see him when you get back. Hopefully he'll be awake and doing better by then," Ken said. "Why don't you go up and get ready. I'm sure they'll be here anytime."

Hanna left the table in a rush, and Arik finished the last of his breakfast. Then he thanked Ken and Patrick and left to get ready to go to the hospital.

Reg's mother and father were going to arrive sometime today, so he made sure he looked decent before leaving the garden house and getting into his car. His anxiety built as he pulled into the hospital lot and parked. He checked with reception and was told that Reg was still in ICU, which meant only family could visit him. He went up anyway and spoke to the woman at the nurses' station there.

"I'm sorry. Unless you're family, I'm not authorized to allow you in. We need to keep visitors to a minimum in this area."

Arik turned to go down to one of the waiting areas. "Excuse me," a voice called from behind him. Arik turned and was shocked. The nurse who'd taken him to see Reg the night before was hurrying toward him. "I remember you were here to see Mr. Thompson last night."

"I'm Arik. His boyfriend. But they said I couldn't see him because I'm not family."

"Mr. Sashinski put you down as an approved visitor." She fixed a steely gaze at the other nurse. "Look at the list." She turned back to Arik. "Come with me." She turned and led Arik back to the area and in to see Reg.

Reg looked very much the same. He did have a little more color in his face, but he was still and his eyes were closed.

"There hasn't been much change," the nurse said.

"Thank you." Arik nodded and sat in the small chair next to the bed. It was like sitting on a block of concrete, and Arik figured Redi-Mix must have been the hospital furniture supplier. He took Reg's hand, caressing the back of it the way Reg always did to soothe

the aches from his injuries. "You need to wake up. I have so many things to tell you." He looked up but no one seemed to be nearby. He watched Reg's eyes, hoping they'd move.

The nurse returned, and Arik quieted.

"Talking to him is good," she said. "Sometimes it helps them find their way back through the drugs and confusion." She used her computer to take down some readings and checked Reg's lines and tubes before smiling and leaving them alone once again.

"What was I saying?" Arik asked himself. "Oh. After I got home, Patrick was there, and he said you were right." There was no movement. "I knew you'd be happy about that. Which is why I'm telling you now, so you can't give me grief about it. He said I have to let go of the past if I want to be happy. He also said I should visualize where I saw myself in five years. When I did, what I saw shocked me." He stopped and waited, watching Reg's eyes, hoping for a sign. "I was surprised, because I was at a party at my house, well, our house. You were there with me. I didn't have to see you to know you were there. But the shocking thing was that my mother was there too." He continued rubbing Reg's hand, willing him to open his eyes. "My mom. I saw my mother in my life in five years. I don't know how that's possible, but she was happy and smiling. She looked good. Not at all like I'm used to seeing, and even better than yesterday."

Arik shifted in his seat, trying to find some comfortable position without letting go of Reg's hand. "What really surprised me was when Bobbie Jo came out of the house, racing into your arms. She was older, a gorgeous young woman, and she called you Pop and me Dad." Arik leaned his head down, kissing Reg's hand. "I know this is all fantasy and wishful thinking, but I see the three of us—you, me, and Bobbie Jo—as a family."

"You do?" Reg rasped, and Arik stilled completely.

"Was that you?" He returned to Reg. "Please open your eyes and let me see them."

"Too bright," Reg whispered, and Arik stood. He found the nurse, and she turned down the lights for him. Arik sat down, took Reg's hand, and watched as he slowly opened his eyes.

"You scared me so much," Arik told him softly. "I figured things out, and then you went and got shot."

"I didn't mean to," Reg said as the nurse brought a cup of ice chips and set them on the table. Arik took one and placed it on Reg's lips.

"Slasher took care of the station and called your mom and dad. They're coming today."

"Okay." Reg closed his eyes, and Arik figured he'd gone back to sleep." "You really want all that?"

"Yes." Arik leaned over the bed. "But is that what you want?" Reg didn't answer, and Arik wasn't going to press him at this moment. He was happy Reg was awake. The rest could wait.

"Never thought about adopting Bobbie Jo," Reg whispered, and Arik gave him another ice chip.

"We'll talk about everything later." Arik continued holding his hand and grew quiet. He gave Reg additional ice chips when he seemed to need them, but otherwise Reg mostly slept.

"You're back among us," the nurse said, and this time Arik made sure to look at the name tag.

"He's been sleeping on and off, Kerry."

She smiled. "That's normal, hon. He'll be in and out of it for a day or two. The medication is still working its way out of him. But the thing is, he'll be waking up soon because the pain is going to kick in. So when it does, just call me, and I'll bring some relief." She leaned over Reg. "You hear me in there?"

"The dead can hear you," Reg murmured, and Kerry chuckled, with Arik right behind her.

"You're feeling okay if you can be feisty," she teased. "On a scale of one to ten, how is the pain?"

"Two," Reg answered, keeping his eyes closed.

"Okay." She fussed in the room, and Reg began to stiffen and move. "How is it now?"

"Seven," Reg answered. Arik was surprised at how fast the pain had returned. Kerry left the room, and Arik could tell the pain was hitting Reg hard and fast. "It's a nine," he said when she returned.

"All right." She injected something into the IV, and a minute later some of the tension slipped away. Arik could feel it in Reg's grip, and the lines around his eyes smoothed away. "On a scale of one to ten, how is the pain now?"

"Four," Reg said.

Arik sat back in the terrible chair. "Just get some sleep. I'll be here when you wake up," he told Reg and placed another ice chip at his lips. Reg sighed and his eyes closed once again.

Arik sat back, sighing softly, releasing the tension that had had him strung as tight as a violin since the incident last night. He closed his own eyes and tried to rest.

Ken and Patrick came in a little later, peering into the room and then stepping inside quietly. Reg didn't even wake up.

"He's doing okay, flying a little on painkillers right now," Arik said. "But he's been his usual smart self, so I think he's going to be okay."

"Have to keep you on your toes," Reg said.

"See?" Arik smiled and stood up and left the room, letting Patrick and Ken visit with Reg. He wandered down to the cafeteria and got some coffee as well as a small snack. He sat at a lone table and ate his cheese and crackers, sipping the awful coffee. But it gave him a chance to think and breathe for a few minutes. Once he was done, Arik threw his trash away and left the cafeteria, happy and relieved. When he got back to the ICU, they were getting ready to move Reg into a regular room. Some of the monitors were being removed, and the staff explained that Reg was doing very well.

ARIK SPENT the rest of the morning sitting with Reg, talking with him when he was awake and otherwise letting him sleep. He used one of those naptimes to get something to eat.

When he returned, he heard voices and walked in to find a man and woman standing near the bed. "Are you Reg's parents? I'm Arik." The woman stared at him blankly for a few seconds and then turned to her husband.

"It's all right. This is a friend of our son's," the man said. "I'm Lars and this is Helena. Unfortunately she's having a little trouble with the strange surroundings."

Helena turned away from him to stare at Reg. "Do I know you?" she asked.

"This is our son, Beauregard," Lars said. "He was injured, and we came to see him and make sure he was okay." He spoke with patience, but he looked tired. "Remember? We talked about this on the way here."

Helena once again seemed lost, but she nodded. Lars guided her to the chair beside the bed, and she sat, hands in her lap, seemingly looking at Reg, but Arik doubted she understood much of what was happening around her.

"Does she ever remember me?" Reg asked his father.

"Sometimes. Now all that exists on a regular basis are me and Marianne. There are times when she doesn't remember me. Physically she's strong and has few problems." Lars took Helena's hand and stood over Reg.

"You need help, Dad," Reg whispered.

"It seems you're going to need some yourself after this ordeal."

"He'll have it," Arik piped up as he moved to the other side of the bed, carefully sliding his hand under Reg's.

Lars swallowed and didn't meet his gaze. "This is… problematic."

"No, it isn't, Dad. You have your life in Florida taking care of Mom, and I have my life here. It's been that way for a long time. Not going to change."

"But this isn't the way you should be living, you know that." There was no heat in his voice, just a statement of fact, which seemed strange to Arik.

"What I know is that I have a mother who wrote me off years ago and rarely remembers who I am in favor of a dead sister she loved more than life itself. I know you need to care for her and you're doing what's right, but you don't get to tell me how to live my life. You forfeited the right to give input years ago." The pain in Reg's voice had nothing to do with his wounds. Arik recognized it clearly. "I have a good life here, with wonderful friends who care about me and watch out for me."

"Then you don't need me?" Lars said.

"No. But I'm glad you're here." It took Arik a few seconds to figure out what Reg was saying. He didn't need his parents, but maybe that made the visit mean more. They didn't have to come, but they were here regardless. "They said I'm doing well, and that I need to rest. I was lucky."

"Did you see who did this?" Arik asked.

"Yes." Reg didn't elaborate.

"I'll call the police and ask Officer Ravenwood to come speak to you."

"I'm surprised they haven't been beating down my door," Reg commented.

"They probably tried, but the staff here are formidable." Arik turned away and made a call, getting right through to Officer Ravenwood. He was excited and said he'd be right there. Arik stayed until the officer arrived, then left the room and showed Reg's parents the way to the cafeteria.

OVER THE next few days, Arik spent part of his time at the hospital and the rest working. He was so full of ideas now, his head couldn't contain them. Reg's parents stayed for three days, and Arik gave them time on their own with their son.

"How are you feeling?" Arik asked when he entered Reg's room. He got a smile in return.

"Bored stiff. My mom and dad went back to Florida. Mom was getting more and more nervous and upset by the day. Dad wasn't sure she could take the flight home if they stayed much longer, so they left." Reg patted the bed next to his feet. The IVs had been removed, along with the machines. His color was back, and while he was still in pain, at least he could eat again. The one problem was mobility, which he was getting back, albeit slowly.

"I hope they had a good visit. Aside from... you know."

"We did, and Officer Ravenwood was just here. They arrested one of Gadrey's cronies for shooting me, and he did what the other two they'd already gotten earlier didn't—he talked. So it seems the contingent of the club that was the problem has been gutted. Slasher came by and said the club is being folded. It will be gone, and he's going to start a new one. He asked if we wanted to join."

"We?" Arik asked. "I don't own a bike."

"No. But you have a permanent seat on mine if you like." Reg took his hand. "If that's what you want. See, I seem to remember someone telling me a story while I was half out of it. I'm hoping it wasn't some hallucination."

"I don't think so," Arik said, smiling.

"I can at least handle the you-and-me part of that story."

"I called Maggie yesterday, and she said that Bobbie Jo's surgery is coming up soon. The little thing is so scared. She apparently asks to see you every day."

"I know, but... I'm.... What kind of father would I make?"

Arik rolled his eyes. "Do you know when I first started not to be afraid of you?" Reg shook his head. "It was when I saw you with Bobbie Jo. She's so small, and you were so gentle with her." Arik paused and waited for Reg to respond. "Let me ask you this. How would you feel if, the next time we visited, Maggie told us that Bobbie Jo was going to be adopted by a couple from—" He picked a city at random. "Detroit. And you would never see her again?" The shock in Reg's eyes told him all he needed to know.

"I should have seen that months ago."

"It's not too late to do something about it." Arik took Reg's hand, looking at him as they sat together.

"Are you sure this is what you want? How you want your life— our life—to be?"

"Yeah." Arik leaned forward and pulled Reg gingerly in his arms, placing his head on his shoulders. "It's exactly what I want."

CHAPTER
Eight

REG STILL ached, and he walked gingerly, holding Bobbie Jo's hand as they crossed Ken and Patrick's lawn to where Arik was standing next to Ken.

"This is how I see it," Arik said. He rushed inside, and Bobbie Jo looked up at Reg.

"We need to stay here for a few minutes," Reg said to her.

"Can I look at the flowers?" Bobbie Jo asked.

"Yes. But don't pick them. They're Mr. Ken's flowers." She nodded, and Reg let go of her hand. He knew Bobbie Jo wouldn't go very far. In the time since he'd gotten out of the hospital, Gert at the children's home had used Reg's excellent record as a volunteer to push through his application to become a foster parent, and once he was approved, Bobbie Jo had been allowed to move into Reg's house during the slow process for formal adoption. Since then, she'd stayed close to him whenever she wasn't at school.

"Hi," Arik called to Reg as he came out, handing Ken a canvas. "We're nearly finished here." Arik ran back inside and came back out with a chair.

"I'm not an invalid," Reg protested even as he sat down. Bobbie Jo ran over and climbed onto his lap after getting a hug from Arik.

"Yeah, yeah." Arik turned back to Ken. "We want this to be about a journey, so if you don't mind, I thought it should start with the painting you bought. That's where I was before all this happened." Arik placed a sketch of Reg next to it, and then one of the colored pencil drawings of him.

"That's you," Bobbie Jo said.

"Yeah, it is."

"I thought then I'd put the garden scene."

"There's a man sleeping in the flowers," Bobbie Jo whispered, and Reg smiled and nodded.

"What about the others?"

"I'm going to do a picture of Bobbie Jo, then Reg and me, or maybe one of the three of us. I haven't worked that out. I'm also going to paint my injured hand and place that here before the sketch of Reg, so the images tell the entire story, but the last one will be a portrait of my mother."

"Why?" Ken asked.

"Because then I'll have come full circle. This isn't as much about my journey back to work and recovery, but about my inner journey to deal with my past and build a future. So I'm painting my mother as an act of forgiveness and leaving my past behind."

Ken nodded. "Then I think you should do a sketch of yourself instead of only your hand, and switch the last two. Put your mother here and then the painting of the three of you, because forgiving your mother allowed you to have the family you and Reg are building."

Arik adjusted his vision and made notes. "And the portrait of the three of us should be in the same garden as the first one. Yes, then everything will flow and we'll have returned to the end.... And the beginning." He could see the huge loop he'd made, both in his work and in his personal life.

"We still have six months, so we can make adjustments as the other works are completed, but I think this will work. Each journey is personal, and this will most definitely be that." Ken smiled.

"What's your journey?" Reg asked Ken.

"What's interesting is that Arik's journey is a piece of mine. I decided to depict my journey as mentor. So I have what I did with my previous student." Ken turned to Arik. "Of course, working with you has been very different than I expected. But we still have time, and from there I'll look into the future to see what I want to do next. I don't think I want a constant parade of people living in my garden house, but I think I might like to teach more formally." Ken gathered Arik in a loose hug. "You taught me that I have something to give."

"Of course you do," Arik said. "I couldn't have done this without you and Patrick." Arik hugged Ken, and then turned to smile at Reg and Bobbie Jo. He came over and lifted Bobbie Jo off Reg's lap. "I couldn't have done this without you either." He hugged her gently. "Do you like it at Reg's?"

She nodded. "I have my own room, and Reg says I can paint it any color I want." Bobbie Jo hadn't gotten to the point where she was calling Reg Dad, but Arik figured that would happen soon. Reg had said that he wasn't going to bring it up, but that he'd let Bobbie Jo decide when she was comfortable.

"Are you ready to go?" Reg asked.

Arik set Bobbie Jo down, and she raced over to him.

"What are you doing today?" Ken asked as he rolled up his and Arik's plans.

"I have to go to work, though I can't do much other than sit, and Bobbie Jo is going to school so she can see some of her friends."

"Actually, I was going to gather some of my things and go in with Reg," Arik said. "I have an idea for a men-at-work series, and I think I'm going to start with the garage. I also need to keep an eye on him to make sure he doesn't try to do things he shouldn't be doing."

"You are, huh?" Reg said.

"Yeah. I also want to work up plans so we can have the place painted and fixed up." Arik turned to Bobbie Jo. "If I bring crayons and colored pencils, do you want to spend the day with us?"

Bobbie Jo nodded.

"Fine. Go get what you need," Reg said indulgently, and Arik raced back inside.

"He's got you wrapped around his finger," Ken said once Bobbie Jo ran inside as well. Reg could hear them chattering away happily.

"The same way Hanna and Patrick have you wrapped around their fingers."

Ken nodded. "It's a great feeling, isn't it?"

"Best in the world," Reg said with a grin. Once Arik came out with his arms full, Reg wondered what exactly Arik had planned for the day. Bobbie Jo had a small case, and when they approached, Reg stood and Arik set down his things and took the chair back inside. He was so full of energy and life, it astonished Reg. Arik's eyes sparkled now, and his lips always seemed either to be in a smile or on the verge of one.

"Go take your case and get in the truck," Reg told Bobbie Jo. Then he thanked Ken for everything and followed her. She got herself buckled in the center of the seat, smiling and swinging her legs. Happiness was definitely in the air.

"WHERE'S BOBBIE JO?" Reg asked a few hours later when he came into the office and sat in his chair. He sighed and wished he'd taken longer to recuperate. Not that he was in pain, particularly, but he was tiring more quickly than he liked. Slasher and Derrick had things well in hand, and he thought about putting his feet up and maybe closing his eyes.

"She went to the bathroom," Arik said, watching as she walked by the repaired windows and came inside. She climbed onto his lap and carefully settled on his left side, where he hadn't been injured. Never in his life had Reg expected to be this contented.

"Remember what we talked about last night?" Reg asked Bobbie Jo. She turned to him, her big eyes shining, and nodded. "Is that okay?"

"Yes."

"Do you want to ask him?" Reg asked, and Bobbie Jo shook her head. "Are you feeling shy now?" She buried her face against Reg's arm. They still had some work to do. Reg had noticed that while Bobbie Jo smiled more and was happier, she rarely asked questions. Reg thought it was because she was always afraid of being told no, or that she'd ask the wrong thing and Reg wouldn't adopt her and instead would take her back to the children's home. Only time would heal those wounds. "Can I ask him?" Bobbie Jo nodded this time.

"Ask me what?" Arik tickled Bobbie Jo lightly, and she giggled and lifted her head away. "What is it you and your daddy want to ask me?"

"I saw your idea for the painting of the three of us, and Bobbie Jo and I talked last night, so I thought we should make it official. So we'd like you to move out of the garden house and in with us." He and Arik had already talked, and Arik had said that he planned to stay in town and rent the garden house from Ken and Patrick.

Arik stopped. "Is that what you really want? We don't have to rush into anything you aren't ready for."

Reg gently tugged Arik down to him. "Of course it's what I want."

"Kissing…," Bobbie Jo crooned and then giggled as Reg took Arik's lips. Heat spread through Reg, and he backed away, not willing to start something he couldn't finish. Recovering from an injury really sucked.

"You'll need to get used to that," Arik said to Bobbie Jo and leaned over the chair, kissing him once again. "I have a feeling we'll be doing it a lot." He gently hugged him, and Bobbie Jo nestled right in. "I love you both."

"Isn't that cute," Slasher said from the doorway and pulled out his phone, taking their first family picture.

Epilogue

A Year Later

"Reg," Arik called as he got out of his Escort. To say it was new would be an exaggeration, but it was a different car and much newer than the one he'd had. Bobbie Jo was in the backseat, and he waited for her. Then they walked across the parking lot at the station together. He couldn't help stopping to look at the building, all freshened up with new paint and a brand-new sign out front that read Thompson's Service. Arik had designed a logo stylized off the art deco design of the building and added it to the sign. Now everyone in town, old customers and new, stopped at Thompson's. Some came to see the building and fill up, others to get their cars serviced. Either way, the place was hopping, and Reg had hired an additional mechanic.

"Hey," Reg said with a grin, wheeling a red bike out of the last bay, its glossy paint shining in the afternoon sun.

"It's a devil," Bobbie Jo squealed and raced up to it, running her hand gently along the gas tank.

"These get better and better." Arik tried not to grin. He'd started working with Reg to help design some of the bike customizations, and this was one he'd done. The gas tank was the devil's head, flames ran down toward the back from the body, and the handle bars had been stylized slightly to resemble horns. It was an amazing sight.

"Fester is going to love it." He was one of the members of the Superior Riders, the new club Reg and Slasher had formed. He looked like the uncle from *The Addams Family*, and he was equally eccentric, but a great guy.

"I bet he is." Arik put his hands on his hips, waiting impatiently. "How much longer are you going to work on a Saturday?"

"Fester is on his way, and then your partner and I will close up here and head to the house," Slasher said. "Reg promised delivery today, so we made it happen."

"Derrick is working today so I can leave," Reg explained.

"But Reg promised me some cake," Derrick said, and Bobbie Jo squealed when Derrick handed her a small wrapped gift. "Happy birthday." Bobbie Jo began tearing at the paper as they all watched her delight.

"Oh, I love it," she said, gaping at the coloring book and crayons before hurrying to give Derrick a thank-you hug. Arik turned away. Whenever Reg got a gift, he always opened it and said how much he loved it. Bobbie Jo had picked up on his habit, and it amused Arik no end. "Thank you." She held them close to her as though they were precious and stood next to Arik.

"Please don't be long, and tell Fester he should stop by." The entire club had been invited, but he wasn't sure how many would show up for a seven-year-old's birthday party. Arik stepped inside with Bobbie Jo and looked around, making sure that everything was as it should be. He and Reg had brought in a Coke cooler they'd found in an antique store. Reg had cleaned it and rebuilt the inside, and now it stood in the corner, adding to the 1920s atmosphere. He'd brought in some vintage-looking shelves for snacks and chips, and they had done very well. The entire station, with the exception of inside the bays and the gas pumps, looked like a step back in time.

"Satisfied?" Reg asked with a half smile.

"Very. It looks awesome. I saw some old road signs and a set of Burma Shave signs the other day. We should go look at them. We could restore them and then mount them on the fencing. That would complete the look."

Reg smiled indulgently. "Okay." He led Arik and Bobbie Jo out of the office and to the car. "Go on and get ready. I'll be there in a minute." Reg kissed him, hugged Bobbie Jo, and scooted both of them into the car.

"Bye, Daddy," Bobbie Jo called as she got in the car. Arik waved and then hurried off toward Reg's, now their house, only a few blocks away.

The neat stone Tudor had been built just a decade after the station. It was plain, but comfortable. The rooms weren't huge, but there was plenty of room for the three of them. Arik's favorite part of the house was the large deck built off the side of the house.

"Do you want to put the tablecloths on the tables?" Arik asked once he'd carried everything inside, and Bobbie Jo began bouncing off the walls with excitement. "Put your present on the shelf in your room and then come back down, and then we'll finish getting ready for your party." Arik began getting the chips into bowls on the kitchen table. He also set out the plates and cups.

The doorbell rang, and he hurried to answer it. Ken and Patrick led a small army of people, including Howard and Gordy, a couple he'd met through Patrick and Ken. Howard was blind, but that didn't slow him down one bit. Their daughter, Sophia, who was about Hanna's age, held Ken's arm.

"The party is out on the deck. I'm still trying to get things set up," Arik said.

"Tom, Greg, and Davey are behind us by about five minutes," Ken said as heavy footsteps sounded on the stairs, and Bobbie Jo squealed happily when she saw her older friends.

"What can we do to help?" Ken asked.

"The girls can put the tablecloths on the tables on the deck and start taking out plates and cups. There are some chairs in the garage to be set up, and the cake should be arriving any minute. Dan and Connor are going to bring it when they get here with Wilson and Garrett."

The girls hurried into the kitchen and then raced outside with the tablecloths fluttering after them. "I'll head up the efforts out there," Ken said, and Patrick motioned that he'd help. Gordy guided Howard through the house and out to the deck, while Ken helped Arik start to bring the food outside and place it on the tables in the shade of the house.

Reg got home and pitched in as other guests arrived, including those bringing the cake, which was the last worry for Arik. Everything was going to be great. Bobbie Jo played with her friends, and the yard was filled with joyous laughter. Davey and his dads arrived, and after being shown around the yard by his father, he joined the others.

"You'd hardly know he can't see," Arik said to Tom as he watched the kids play.

"He's remarkable, but the kids all watch out for him."

Arik nodded. He looked over their ever-increasing throng of guests and marveled at the collection of amazing individuals within their circle of friends. There were deaf adults and children, blind people, even some in wheelchairs. He looked down at his hand and smiled. He was lucky…. They were all lucky. Bobbie Jo's own hand had been corrected, and now other than the fading scars, you'd never know there had been anything wrong. She was a perfect, happy little girl who now sat on the lawn with a group of her friends playing dolls and learning sign language from Dan and Connor's daughter Janey.

"I wasn't going to start the grill for a while yet," Reg said.

"Perfect. Does everyone have everything they need?" Arik asked as a rumble shook the air and got louder before cutting off in front of the house. A dozen men in leather entered the yard, taking off their jackets and other biking gear. Reg led them inside to explain where they could hang their gear, and the party got larger and the table with gifts for Bobbie Jo got even fuller.

Arik wandered out into the yard and sat on the grass next to Dan and Connor's son Jerry's wheelchair. He'd started collecting the young artist's work and had it all on one wall of his studio off the garage. The drawings served as a constant inspiration to him never to let anything or anyone hold him back. Jerry's work was a great reminder that anything was possible. "I was wondering if you'd like to work with me sometime."

Jerry's eyes brightened like the sun. "Sure." He rocked back and forth in his chair, a sign Arik had learned meant he was really excited.

Footsteps approached behind him, which Arik felt rather than heard. Arik knew it was Reg, and he turned and lifted his gaze to his partner's. Behind Reg he saw someone he hadn't been expecting—his mother. It hadn't been five years or anything, but maybe he was lucky and the things he truly wanted had started to come true earlier. She looked good, her eyes clear. She wore a scarf over her head, but other than that no one would know the dragon she'd done battle with and had, at least for now, vanquished.

"Mom." Arik stood and took her hands. He wasn't sure how to react. "I'm so glad you're here."

"Grandma," Bobbie Jo cried and raced to her for a hug. Arik sighed and smiled as Reg wound an arm around his waist.

"Did you ever imagine this last year when you first came here?"

"You mean when I was so scared of you I hid behind something?" Arik felt a little dumb about that now. "No. Now I have it all." Sometimes he was afraid to say the words for fear that something awful would happen. He looked up at the blue sky, waiting for the flash of lightning to strike anyway, but the only thing he saw were the birds playing in the trees.

"Jerry, come play ball with us," Janey called, and Jerry's chair hummed as he rolled across the grass.

Arik looked up at the deck with all the people talking and milling around, laughter and overlapping conversations carried on the breeze, mixing with the laughter and joy from the kids as they played. "Sometimes I can't believe all that's happened." Arik rested his head on Reg's shoulder for a few seconds, soaking up contentment and happiness as his mother played catch with her granddaughter.

"She isn't the same woman you knew," Reg said.

"I don't think anything is the same as what I knew before coming here, meeting you, and falling in love with you." Arik shared a kiss with Reg, and some of the guys on the deck applauded. Arik pulled away, his cheeks heating.

"Things aren't the same for any of us." They watched their guests and smiled. "They're way better than I could ever have imagined."

"Me too." Arik soaked in the joy of being with the man he loved for a few minutes, and then they walked toward the deck to join their guests, becoming part of the party, enveloped by the joy of their love for each other and the warmth and light of dear friends.

Stay tuned for an excerpt from

Love Comes Silently

A Senses Series Story

By Andrew Grey

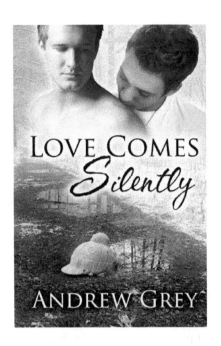

Caring for a loved one with cancer is tough. Doing it alone is overwhelming—especially when that loved one is a child. But ever since Ken Brighton's partner left him, Ken has spent his days at the hospital with his daughter, Hanna, hoping for a miracle. Maybe the mysterious care packages that appear for Hanna don't qualify, but they bring a spark of hope into his and Hanna's tired life—and so does Ken's neighbor, former singer Patrick Flaherty.

For two years Patrick hasn't been able to focus on anything but the life he should have had. An injury robbed him of his voice, and the idea of introducing himself to new people intimidates him. But over the past months, he's watched as his neighbor nursed his sick child, and once he meets Ken, Patrick starts to crave a life with him—a life he isn't sure he can have.

Ken doesn't realize he's fallen in love until the doctors send Hanna home, saying there's nothing more they can do: Hanna will either recover or succumb. Ken's heart is set on a new beginning—with both Patrick and Hanna. But Patrick's silence leaves Ken wondering what Patrick wants.

www.dreamspinnerpress.com

Prologue

KEN MOVED quietly through the small house, darting around boxes as his insides twisted and turned with every sound that came from Hanna's room. He'd have sworn on a stack of Bibles that he'd unpacked all the bathroom stuff, but he couldn't find the goddamned thermometer. When he'd touched her head, she was hot, and he desperately needed to know how high her fever was. "Daddy," he heard Hanna call weakly, and Ken hurried back up the stairs to her room. Hanna had kicked off her covers and was shivering in her bed, so Ken pulled them back around her, touching her forehead once more before getting a glass of water and a cool cloth that he placed behind her neck as he held the glass for her.

"Is that better, sweetheart?" Ken asked worriedly.

"Yes," she answered as she settled back on the bed, her eyes closing. Ken transferred the cloth to her forehead and then hurried back downstairs. He'd already checked every remaining box upstairs, so he rushed into the small dining room that he was using as unopened box storage and began systematically looking for the missing box.

He finally found it stuck in with the boxes of china that would eventually go in the cabinet that sat empty along the dining room wall. Ken picked up the box, carried it upstairs, and set it on the toilet in the bathroom. He rummaged around inside, not caring what fell on the floor, and finally found the object of his quest. And the fucking thing was dead. He wanted to scream, but began rummaging again until he found the battery charger. He carried everything into Hanna's room, plugged in the thermometer, and let it charge for a minute before placing the tip just inside Hanna's ear. Ken waited impatiently for the soft beep and then lifted it away—103 degrees. That settled it. Ken went to Hanna's dresser and found her tiny robe, placing it on the bed. Hunting around, he found the bunny slippers his parents had gotten her for Christmas the previous year, along with Emily, the doll six-year-old Hanna was rarely without except when she was at school.

"Honey, can you open your eyes for me?" Ken said as he lifted her up. He set her on the edge of the bed as he worked her arms into the robe and got the slippers onto her feet. "I'll be right back," he said and hurried out into the hall, then returned with a blanket. Ken wrapped it around her and then lifted her off the bed, making sure she was covered and warm before leaving the room. He turned out the light with his elbow before descending the stairs.

Ken laid Hanna on the sofa in the half-put-together living room before locating his keys and wallet, coat, and gloves. Then he lifted her into his arms once again. Ken felt Hanna's head rest on his shoulder as he opened the front door.

The frigid air assaulted them both as Ken stepped out into the evening. He closed the door behind him and moved as quickly as he could down the walk to his car. Reaching his keys was another matter, and he couldn't unlock the doors. He didn't have a place to set Hanna down and he could feel her getting cold. By moving Hanna carefully, he managed to pull his keys out of his pocket and click the car doors unlocked. Ken was about to grab for the door when he saw someone reach for the door handle and slowly pull open the back door of his car. Ken glanced at the man quickly before setting Hanna in her booster seat. Ken buckled her in and then closed the door. "Thank you," he said hastily and was able to actually look at the man, who appeared to be about his age, although it was hard to tell under all the winter gear.

The man smiled and nodded, stepping back from the car as Ken opened his door and got inside. The car was ice cold, and he wished he'd have thought to warm it up before bringing Hanna outside. "We'll be warm in a few minutes," he told her as he turned the key in the ignition. Using the wipers to brush away the inch or so of snow, Ken slowly pulled down his driveway and out onto the street. Thankfully, it wasn't snowing right now, and Ken turned on the radio to get the weather forecast as they moved along the plowed street toward the highway. There were very few freeways in Michigan's Upper Peninsula, which had been part of the allure of moving here. One of the things he should have done was choose a house closer to a hospital. Not that he could have expected Hanna to get sick within two weeks of moving into their new home. They reached the highway, and Ken felt heat begin to come out of the vents, so he turned the fan on maximum. After turning onto the recently plowed and nearly clear road, Ken sped up as he drove toward Marquette.

The nerve-racking drive didn't take all that long, not really. It was simply the anxiety of having Hanna sick in the backseat that made the miles seem dozens of times longer than they actually were. Ken had been to Marquette a few times since he and Hanna had moved to Pleasanton a few weeks earlier, and by happy coincidence he happened to have passed by the hospital, so he was actually able to find it. "We're almost there."

"Daddy, I'm thirsty," Hanna said weakly.

"I know. When we get to the hospital, they'll give you whatever you want," Ken promised, his entire being focused on turning into the emergency entrance and then maneuvering the car under the small portico. Ken stopped the car, turned off the engine, and got out. He opened Hanna's door, lifted her out, and then carried her into the emergency entrance and right up to the desk, where a middle-aged woman looked at him with concern.

"She's been sick for a few days and her temperature was 103 when I left the house," Ken began before the woman could ask questions. "I need someone to look at her right away." Ken was feeling frantic. He could feel the heat washing off Hanna and he was afraid her temperature was even higher now than it had been when he'd taken it at home.

"Bring her around to the door," she said as she pointed, and Ken carried Hanna to where the lady had indicated. He heard a buzzing, and then the door opened and a nurse met him and led him through to the emergency treatment area, where he laid Hanna on a bed. He expected to be given a hard time and told to wait, but the nurse began immediately taking Hanna's temperature and vital signs, and then wrote them on a chart as she asked questions.

Ken answered every question. No, she didn't have allergies. She'd been fine a week ago, but she'd gotten a cold that had steadily gotten worse. Ken explained what he'd been giving her and everything he'd done since Hanna had gotten ill. "I'll have the doctor stop by right away," she said and then hurried away.

"Honey, I need to move the car so other people can get help. I won't leave you for very long, I promise," he said, holding her small hand in his. Hanna nodded, and Ken hurried out toward the entrance after telling the receptionist where he was going and that he'd be right back.

Ken flew to the car, parked it, and was back inside in two minutes flat. The doors opened, and he walked to Hanna's bed at the same time as the doctor. "We're going to start an IV to get her rehydrated and see if we can't bring that fever down," he told Ken after looking Hanna over thoroughly. "We're going to run some tests to see exactly what's wrong." The doctor stroked Hanna's hair out of her eyes. "I'll order a bed, and we'll get her into a room as quickly as we can."

Ken nodded as he reached for Hanna's pale hand and held it in his. This little girl, who he'd adopted just two years ago, when Hanna was four, had quickly become the center of Ken's whole world. They'd been looking for a place away from the city where he could raise Hanna in a more rural, down-to-earth setting when he'd found Pleasanton. The town looked ideal, nestled against a small, protected cove on Lake Superior. The views and landscapes were breathtaking, and Ken had been looking forward to painting everything around him. Maybe he would, but first he had to get Hanna better. Little else mattered right now except her.

His phone rang, and when Ken snatched it out of his pocket, he saw it was Mark. He answered in a rush. "I'm at the hospital in Marquette with Hanna," Ken began without preamble.

"What happened?" Mark asked, and Ken heard what sounded like a crowd of people in the background.

"Her temperature spiked and she hasn't been getting better, so I brought her in. They're going to admit her and run some tests." The thought chilled Ken faster than the air outside. She'd been sick for a while and she hadn't been getting better. What if something happened to her and he should have brought her to the hospital sooner?

The noise behind Mark quieted. "She's going to be all right. You did the right thing, and they'll be able to help her," Mark explained logically in his usual reasonable tone. "I stopped for dinner with some friends and I'm heading your way. I have everything packed and I'll be getting on the road in a few minutes. I'll get a hotel tonight and I should be there by early afternoon at the latest."

"Thanks, I'll see you then," Ken said, feeling a bit better knowing Mark was on his way. "I have to go. The doctor just returned. Call me later tonight." Mark agreed, and Ken hung up, shoving the phone back in his pocket. Ken returned to Hanna's side, holding her hand and watching as the nurse spread pain-deadening cream on her arm and put in the port for the IV. Hanna gasped and then began to cry. "I know, honey, but it's almost over and this will help you feel better." He continued holding her hand as the nurse rolled a machine to Hanna's bed and proceeded to attach it to the port.

"You were a very good girl," the nurse said in a level voice before leaving. She returned almost immediately with what looked like a blood kit and began to prepare Hanna's arm. Hanna rolled her head toward him, and Ken saw the fear and confusion in his daughter's eyes. He knew he'd do anything to prevent this. Hell, he'd let them poke him with needles for days if it meant Hanna didn't have to endure it. "I'll be gentle, I promise," the nurse said. "I have a daughter about your age, and she has a doll just like yours," the nurse said as she continued working. "What's her name?"

"Emily," Hanna answered, and Ken let go of Hanna's hand so she could cuddle her doll. The nurse inserted the needle and began drawing the blood.

"Did you get her for Christmas?" the nurse asked as she switched vials.

"Daddy got her for me," Hanna explained in her weak voice as the nurse withdrew the needle, putting a Band-Aid with Oscar the Grouch in its place.

"That's wonderful. You hold her tight. I know this is a strange place, but as long as Emily and Daddy are with you, there's nothing be afraid of." The nurse stood up, and Ken gave her a smile. "All done," the nurse pronounced and left the room once again, leaving Ken and Hanna alone.

"Close your eyes, honey, and try to rest. They should be in soon to take you up to your room. You won't have to get out of bed or anything," Ken explained, and Hanna held her doll closer with one arm, the other hooked to a machine. Eventually, Hanna closed her eyes and fell asleep. Almost as soon as she did, they arrived to take her to her room. Ken gathered their things and walked alongside the bed; Hanna never opened her eyes.

The room was nice, if sparse, and to Ken's surprise, there was a sofa that the orderly explained folded down into a bed. "Parents often spend the night with their children. I'll be back in a few minutes to make up the bed for you."

"Thanks, I really appreciate that," Ken said before sitting down. He stared at his sleeping daughter, his heart pounding as he thought of all the possible things that could be wrong with her. He hated that she was sick and that Mark wasn't here when he needed him. Ken stood up and walked toward the door, dimming the lights before stepping out into the hall to call the one person he knew would understand.

"Carrie?" Ken said when his call was answered.

"What is it?" his friend asked immediately. She was the person he most regretted leaving behind. "Something's wrong—I can hear it in your voice."

"Hanna's in the hospital. She's been sick and wasn't getting better, and when I took her temperature, it was really high. I'm so worried. She just lies there."

"Is she sleeping?" she asked.

"Yes. They're running tests and won't know anything until tomorrow. They're making arrangements for me to sleep in the room with her." Ken swallowed hard, but the lump stayed firmly lodged where it was.

"It's okay. She probably has a bad case of the flu and the tests will confirm that," Carrie soothed. "Just get some rest and make sure she's comfortable. That's all you can do, and when you hear something, call me right away. I can be there if you need me," she said, and Ken appreciated that, but he knew it wasn't that easy for her to get away from her own family. Talking to her, while helpful and what he needed to hear, only reinforced how alone he felt.

"I'll call as soon as I hear anything," Ken promised, hanging up as the orderly approached. He made up the bed and brought a few blankets and a pillow for him. "Get some rest if you can," he said with an encouraging smile before leaving the room. Somehow, bed or not, Ken knew this was going to be a long night.

KEN WOKE with a start, wondering where he was. Hanna lay quietly in the bed, and he remembered where they were and why they were here. He stood up, walked to his daughter's bed, and placed his hand on her forehead. At least the fever seemed to be down, and Hanna appeared to be resting comfortably. Opening the door to the room, Ken quietly stepped out and wandered down the dimmed hallway to the nurse's station, where the night shift was working, talking in hushed tones. One of the nurses saw him approach and smiled.

"We have coffee if you'd like some," she told him in a hushed tone.

"Thank you," Ken said. "Hanna's fever seems to be down."

"That's good. I'll be in soon to check on her," the nurse explained, and then she stood up and disappeared into a small room off the desk, then returned with a paper cup. "Here you go."

Ken smiled worriedly and nodded, sipping from the cup. The smooth coffee slid down his throat, soothing him with the familiar in a place that scared him, purely because Hanna had to be there. The nurse went back to work, and Ken wandered back to Hanna's room, leaving the door open slightly for a bit of fresh air before sitting on what he'd used for a bed, sipping the coffee and watching Hanna as she slept. The nurse came in and checked her, and confirmed that Hanna's fever was indeed down before leaving again.

Caffeine or not, after he finished the coffee, Ken must have dozed off again because he awakened when the door to the room opened. "I'm Dr. Helen Pierson, and I've been assigned your daughter as a patient," she said remarkably pleasantly before lightly touching Hanna. "Sweetheart, I'm the doctor and I need to listen to your lungs and heart." Hanna opened her eyes, and Dr. Pierson helped her sit up. She listened to both her chest and back before laying her back down. "Thank you," she told Hanna, who closed her eyes again. "The results of the tests haven't come back yet, but I expect them in the next couple of hours."

"You suspect something," Ken stated, and he could see a flicker in the doctor's eyes.

"We need to wait until we have the test results, and then I'll be happy to discuss anything you'd like. I don't want to speculate at this point. She's resting well, which is excellent, and her fever is definitely down, so that's a good sign. We'll just have to wait a little while longer," she explained. "I'll be by with the results as soon as I have them." She gave Ken a reassuring smile and then left the room.

His phone vibrated in his pocket, and Ken fished it out and walked into the hallway to talk so he wouldn't disturb Hanna. "I just got on the road and I'll cross the Mackinac Bridge in less than an hour," Mark told him.

"I'll be at the hospital in Marquette. When you stop by the house, would you please grab some fresh clothes and my shaving kit for me?" Ken asked, peering into the room because he thought he heard Hanna, but she was still asleep.

Mark didn't answer right away but after a moment he said, "Okay. I'll see you in a few hours." Mark disconnected, and Ken shoved the phone back into his pocket. He didn't have time or the energy for Mark's drama at the moment. He knew Mark hated running errands for anyone, but at the moment, Ken really didn't care. He also knew Mark had a good heart and he'd realize that Ken needed the help about two minutes after hanging up, and then he'd feel guilty.

Ken went back into the room and was greeted by Hanna's blue eyes. She still looked tired, but she was awake. "Are you hungry?" he asked her, and she nodded slightly. "Let me call and get you something to eat," Ken told her before picking up the phone. He talked with the person who answered, and he promised to send up a tray. "You can watch television if you want," Ken told Hanna before turning it on and finding the Disney Channel. Ken didn't normally allow Hanna to watch much television. When they lived in Grand Rapids, they'd spent their time outside, or doing things together. Hanna would draw and color her pictures while Ken painted his. Hanna wasn't his biological daughter, but their interests and talents couldn't have been better aligned. Hanna had the makings of a talented artist; Ken could see it already. She drew beautifully, but she also saw things that other people didn't.

"Can I color?" Hanna asked as she looked away from the television.

"Mark is on the way, and once he gets here, he'll sit with you for a little while and I'll go get your art stuff for you," Ken said. He'd gotten her everything he could think of that was appropriate for her age. Ken settled in the chair next to her bed, and they watched the television together until Hanna's breakfast came. She ate a little and then pushed it aside.

"Aren't you hungry?" Ken asked.

"It's icky," Hanna answered, making the "I'd rather go hungry than eat that" face that Ken knew well. The nurse chose that moment to make an appearance.

"I have some fruit cups, would you like one of those?" she asked, and Hanna nodded. The nurse left and then returned with two small packaged fruit cups. She handed one to Hanna and the other to Ken, who set it aside for later.

"What do you say?" Ken prompted.

"Thank you," Hanna said as she pulled off the cover. The nurse then took Hanna's temperature and vitals before saying good-bye and leaving the room.

Hanna was just finishing the mandarin oranges when the doctor returned. Ken tried to read her face, but he couldn't. "It looks like you're one sick little girl, but we're going to make you better," the doctor said with a smile for Hanna. "Would it be okay if I talked to your daddy for a few minutes? I promise not to keep him too long."

"Okay," Hanna said innocently as she looked at Ken, who pasted as sincere a smile on his face as he could, even though his heart pounded in his chest and his stomach clenched. Ken left the room and followed the doctor down the hall to a small office around the corner. The doctor motioned Ken to a chair and then sat next to him.

"The reason Hanna has been sick is because she has the flu, as you probably suspected," the doctor began. "But the reason she isn't getting better is because we found that she has pediatric leukemia, which has weakened her immune system. We don't know how advanced the disease is at this point. We'll need to run more tests."

The news hit Ken like a sucker punch to the gut. He could barely breathe at all. Closing his eyes, he tried to push away the thoughts that flooded his mind. Never in a million years had he considered that Hanna might have cancer. Ken tried to hold back the tears that threatened to overwhelm him, especially as images of attending Hanna's funeral flashed in his mind.

"Mr. Brighton," the doctor said quietly, and Ken took a deep breath to try to help get his rampant emotions under control. "Take whatever time you need."

Ken reached for a tissue and wiped his running nose. "Where do we go from here?"

"We'll begin with tests and then develop a treatment plan," the doctor explained.

"Should we have her transferred to Ann Arbor?" Ken asked. He was willing to do whatever it took to make sure Hanna had the best care possible.

"You could," the doctor told him. "I don't want to blow my own horn, but you need to know the facts. My family and I moved here from Ann Arbor because my sons wanted to go to Michigan Tech. My husband and I moved with them because we both grew up in the area and because we thought we could do some good for the community. My specialty is oncology, and his is cardiac care." The doctor paused, and Ken blinked a few times, trying to will away the tears, using a tissue to wipe his eyes. "I would be pleased to have Hanna as my patient. I was a senior member of the oncology department in Ann Arbor, and I'm the head of the department here. This little hospital is one of the best in this part of the country. I'm not trying to make your decision for you, though, and I'll support your decision if you want to transfer her."

"Thank you," Ken said with a bit of relief.

"If you stay, she'll also be closer to home, which, when we get to the treatment phase, can make all the difference in the world." The doctor was silent for a few minutes. "Do you have any questions for me right now?" Ken shook his head. He knew he would in the future, but he couldn't think very well right now. "I'm going to go ahead and get the next round of tests ordered. You can let me know what you'd like to do," she said, and Ken nodded. The doctor stood up and left the room quietly.

Ken stayed in the chair, wondering what he was going to do. Hanna had cancer. His precious little girl could die. The doctor hadn't said that, but Ken knew it was true. Ken could almost feel his entire emotional world coming apart at the seams. More than anything right now, he wished Mark were here, just to hear him say that everything would be okay. He needed to hear that even if neither of them knew it was true.

Ken stood, steadying his wobbly legs. Somehow he had to go back to Hanna's room and make believe everything was okay until he got more information from the doctor. Then he could explain to her what was going to happen. For now, she was better off not knowing.

His phone vibrated in his pocket, and he pulled it out and saw the call was from his parents. "Hi, Mom," Ken said, knowing she was the one who always called for both of them.

"How's my precious granddaughter?" she asked, and Ken fell back into the chair.

"Hanna has cancer, Mom," he said, and he heard his mother gasp and then begin to weep softly. Ken placed his head on the desk the doctor had used, unable to hold it in any longer, breaking down into tears as well, and he and his mother shared a long-distance cry.

CHAPTER
One

THE SUN shone off everything as Ken walked next to Hanna's wheelchair as the orderly pushed her out of the hospital. Months of treatment that had at times left Hanna almost too weak to lift her head were now behind them. Hanna was showing steady improvement and getting a little bit stronger each day. The air was still cold, so Hanna was bundled up under blankets, but Ken couldn't help hoping that the sunshine that had been so scarce through the winter this close to Lake Superior was a good omen. At the car, Hanna stood up, and Ken rushed around to hold open the door. She was about to get in when the hospital doors slid open and Dr. Pierson walked out in her lab coat, and embraced Hanna. Over the past few months, Hanna had won the hearts of most of the hospital staff, from the doctors to the nurses who brought in special treats so she wouldn't have to eat the hospital food all the time. "You do what your daddy says, and I'll see you in a few weeks," Dr. Pierson said. "And I want another of your special drawings for my office wall."

Hanna smiled. "I promise," she said happily before climbing into the backseat of the car.

"You take care of yourself," Dr. Pierson said as she turned to Ken. "You aren't any good to her if you let yourself get run down. Call me if you have questions or concerns, and if you need help, I'm good at battling with insurance companies." Dr. Pierson smiled, and then, to Ken's surprise, she pulled him into a hug as well. "You're an amazing father and her best chance at a full recovery." She released him and stepped back, waving with the others as Ken got in the car.

"Is your seat belt fastened?" Ken asked, and Hanna belted herself in before turning toward the window to wave at everyone as he put the warm car into gear and slowly pulled away. As helpful and understanding as everyone had been, he was glad to see the hospital disappear in the rearview mirror.

"Daddy, is my hair going to grow back?"

"Yes," Ken said with relief. "You have a few more treatments, and then once they stop and the medicine works out of your body, your hair will start to grow again." When they'd started the treatments, Hanna's hair had begun to fall out pretty quickly. Ken had taken it harder than Hanna had. The doctor had explained it to Hanna and had even given her a pink hat that she'd made from the softest yarn possible. Hanna had thanked her with a hug, and Ken had nearly cried at the thoughtfulness. The doctor had gone on to explain that she had knitted for years and loved making the things for little girls she'd never had the opportunity to do with her two sons. Hanna had worn the hat almost every day since, only taking it off when Ken insisted on washing it.

"Will I be able to go swimming this summer?" Hanna asked as they passed a clearing where they could see Lake Superior, still pretty much iced over.

"I hope so. Lake Superior is probably too cold, but there's a community pool we might be able to use." Ken knew that depended upon the state of Hanna's immune system, which had taken a real beating over the past few months. Hopefully, by then she'd be stronger. "Why don't you ask Dr. Pierson the next time you see her," Ken said, and he saw Hanna nod as she looked out the window.

"Will it be warm soon?" Hanna asked, bare trees passing outside the car.

"Yes. The leaves should start coming out in a few months, and once it gets warm, you and I can go on one of our art walks," Ken told her, and Hanna smiled. Before they'd moved, he and Hanna would spend summer afternoons in the park. Ken would take a sketchbook and Hanna her art set, and they would spend the day drawing and coloring the world around them.

"Will Dr. Pierson come too?" Hanna asked.

"She can if she wants. You can invite her when it gets closer." Ken knew Dr. Pierson was very busy.

"Are you going to marry her?" Hanna asked, and Ken nearly jammed on the brakes in his shock. "I saw you hug her and she hugged you. Does that mean you're going to get married?"

"No. Dr. Pierson is already married and has grown children." There were so many things wrong with that question that Ken didn't quite know where to start. "Where did you get that idea?" Ken asked as he peered quickly into the rearview mirror.

"Callie said once that she came into her mommy and daddy's bedroom and they were hugging, or at least her daddy was hugging her mommy really tight. They told her that hugging is what mommies and daddies do when they love each other," Hanna said happily, as though she understood the mysteries of the universe. Callie definitely knew and saw way too much for her own good.

"Dr. Pierson is my friend just like she's your friend," Ken explained. "Besides, you know I love Mark."

"Because you're gay?" Hanna asked.

"Yes. We've talked about this," Ken reminded her. "I don't fall in love with girls, but I do with boys."

"You love me," Hanna countered.

"Yes. Very much," Ken reassured her.

"But I'm a girl," Hanna countered seriously.

"Yes. You're a girl and I love you. But I'm not going to marry you." Ken had struggled to explain being gay to his daughter, and he'd obviously failed up till now. "Think of it this way. Most men want to marry women and have babies. Instead, I adopted you and I want to marry Mark." Good God, Ken hoped that explained it well enough for her. It seemed to, because Hanna was quiet for a while. Ken knew that could be good, because she was satisfied, or bad, because she was pondering something else.

"What's the difference between boys and girls?" Hanna asked, and Ken found himself pressing down just a little more on the accelerator. This conversation couldn't get over with fast enough.

"What do you think the difference is?" Ken asked, feeling clever that he'd turned the question back on her.

"Boys have penises and girls have 'ginas," Hanna said, and Ken breathed a sigh of relief. "Girls also get boobs, but some men do too. Daddy, will you get boobs?"

Ken laughed. "No. Not if I can help it?"

"Will I get boobs?" Hanna asked.

"Yes," Ken answered, starting to laugh. If Hanna asked one more question about boobs, penises, or vaginas, Ken was going to run screaming from the car. "How about we see who can be quietest the longest. I'll bet you ice cream I can beat you."

Hanna opened her mouth to argue with him, but then she slapped her hands over her mouth, and Ken could see she was smiling. The rest of the trip was quiet, and ten minutes later, Ken pulled up in front of the house. "You win. After dinner, you can have ice cream," Ken said, and Hanna laughed as Ken turned off the car before getting out. He opened the door for Hanna, and she unhooked her seat belt before climbing out of the car.

Ken got out as well, popping the trunk so he could grab their bags before following her up the walk. It had been months since Hanna had been home, and Ken doubted she really remembered their house.

Hanna was halfway up the walk when a gust of wind, cold and straight off the lake, blew across the yard. Hanna shivered at the cold and hurried toward the house. She'd just reached the steps when her hat blew off her head, the air lifting it for a few seconds before carrying it across the lawn. "Daddy," Hanna cried, and Ken hurried to where Hanna stood. He set down the bags and hurried after it, but didn't reach it before the wind picked the hat up again, blowing it across the street, and Hanna's favorite pink hat ended up in a mud puddle. Hanna began to cry, and Ken hurried to her, lifting her into his arms.

"I'll get it, and once it's washed it'll be as good as new, I promise," Ken said as he carried her into the house out of the wind. He set her on the sofa and heard Mark walking through the house. Hanna was still upset as Mark came in the room. "Would you stay with her for a minute?" Ken asked and then hurried back outside.

As he descended the steps, Ken saw his neighbor walking toward him, carrying the sodden hat with an almost sorrowful look on his face. He didn't speak as he handed over the once pink hat, now brown, with twigs stuck to it. He'd obviously wrung it out, but he didn't say anything.

"Thank you," Ken said. "My daughter just got home from the hospital and this is her favorite hat." Ken waited for him to say something, but the man didn't. Instead, his eyes conveyed that he felt badly for Hanna. "She has to wear hats all the time because she lost her hair." Why Ken was telling him this he didn't know, but the man looked as though he was hanging on every word.

"Daddy," Hanna called from the door.

"I have to go," Ken explained. "Thank you so much," Ken said, and the man smiled and waved before turning to walk back down the sidewalk. Ken watched him leave for a few seconds, sort of getting lost in the way he moved. Then he realized what he was doing and hurried back toward the house, hoping Mark hadn't seen him watching someone else.

"Is it okay?" Hanna asked as Ken approached.

"It will be, honey. Go on inside. I'll bring the things in and wash it right away for you," Ken explained, and he stopped to pick up the bags. Hanna disappeared into the house, and Ken couldn't stop himself from looking to where his neighbor had gone. He saw him standing a few houses down watching him. He waved, and Ken did his best to wave back before walking into the house.

"I need to talk to you," Mark said almost as soon as he'd closed the front door.

"Okay," Ken said. "But I have to get Hanna settled in her room and then do some laundry." He held up the sodden hat. "We can talk once I get her to sleep." Ken moved away and hurried to get to work. Getting Hanna settled was the most important thing right now.

Ken got Hanna situated on the sofa under a blanket and let her watch television as he hurried through the house trying to get things done. He unpacked the things they'd brought home from the hospital, made Hanna something to eat and drink, and took them in to her before descending the stairs to the basement so he could get the laundry started. He had a lot to do, but he was still happy. Hanna was home with him once again and hopefully on the mend.

In the laundry area, Ken sorted the dirty clothes and got the washer started. "You haven't hummed in quite a while," Mark said from behind him. Ken finished loading the clothes before closing the lid on the washing machine.

When Ken turned around, he didn't see the happy, open expression he expected. Rather, Mark's features were pinched, he had bags under his eyes, and Ken even noticed a few wrinkles that hadn't been there a few weeks ago. They'd both been through a lot in the past few months, and Ken moved closer, ready to pull Mark into his arms, but Mark took a small step backward, and Ken stiffened. "We need to talk," Mark told him, and Ken sighed, nodding slightly.

"I'll meet you in my studio in a few minutes," Ken said, and Mark nodded before walking away. Ken heard his footsteps on the stairs as he finished up with the laundry. Once he was done, Ken climbed the stairs, turning off the lights before checking on Hanna. She was quietly watching television, resting under a pink blanket. She looked a little pale, but still as precious as ever. Looking away from the television, she smiled at him, and Ken walked over to the sofa, kissing her on the forehead.

"Are you okay, Daddy?" Hanna asked.

"I'm fine. I'll be out in my studio if you need anything," Ken said, and Hanna nodded, returning her attention to the television. Before leaving the room, Ken picked up Hanna's art case from the hall and placed it near the sofa. She'd been watching a lot of television in the hospital, and Ken was hoping to entice her back to the things she'd always loved before she'd gotten sick. "Don't forget the picture for Dr. Pierson," Ken told her softly.

"I won't," Hanna answered, and Ken left the room, walking down the hall and out to the small room that had been added onto the house by the previous owner.

Mark sat on the old sofa the movers had placed against the one wall, a sofa Ken had never moved. There were still boxes that had never been unpacked and canvasses leaning along the other wall. Ken hadn't painted in months; his heart and mind hadn't been in it. He'd been fully occupied with Hanna.

"Sit down, Ken," Mark said as he stood up, and Ken sat on the edge of the sofa. "I'm not quite sure how to say what I need to say," Mark began as he wandered slowly through the room. "Things aren't working between us anymore. They haven't in a while," Mark said, and Ken stared at him as he moved. "You've been taking care of Hanna, I know that, and you needed to. I don't begrudge her your attention. But even before she got sick, things weren't particularly good between us. We slept together and lived in the same house, but we're moving in different directions." Mark's voice trailed off, but he continued pacing the room.

Ken opened his mouth to deny what Mark was saying, but he couldn't, not really. He'd been living at the hospital almost constantly for months, and though he'd called Mark every day, in two months they hadn't talked about anything other than Hanna and how she was doing.

"You know I'm right, and I'm not doing this to hurt you," Mark continued.

"I know," Ken finally managed to say. "You never did anything hurtful the entire time I've known you." Ken sighed, wondering if there was anything he could say. "Why did you move with us, then?"

Mark stopped pacing and sat down next to Ken on the sofa. "I honestly thought that things might change between us once we moved. We would be working together to set up our new home, making new friends together. I really thought building a new life in a new place would bring us closer, like we were right after you got Hanna, but it hasn't worked, and I don't think it will. Circumstances got in the way, and I don't think our relationship is reparable. Do you?"

Ken thought about it for a long time and then shook his head. "You're probably right," he whispered. Ken had honestly thought Mark was the man he'd spend the rest of his life with. Ken had been in the early stages of adopting Hanna when he met Mark, and he'd been supportive and loving through the ups and downs of the entire process.

"Don't get me wrong. I love both you and Hanna and I always will. But I've been giving this a lot of thought over the past few months, and to be honest, we probably would have had this conversation a while ago if it hadn't been for Hanna getting cancer. I couldn't have this talk with you then, and I'm trying to not be a dick about things."

"What are you going to do?" Ken asked, feeling both hurt and a bit relieved. The more he thought about it, the more he realized that Mark was probably right. It was time they got on with their lives, and while that would have once meant working through everything together, now it meant going their separate ways.

Mark humphed softly. "Kenny, we've drifted apart to the point where you haven't even noticed that most of my things are already gone. I have an apartment in town, and I'll move the last of my things out later today."

"Is there someone else?" Ken asked, and Mark shook his head.

"I'd never do that to you or Hanna, you know that," he answered with a touch of hurt in his voice, and Ken nodded.

"I do know that. You're a good man, you always were," Ken began. "I'm going to miss you, and so is Hanna."

"I'm going to miss you too. I'll still be in town, and we can still see each other and talk. I want us to be friends, and I still care about both you and Hanna. I just think it's time we look at things logically and make a break of it before we come to resent and hate each other, and we will. You need all your efforts concentrated on your work and Hanna. I need to start building my own life." Ken felt Mark's hand slide into his. "I do love you, Kenny, I probably always will, but this is for the best. I think we'll both realize it pretty quickly." Mark let go of his hand and walked toward the studio door. "I'm going to load the last of my things into the car and say good-bye to Hanna. Maybe in a few weeks, we can all have dinner together or something."

"Okay," Ken answered, standing up himself.

"You'll see that I'm right," Mark whispered before leaving the room. Ken stayed where he was, glancing around the empty studio, waiting for the hurt and rejection to hit, but they didn't. At times like this, he'd normally feel the need to paint, but that didn't materialize either. Ken closed the door behind him as he left the studio, walking through the house until he heard Mark softly talking to Hanna. Leaving them alone, Ken went into the kitchen to start something for their dinner, but he didn't really feel like doing anything at all. Eventually, he heard footsteps and knew Mark was getting the last of his things. Ken joined Hanna in the living room. The television was off and she had a pad resting on her legs as she colored, her tongue sticking out slightly between her lips as she concentrated.

"What are you doing?" Ken asked, sitting next to her on the edge of the sofa. He half expected to be bombarded with questions, but Hanna kept working.

"I'm drawing a picture for Mark," she explained without looking up, and Ken watched her for a second. She didn't ask him anything, so Ken stood up and sat in one of the nearby chairs. Mark came into the house and walked down the hall and up the stairs, returning a few minutes later with his suitcase.

"I'll call you in a few weeks," Mark promised as he headed for the door. After setting down the suitcases, Mark walked over to Hanna, saying good-bye to her before kissing her forehead.

"This is for you," Hanna said, handing Mark the drawing. "So you don't forget Daddy and me."

Ken blinked away the tears that threatened as Mark thanked Hanna. "I could never forget you, munchkin." Hanna threw her arms around Mark's neck, giving him a hug. "Things didn't work out between your daddy and me, but that doesn't mean either of us love you any less." Then Mark stepped away and looked at him. Ken took a deep breath and gave Mark a hug.

"Take care of yourself," Ken whispered before releasing Mark and watching his lover and partner of almost three years leave the house for the last time. Ken closed the door behind Mark and then walked back into the living room. He refused to allow himself to do anything as maudlin as watch his car drive away for the last time.

"Daddy, does this mean Mark isn't your boyfriend anymore?" Hanna asked, her eyes widening.

"Yes. That's exactly what it means," Ken explained with a sigh. Mark was probably right. They had been drifting apart for a while, but that didn't mean he didn't feel the loss or the loneliness. He might not have been with Mark while he was spending those long hours at the hospital, but that didn't mean he hadn't missed him or wasn't comforted simply by the fact that Mark was there. Now he and Hanna were alone, and he wasn't sure how he felt about that. Maybe he wouldn't know for quite a while.

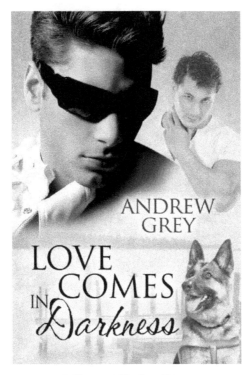

ANDREW GREY

LOVE COMES IN Darkness

A Senses Series Story

Howard Justinian has always had to fight for his freedom. Because he was born blind, everyone is always trying to shelter him, but he's determined to live his life on his own terms.

When an argument with his boyfriend over that hard-won self-reliance leaves Howard stranded by the side of the road, assistance arrives in the form of Gordy Jarrett. Gordy is a missionary's son, so helping others is second nature—and he does it in such an unassuming manner that Howard can't say no.

Life is barely back on track when Howard receives shocking news: his sister died, leaving him her daughter to care for. Howard now faces his greatest challenge yet: for Sophia's safety, he'll need to accept help, but will he learn to accept it from Gordy, the one man who will not curb his independence?

www.dreamspinnerpress.com

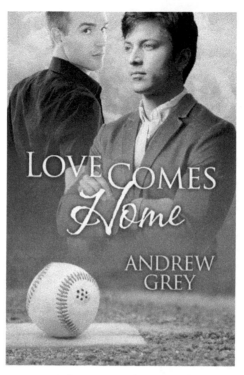

A Senses Series Story

When architect Gregory Hampton's son, Davey, starts having trouble in Little League, Greg takes him to an eye doctor. The diagnosis hits them hard. Davey's sight is degenerating rapidly, and eventually he'll go blind.

Tom Spangler is used to getting what he wants. When Greg captures his attention, he asks Greg for a date. They have a good time until Greg gets a call from the friends watching his son, telling him Davey has fallen. Greg and Tom return to find the worst has happened—Davey can no longer see.

With so much going on in his life, Greg doubts he'll see Tom again. But Tom has researched beep baseball, where balls and bases make sounds to enable the visually impaired to participate in Little League. Tom spearheads an effort to form a team so Davey can continue to play the game he loves. But when Greg's ex-wife shows up with her doctor boyfriend, offering a possible cure through a radical procedure, Greg must decide how far he'll go to give Davey a chance at getting his sight back.

www.dreamspinnerpress.com

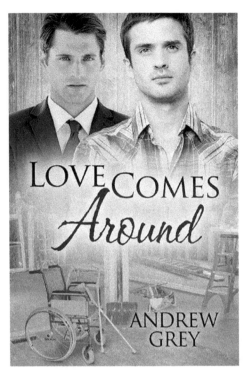

A Senses Series Story

Dan was a throwaway child and learned to take care of himself in foster care. As an adult, he devotes his life to the business he started and his heart to raising children no one else wants. Dan has already adopted six-year-old Lila, who walks on crutches, and then decides to adopt eight-year-old Jerry, who suffers from MD and is confined to a wheelchair.

Also abandoned as a child, Connor ended up on his own and retreated into himself. He works as a carpenter and woodcarver and is the perfect man to ensure Dan's home becomes wheelchair accessible.

When Dan hires Connor, neither of the men are ready to open their hearts to the possibility of love. As they learn how much they have in common, both of them must weigh the possibility of family and a future against the risks of getting hurt again.

www.dreamspinnerpress.com

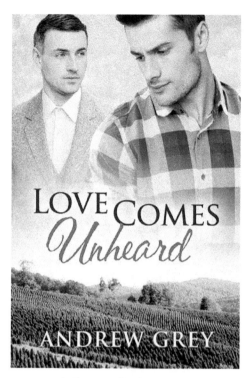

A Senses Series Story

Garrett Bowman is shocked that fate has brought him to a family who can sign. He's spent much of his life on the outside looking in, even within his biological family, and to be accepted and employed is more than he could have hoped for. With Connor, who's included him in his family, Garrett has found a true friend, but with the distant Brit Wilson Haskins, Garrett may have found something more. In no time, Garrett gets under Wilson's skin and finds his way into Wilson's heart, and over shared turbulent family histories, Wilson and Garrett form a strong bond.

Wilson's especially impressed with the way Garrett's so helpful to Janey, Connor and Dan's daughter, who is also deaf. When Wilson's past shows up in the form of his brother Reggie, bringing unscrupulous people to whom Reggie owes money, life begins to unravel. These thugs don't care how they get their money, what they have to do, or who they might hurt. Without the strength of love and the bonds of family and friends, Garrett and Wilson could pay the ultimate price.

www.dreamspinnerpress.com

ANDREW GREY grew up in western Michigan with a father who loved to tell stories and a mother who loved to read them. Since then he has lived all over the country and traveled throughout the world. He has a master's degree from the University of Wisconsin-Milwaukee and now works full-time on his writing. Andrew's hobbies include collecting antiques, gardening, and leaving his dirty dishes anywhere but in the sink (particularly when writing). He considers himself blessed with an accepting family, fantastic friends, and the world's most supportive and loving husband. Andrew currently lives in beautiful historic Carlisle, Pennsylvania.

E-mail: andrewgrey@comcast.net
Website: www.andrewgreybooks.com